KINGSTON NOIR

KINGSTON NOIR

EDITED BY COLIN CHANNER

Published by Akashic Books
©2012 Akashic Books

Series concept by Tim McLoughlin and Johnny Temple
Kingston map by Aaron Petrovich

ISBN-13: 978-1-61775-074-8
Library of Congress Control Number: 2011960945

Akashic Books
PO Box 1456
New York, NY 10009
info@akashicbooks.com
www.akashicbooks.com

ALSO IN THE AKASHIC BOOKS NOIR SERIES

FORTHCOMING

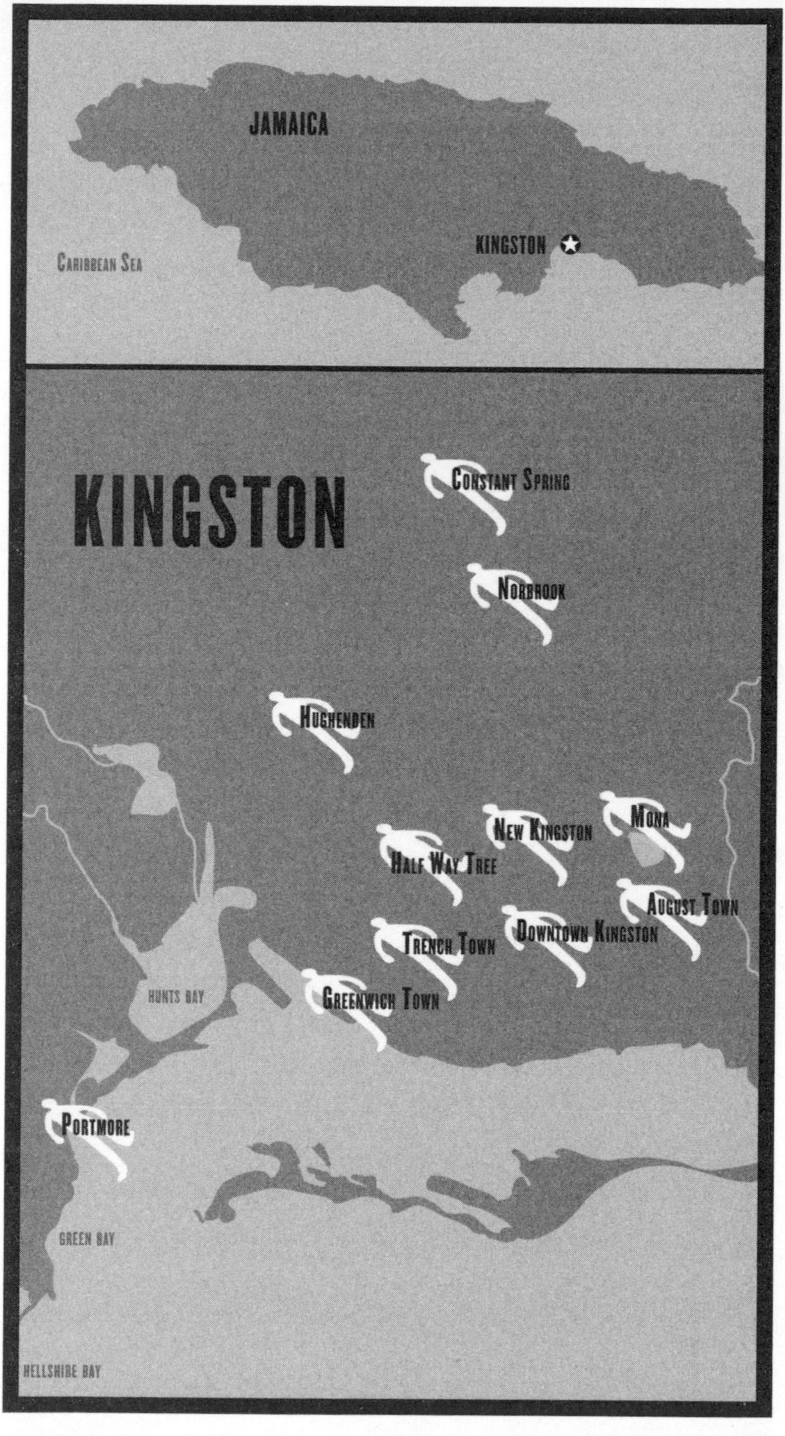
JAMAICA
KINGSTON
CARIBBEAN SEA
KINGSTON
CONSTANT SPRING
NORBROOK
HUGHENDEN
NEW KINGSTON
MONA
HALF WAY TREE
AUGUST TOWN
DOWNTOWN KINGSTON
TRENCH TOWN
GREENWICH TOWN
HUNTS BAY
PORTMORE
GREEN BAY
HELLSHIRE BAY

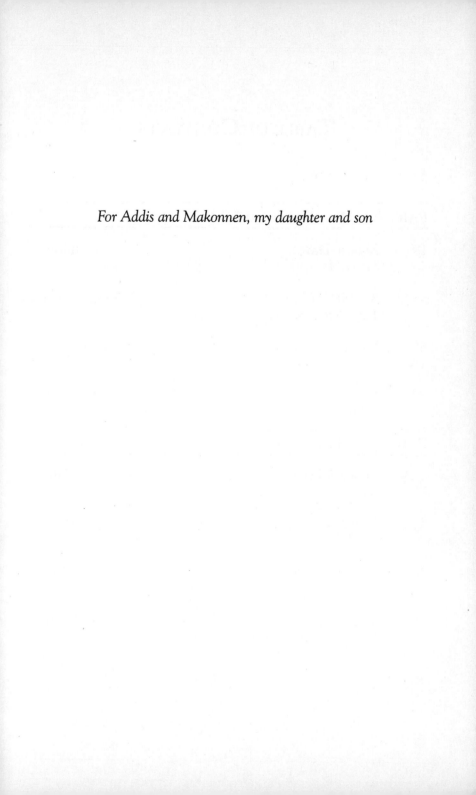

For Addis and Makonnen, my daughter and son

TABLE OF CONTENTS

PART III: PRESSURE DROP

INTRODUCTION
WHAT IF? WHY WOULD?

I lived in Kingston from 1963 to 1982. I was born there—at St. Joseph's on Deanery Road, delivered by Dr. Parboosingh. I was christened there as well, by Reverend Campbell at Christ Church on Antrim Road. My hometown was also where I first had sex. This happened in the small room I shared with my brother in a hot prefabricated house in Hughenden. No—I'm not going to share her name.

One of the things I remember most about my years in Kingston, in addition to the fact that I'd faked my orgasm that first time so I could go back to reading a comic book, is that this metropolis of half a million in those days had no directional signs. As such, people would get lost all the time, even those who'd grown up there, but especially those who had not.

Which way to public horse-pit-all? Which part you turn fo' reach the zoo? Carib theater—is where that is?

And the answer to these questions always seemed to go along the following (squiggly) line: "Okay . . . you going go down so where I pointing, then you going see a man with a coconut cart. When you see him now, you going turn, but not turn all the way, just part way, cause you going see a fence that kinda break down. But you not going stop there at the fence, y'know. You only going see it. You going see it, then you going pass. You going pass it till you reach the gully. But when you reach the gully now, what you going do is wheel round till you see the big tree. Listen me good here now. Cross the street when you see the big tree, because you have some man out there who will hold you up. Then after you cross the street now, go on and go on, and go on, then turn again, then turn again, then stay straight. Stay straight until you see where the road turn. But you mustn't turn. You must stay straight . . . and then if you still can't find where you going, just aks again."

Today, the largest English-speaking city between Miami and Buenos Aires has lots of signs. Even so, if you're not from there it's still easy to get lost.

This is one of many ways in which Kingston reminds me of New Orleans. Like its cultural cousin on the Mississippi, Kingston is a liquor-loving, music-maddened, seafood-smitten, class-addicted place. Dangerous as a *mutha*, but also—especially when you feel a cool wind coming off the harbor, or see a cape of mist on the shoulders of the northern hills, or hear a bongo natty singing praises to the Father as some herb smoke warms his heart—a place of Benedictine peace.

Every story in this collection was written (and rewritten, and rewritten, and *damn rewritten, Colin*) by an author who knows and understands this charismatic, badass city very well. In addition to having this intimate knowledge, the eleven writers share something else—a fascination with the city's turbulent dynamics, with the way its boundaries of color, class, race, gender, ideology, and sexual privilege crisscross like storm-tangled power lines.

Still, each story is driven by its unique *why would* or *what if*.

Why would a man sleep with a woman knowing she has HIV? Why would anyone throw a school girl's corpse beneath a bus? What if a European photographer takes it on herself to document a neighborhood controlled by gangs? What if an American actress wakes up to find herself gagged and bound in a stranger's bed?

Speaking of questions. As editor there were a few big ones I had to ask. Perhaps the most important one was, *How will I proceed?*

Some editors think of anthologies as potluck dinners. They send out general invitations. Encourage everyone to bring a favorite dish.

I've been to that dinner party. I know how it goes. Some things are great. Some things are awful. But most things are so-so.

Now why would I want to do something like that? I thought. At the same time I thought, *What if?* What if I thought of *Kingston Noir* as a great LP? Ahhhhh . . .

As I did with *Iron Balloons*, my first anthology for Akashic, I began with a simple understanding: few writers would be called, and even fewer would be chosen. Because nothing less than a classic would do.

Colin Channer
May 2012

PART I

Hard Road to Travel

MY LORD

BY KWAME DAWES

Portmore

A lot of people say they want to leave this city to go somewhere else. Not me. I love this place for what it is. Ugly and pretty. Rough and tender. Chaotic and smooth. Loving and murderous. All of it.

I love it like I love things you maybe shouldn't love.

When I was growing up off Red Hills Road, on Whitehall Avenue, I used to wake up in the morning, step into the yard, hear rooster crowing, smell the wood fire burning, hear *Swap Shop* on the radio, and just smile and say, "Yes, my people. Yes, my country." But I didn't really know love till around '78 when I remove to where I live now at the bottom of Stony Hill. Yeah man. Long time.

This is a house with history. The first time I see this place was in the early '70s. That time no house wasn't even here. It was just a little spot after you cross over the bridge from Constant Spring Road, and before you start to properly climb the hill, where a man had a small shop where he used to fix bicycle.

Most people, myself included, thought is squat the man was squatting there. After all, who would *buy* a piece of narrow land right side of a wide concrete gully and surround by macka bush and bramble, right?

But the man had bought the land. And soon he built a small cottage like one of them you find on a country road in cool Mandeville—tidy, nice filigree woodwork, and a full covered veranda. He paint the whole thing yellow and green. And the man live in that house even when everywhere around him they was building those flat-roof bungalow on the lower parts of the hill and the fancy house on the upper slopes. The man wouldn't sell a inch of the property. So, what you have in the middle of the area is like a piece of the country.

Well, the man dead and his people decide to go to foreign with every other brown-skin Jamaican who was absconding to Miami in those days. And is so I get to buy this place cheap-cheap.

This is where I brought Deloris. She was my wife.

Kingston is rough. My work is dirty work. And most night, when I am driving northward from the congested city by the sea, through the crazy traffic and smoke and noise (with the window down cause I like to hear and smell my city—and anyway, I waiting for the right time to fix the damned air conditioner in the car), I am just thinking about the way the whole place start to get greener with trees and more residential house as we climbing the hill toward Constant Spring. Past the stoosh Immaculate Conception High School for girls, past the horse farm on the left, past the stretch of the golf course, past the old market after the traffic light, then past the plaza where my office is, and then turn left to cross the bridge, and right there so, right at the foot of the mountain itself, my cottage, my castle, my refuge.

As I am driving I feel the sweet heaviness of heartbreak and desire, like a great Alton Ellis tune seeping out of a rum bar around six thirty, when the sun going down—the kinda tune that make you want to cry, and laugh, and screw, and hug-up, and pray at the same time. Yes, this city will break my heart every time, and the city come in like the women—tough, sweet, soft, dangerous, pragmatic, and fleshy. This city is my bread and wine, my bitters and gall, my honey and milk.

Deloris gone, Cynthia Alvaranga gone, and the place feeling sadder and sadder these days, but it is what I have, it is my comfort, it is my familiarity. I will dead here. That is the simple truth of the matter. Right here. Right here.

When Cynthia Alvaranga came to my office that first time, she wasn't coming to see me. She wasn't coming to hire me. She was coming to see Deloris. See, that was around the time when Deloris decide to start her dressmaking business.

It was Deloris idea to set up the place—what she call a "one-stop shop." You know, dressmaking, wedding planning, detective agency—one-stop shop. She said that is how they doing it in America now. Well, I never hear of it, but it make sense to me. So it was her idea, not mine. She said to me that if I did that I could start to branch out to more things—handyman finder ("If you can find people, you must can find a man to fix anything quicker than most people"), rent-a-house finder, that kinda thing—and she wanted to start a dressmaking place near me, but wasn't ready yet, but said it was a good way to start a business mentality, and when a couple go into business partnership and work together, she say, it strengthen their marriage. If you ask me, she just wanted to keep her eye on me. You know woman.

Be that as it may, our place was at the corner of the plaza and my glass door was nicely shaded by a big pretty flamboyant tree. The people who used to have the space before had what they call a gourmet Jamaican restaurant—a place name Nyame's that some Dutch couple used to own. It never work out—the woman find a rastaman and run away to Portland, so the man pack up and go back to Europe with the children. I get it cheap-cheap. Tragedy can be a blessing.

The way my office set up, it is hard for me to not see who coming in even if they are not coming to me. You see, I work in a cubicle to one side of the office, which use to be the manager office for the restaurant, I think. But in fact is not really a cubicle, because *cubicle* make it sound like it small. My door is open most of the time, so I can see when people coming into the office; and when the front door open, a buzzer go off so I can be ready for anything.

Deloris has her working area around the back where the kitchen used to be. It is a big space and she have machine and two big cutting table and whole heap of mannequin and that kinda thing there. She keep bolt and bolt of cloth in there too, and she have a rusty fridge and restaurant-grade stove so she can cook for us sometimes.

Be that as it may, Cynthia Alvaranga came in around two o'clock, so the place still smelling of oxtail and butter beans from our lunch. I see her hesitate at the door, but maybe it was me who hesitate. Maybe it was my head that hesitate, because I still remember that what I saw was a tall woman, a strong woman, a dark beautiful woman, who, I could tell, must have been some kinda athlete, because her body moved under what Deloris like to call a A-line frock, like a machine. Her face had that clean, fresh look. No makeup. Eyelash thick and long, lips full and pouting, and her eyes looked so tired, so sad, so broken down.

Normally for me, what I look for is a weakness in a woman, a flaw, a thing that can make me feel sorry for her. That is why fat woman was always my target when I was misbehaving.

And is not just because me fat too.

Most of the PI I know are fat like me, but they got fat recently, you know. I was always fat. And my fat is a fit kinda fat. I carry fat well. Them, is like they wear their clothes tight because they don't know they are fat. For instance, they like wear their shirt tuck in. So their belly is always hanging over. And guess what? They feel they looking neat because they always used to wear their shirt in their pants from when they never had a belly.

Me, from I was in technical school, I was wearing my shirt out of my pants to hide my belly. So I know how to dress like a fat man.

Yes, I am a fat man, but don't sorry for me. In Jamaica a woman like a big man. She can see he is prosperous, and that he can be in charge. People call you "boss" before they even know who you are. "Big man," "Boss," "Officer," "King," and my favorite, "My Lord." When a woman call you "My Lord," that is a sweetness.

Be that as it may, fat woman use to be my target. Though sometimes it is not just the fat, sometimes it might be something else. As I said, my secret is to find something in a woman, a limp, a sickness, something she ashamed of—a secret, you know, some nastiness in her life. When I can find that, maybe it makes me feel superior, but mostly it makes me feel that I can do something for her that she will appreciate, and that is how they come to love me, and that is how I can make a move.

I could see that Cynthia had a tiredness hanging off her. The expensive darkers on her forehead didn't fool me. Yeah, she was wearing nice things. She even had a Prada bag in her hand. But the things had an oldness and a beat-up quality to them so I know she was a woman in distress. And I began to think: A wonder what she want from me.

But it wasn't me she came to. It was Deloris. She came about a dress. I just happened to be the person she saw. Though I still wonder about this sometimes.

"The dressmaker is in here?" This is the first thing she said. She was standing at the door to my office. I had buzz her inside. She stare into my face like she was looking for something. Hard high cheekbone, almond-shape eye, and a small mole by her right temple. One second I register it as a flaw, next second I change my mind. Her hair cut low-low and neat and shining with oil. I wanted to touch it, feel how it feel on my palm.

"Yes, she in the back," I said. Then I shouted, "Deloris, customer!"

She walk by, and I wait for a second and then stand up and walk to my door to see her from the back. Lord, what I thought I saw to be beautiful from the front was a joke. Talk about thighs. And bottom. Firm. Lift up. Savior!

I had to step back into my office because the way I was looking at her, I felt dirty, like I was violating her with my eyes. No, no. I didn't want to do that. So I stay inside my office and blank out every other sound and listen. She wanted a dress. Black.

"It is for a funeral. I want it to be nice—stylish. Then I want you to make the same exact one, but this time for a eleven-year-old girl."

Her voice tell me she went to a good high school, but I couldn't tell anything else. I know she wasn't a Stony Hills money woman. This woman was like me and Deloris. Poor, but with education, and she must have worked in a nice office or something. Or maybe she was one of those woman who went to America on sports scholarship.

Show you how good I am. On every one of those, come to find out later on, it turned out I was right. St. Jago High. Sprinter. One. Two and hurdles. I even knew her name. I remembered her name from Champs. Yeah man. Had seen her from the stands but never up close. Even see her run for Jamaica couple time a few years back. A vague memory came to me about how she got injured or something like that—that's why she never made it big. Maybe I just filling that part in now. Yeah, but she was a big name in high school, for sure. Career done early. Promising for a while. A muscle tear or bone fracture break the promise, and that was that.

Be that as it may, as I was leaning back in my chair with my hands cross behind my head and listening, I began to wonder who died. Same time I hear Deloris say, "Sorry for your loss. My condolences."

And then Cynthia, like she answering me too, say, "No one has died yet. This is for us. This is to bury me and my girl."

I keep saying *Cynthia*, but it wasn't until I took her out that I learned her name. Yeah, I took her out. But that was not my original intention. In a sense it was Deloris fault.

When Cynthia left, I felt very worried. From the footsteps and the buzzer at the door I could tell that Deloris had gone to walk her outside. But that is neither here nor there. I was worried because I was sure Deloris had somehow seen the way I was staring at Cynthia and even had some sense of the thoughts I was fighting in my head. Is like I felt the thoughts were so loud that anyone close to me could hear.

I feel shame to say it now, but somehow in that short space of time—the time in which the two of them went outside the door and Deloris come back by herself—I imagined one of them passing. Which one? I feel shame to say . . . my wife. Yeah, in that short space of time of listening to Cynthia and watching her, I imagined my Deloris passing, imagined Cynthia coming to give me comfort, imagined us finding a romantic connection, deep as the deepest ocean between us in our loss and need.

Yes, I even imagined what it would be like to make love to a woman with tall legs like that. How she would squat over me, how she would move, how different it would be to see her thighs ripple as she rose and sat on me.

Deloris, you see, have some short legs, and for a while she had stopped getting into acrobatics or anything that would make her sweat even a little.

And I don't want to disrespect Deloris because she help build me in life and she teach me plenty things. For instance, is she who teach me about A-line dress. She used to say that they were flattering and forgiving to short woman like her who were well-endowed. Well, truth be told, by the time I met Cynthia not even A-line could help Deloris, if you know what I mean. But she was my wife and I love her, so I never ever tell her anything like that.

But it kinda hard when you marry a woman and you think she going just get a little grayer and maybe get two wrinkle when she get old. Yeah man, when I married her, I was thinking that all woman with Indian blood would stay fine-fine like stick.

Now I am not complaining, but Cynthia, I have to admit, made me have these very unfair imaginings.

When Deloris came back from walking Cynthia outside, I was waiting to hear it from her. I was waiting for her to ask me why I was staring at that woman like that. I was waiting for her to say, in the way only Deloris can, "I don't like that woman." But I swear, what I heard was the exact opposite. Exact.

"I like her," Deloris tell me. "I feel for her. You have to find a way to help her."

That is what Deloris said, with this look in her face of such care and pity and compassion. So is not like it was me who get myself involved.

I got up out of my chair and walk to my wife. I looked her straight in her face but I didn't touch her. I looked in her eyes. Then I recognized it. I knew the expression. It was the one she showed for people she liked but felt sorry for. I can't describe it but when you live with a woman long time you know these things.

And then I saw another look under the first look. Is like when women used to wear slip under them frock and piece of the pinkness hang down. Deloris was enjoying the pity. To her look there was something you'd call *relish*.

And I knew in the moment what it was about. Come on, people, I am a detective. I am people literate. I can read. Something Cynthia must have told her outside was allowing Deloris to feel sorry for her in ways that made her feel good, feel better than her. Cynthia, who was so much more beautiful that Deloris was, had ever been, or would ever be. This was more than being sorry for a woman who is afraid to die. It went deeper.

"She want to kill that man," Deloris said, shaking her head.

"Which man?" I ask.

"Her husband. Him is a dirty bitch." Deloris stomp her foot as she walk to the back of the shop. "You going to have to help her."

Now, I should have stopped it there. I should have put a stop to that kinda discussion right there. It was clear that Deloris had not noticed my thoughts, and I had already gotten away with murder, so to speak. Now was the time to end it. Now was the time to pull away from it and not entertain a discussion.

It did occur to me in that instance that maybe this was a trap. That maybe Deloris was testing me to see how I would react. But something in her tone, something in the way she did not focus on me when she was speaking, something about the distracted interest she had in this woman, made me think that this was no trap—Deloris was not even thinking about me at all. Deloris wanted to help this woman. Deloris wanted to join forces with me to help her. Deloris wanted US to like this woman. Which means that Deloris was giving me permission. Did she not understand what she was doing here?

I followed her to the back room and watched her picking out some black material.

I asked her, "So, you going to make the dresses?"

"Yes, man. Have to make it for her. I understand what she trying to do, and she must get the dress and look good in it."

"For her funeral?"

"No, man. For *his* funeral. She wearing it to his funeral." Deloris stared at me when she said this. "Dat man haffe dead."

"That is a serious thing to say." I was trying to stave off what

I could sense was lurking in the shadows ready to consume me.

"You going to have to help her," Deloris said. "She say she want you to help her finish things proper. You can't say no. I don't like to get into your business, as you know, but this is one time I am going to beg you to do me the favor. Meet with her. Find out. And finish it for her."

There was a lot of things I wanted to say to Deloris, but the thing I said was, "Finish what?"

Deloris told me what the woman said.

"But you don't even know her," I responded, trying to muster up some good reason that even I did not believe. "What if she lying?" I asked this question knowing that she was not. I threw out several scenarios. Five or so, including, "What if she had another man?" Deloris threw up her hands. I said to her, "This kinda thing happens all the time."

"I know women," Deloris said. "I know when a woman lying."

"I will have to talk to her first, then." And that was my first act of deception. But I was pushed into it. As Deloris and I talked, I was already picturing where Cynthia and I would meet. It would not be in the office. It would be in the Shanghai restaurant in the Mall Plaza down in Half Way Tree, an hour's drive in the usual traffic. I pictured the dark cubicles in the back. I pictured myself choosing the food for her because she wouldn't know that they have a beautiful steamed sea bass on the menu that they do specially for me. I pictured myself asking her about her life, about her family, her dreams and her fears. I pictured her asking me about my dreams, and me telling her how much I want to visit China—the northern part—to find a nice Chinese woman to marry. I pictured her laughing at my foolish dream and me using that opening to ask her to tell me her biggest secret, and her telling me, and the two of us knowing at once that we are locked. I heard myself tell her while we are pulling the flesh off the fish that I would do anything for her, anything at all.

Maybe it could have all stayed in fantasy if Deloris didn't push me. Yeah, she definitely did. Look, I didn't know how to get in touch with Cynthia. At that point I didn't even know her name. But Deloris, frigging Deloris: "Call her for me. Do. Make it soon. See her number here."

I examined the paper. Cynthia's neat and tiny scrawl. Her fat *a*'s were made with peculiar loops in them, with a distinct backward lean in her lettering. She wrote like a little child.

I shouldn't have taken that job. I didn't know what I was doing. Although in a sense I did. Which is also why I should have told Deloris no.

Deloris never knew me to take a case if murder was involved. Most of the work that comes to our little firm is boring stuff. I came into the PI business different from all the other PIs I know in Jamaica. Most of them are ex-policemen who realized they could make more money working private than working for the government. But what they are good at is doing the work police are supposed to do for the legal system. They find witnesses, protect them; or they find a criminal that the police really want and arrange for them to be "caught"—that kinda work. Then, in addition to that, they do a little work for businesses.

Almost all my work is for businesses. You wouldn't believe how much spying go on for corporations in this country. Is boring work. Easy work. But I make it look hard to the clients them. Make them imagine me breaking into places at night and all that to find files, when most times I just find the cleaning lady and sweet her up and on a Saturday morning she let me in.

Be that as it may, I have a side business. When somebody looking for somebody else, anything liable to happen to the person who they are looking for. So I make it my side business to find the one they are looking for, and to find the one they want that one to meet, if you understand my meaning.

Killing is not really in me. It is around me though.

We Jamaicans are a truly murderous people. Can't deny it. We are. And in my work I see everything. My friends, the ex-policemen, the ones I used to work with before I form my own thing, they still give me the inside tip before anything reach the papers. Some things never reach the newspaper. So I know both the known and the unknown. I know about the people who nearly dead, as much as about the people who dead-dead.

I love this country, as I say, but it is a murderous place. When them boys murder that professor up in the hills some months ago, take that for instance. The man had his own cocky in his mouth when they find him. Two hundred and twenty-one stab wounds. None of it in the papers. "Police suspect foul play." Foul play is right.

People dead in this country for the simplest reasons. You can pay somebody five thousand Jamaican dollars—what, that is like ten dollars American, a few pound sterling—and he will kill a person for you, no questions asked. That is how easy it is.

That shake me up sometimes. How much killing goes on. But you know what work my brain the most? And maybe "work my brain" is not the right way to say it, but you will get what I mean. What always hold me is how much people don't know that killing is not easy.

You know how many people escape murder just because the killer get tired, or the killer change his mind, or the killer just can't understand how somebody is still living after they chop and beat him. Sometime the victim just run and run and get away. Sometime the victim beg for her life and get it. Sometime the killer find out that the victim is somebody they really know and so change their mind. One man had a gun and was to kill this woman, but he couldn't shoot her in the head because he felt it would hurt her, so he shot her in the stomach. Well, she never dead. That is how she lived. She said to him, "Not in my head, it will hurt too much." That is how she lived. So even though we are a murderous nation, the whole business is more complicated than people might think.

And even though I have been around a lot of murder in my life—dead body, killers, courtroom, police, that kinda thing—I never thought I could actually kill a person just so, not without some hatred or anger inside me. That is something I always thought about. I couldn't kill a person just like that, cold, calculated, and walk off. Not me.

But when Cynthia and I sat down in that restaurant smelling heavy with soy sauce and all kind of spices, I knew right then and there that I could kill without vexation, without being provoked. That I could kill for something like love.

Maybe this isn't coming out right. What I maybe mean to say is that I realized that I could kill for Cynthia.

I wouldn't kill for Deloris—not like that. This was clear to me. For Deloris, I would have to be vex, I would have to be under threat—like a man about to hurt me or her, and then maybe I would fight back and maybe that would kill the person. But for Cynthia Kendra Alvaranga, I knew I could kill a man, no questions asked, no fear. I could just kill him. And I would do that for love. Because what I was feeling for this woman, in that dark Chinese restaurant, was something like love.

Now, you might wonder how I know is love, but love is the thing that you can't really understand. I don't know this woman but already she was in my head, in my nose, in my mouth. Don't that must be love? Well, whatever it is, I could kill for that. And even though I didn't tell her this, I could tell that she knew. She knew.

The waitress asked us nice-nice, "Anything to drink,

please?" And I look at her and raise my eyebrow and wait. And she said, without even hesitation, "Gin and tonic."

I couldn't help myself, because I same time look at my watch and see it was one p.m., and I feel a sweetness in me. When the waitress look at me, I decided to try something, so I said, "Ting." And I look at Ms. Alvaranga like I was waiting for her to change her mind out of embarrassment or decorum or whatever, but all I get was dimple. Deep, beautiful dimple. So I smile and say, "With a lickle drop of rum." And we laugh for five seconds before the sadness and serious come back into her face. But I felt good because maybe what I had here was a drinker, and maybe that would be the way home for me.

The thing is, though, she only took one sip of that gin and tonic, and then no more for the whole two hours we sat there talking.

At first she didn't talk about herself. She wanted to know about me. What did she want to know? How I got into the business. She listened as I talked. I could see she was taking mental notes. By the time I finished blabbing she knew more than I thought I could tell anybody in such a short time. What she knew, well, she shouldn't know. Some things not even Deloris knew.

And I wasn't no police, or anything. The opposite. From I leave St. Andrew Technical in fifth form, after I never made the national youth cricket team, I realize that my life would only work hustling for everything I could get. So my background is criminal, of course. Well, I wouldn't directly call it criminal. Better to say illegal. I start supply the higglers with things from Panama, Dominican Republic, and eventually Miami. Soon I was traveling back and forth, buying and selling back, and that was fine. But then I start to manage the higgler and protect them. And next thing, elections coming around and a politician ask me to help him. So I touch up people, you know, but mostly I find the people anybody looking for. At first I was working for a politician in my area, and then somebody died. I was involve. I never do it but I was there. I was the one to find him, if you know what I mean. Well, things got too hot so they ship me to London for three years until things cool down. What actually happen was the politician lose the election and so he stopped sending me money, so I had to get back to Jamaica. When I reach back, a new party was in and they knew me as a man from the other party, so I couldn't find work.

Well, I run into one of my friend from school and that guy was working with his father business—selling panty or something such. It was one of the red boys who could do whatever he wanted in school because he had a work guaranteed for him after school. Anyway, the boy was just plain dunce. He was duncer than me, so you must know how bad it was. Anyway, when I run into him he ask me what I was doing, and I tell him I was just hustling, and I don't know what made me say it but I just put it to him simple: "Look, if you want to find anybody, anybody at all, just shout me. I can handle it cheap."

I was a fair man. I charge extra if I know what is going to happen to the person. I get pay in cash until I had an account set up.

By the time she told me *her* story, the ice in her glass had melted, my rum and Ting was done, my ice cubes chewed up as we talked, and all I could feel like was the most unworthy man in the world. She was no drunk, she was in control, and she was beautiful, and by the time we were finished, I knew that I would have to do whatever she asked me to do because, in truth, it would be the only instant in which she would need me. You wouldn't call that love?

Cynthia did not present her situation as a problem for me to solve. Nobody can claim that. She never ask me to do anything but one thing. She wanted me to find her husband. That was all she ask for.

But even though we sit down there eating and talking about serious things, the woman was so at ease with me. She laugh and smile. One time she ask me what she must call me.

As I say before, in Jamaica a woman like a big man. One who is prosperous, and show that he can be in charge. What I said was something like, "Call me what you want to call me," and leaned back with a smile to show her my confidence.

"But I don't know what to call you," she say, laughing again.

"All right, so what you think people call me normally," I ask her, like a tease.

"You mean, like, who?" She look a little confuse.

"Well, like the woman we see outside the restaurant selling orange."

"I don't know. I will just call you Mr. Detective, then," and I swear she was flirting with me.

Now she tell me a lot of things. I sat there and listen to everything she was saying—everything. The truth is that the whole situation was a piece of nastiness, and the man was the problem. But the way she tell me the whole thing, she made it sound like she want me to find him because he did not know what he was doing, and he need her to save him from himself.

"I have to tell you something that I can't tell anybody else," she said. And I tried not to look as if Deloris had already told the story to me. I didn't want the thought of Deloris in the room. "I have AIDS. Well, I am HIV positive. Me and my daughter. He gave it to us. Now you must know that I can't blame him for it. I mean, he said he only found out when I got tested for my application for the police training school. The coaching business I was doing at Ardenne High School gave me a little something, but it wasn't enough. And before the child, and before he lost his work, my teaching job at the business college was enough. You know, I teach a little math and accounting, and I was getting enough from that to make ends meet. And on top of that

I started to do a little investing. I was doing so well, you know. Careful, taking small risk. But honestly, I got a little greedy— that is how I would put it. You remember that scheme? They came to our church and told us that God was blessing people left, right, and center, and these people, people I trusted, people I went to school with, people from my church—all of them stood up at the altar and talk about how God bless them with this investment. Pressed down, shaken up, and flowing over. So I decided to put in my savings. And everything crash. Everything crash. Which is when I decided maybe the police was something I could try. I would get a little more money than the teaching and I could still coach.

"Well, they tested me, and I was positive. And I told him, and he started to get vex with me. He got tested and he was positive, and he continued with the vexation. But he knew the truth. And I told him, I told him to his face. I said, *Clarence, I come from nothing. You know where I grow up, you know how poor my people were, you know how I take my talent and run for my school and run for Jamaica and get scholarship to Nebraska and how I got my degree, and how I went and got pregnant careless and I had to come back to Jamaica. And you know how that whole thing took away my career as a sprinter. And you know how much I fought you when you said you want to marry me. How you tried and tried and begged and begged before I said yes. And I married you, and I decide to make my life with you. You know what I gave up for this, and you know that I have no reason to lie to you. You know that is not my style. You know I am not afraid of you, or any man. You know I don't take crap from nobody, especially you. So don't you dare lie to me, and worse, come accuse me of something you know I didn't do.*

"Well, he admitted it. What else was he going to do? She was a woman living in St. Elizabeth. He said she was sick. He found out she was sick, and he was worried but was afraid to check himself. He bawled, bawled the living eye water. And

I told him it was all right. And we decided to make it work. But after about a week, he started to talk the same foolishness again. Started to say that I deceived him, and that I brought this thing on him. I can't explain to you how two people could start to hate each other in such a short time. I can't explain how much nastiness came out of that man's mouth to me. I can't explain how he put his hand on me. I can't explain how he started to mistreat that girl, the same girl who he claimed he loved like his own daughter. The kinda nasty things he said to her, talking about how she is a dirty white bastard, and all kinds of sickness. And then what he did to her—touch her, force himself on her, and told her, told her to her face that he was doing it because I gave him this sickness and he wasn't going to let anybody that I love ever have a peaceful life."

She stopped talking at that point and just stared out the door to the parking lot like she was waiting for someone to walk in. When she start to talk again, it was like she was talking to herself.

"I have never told anybody this thing. Never. But that is what he did. That was the last thing he did before he left. He left me a note. He said he was going to kill himself and that I shouldn't look for him. He said that he had destroyed his life, destroyed the only person who ever loved him, and now he had destroyed the life of an innocent child. Mr. Brown, I can't tell you how hard it is for me to look at my daughter knowing that I brought this thing into her life. I brought this darkness into her life. She is positive. She might live a longer life than me. She might. But what kinda life is that?

"So tell me, am I so sick to start to worry about him, to wonder where he is, to wonder if he really is going to kill himself, to wonder who going to look after him when he gets sick? I can't tell anybody this thing. How can I tell anybody that I still love this man? Maybe it is not love, maybe it is something like a sickness that makes me think that me and him are now tied up in a way and we can't be separated. Me and him and my daughter. All I know is that I need to find him, and I want you to help me find him."

"Deloris say you want me to kill him," I said, the word coming out with difficulty because my throat was dry-dry.

"I never said that. I just said to her that he has done some things that no woman can forgive. I told her me and my daughter was sick because of him. I told her I needed you to help me find him. I never said I want to help him. I couldn't explain that to another woman. She heard what I said, and maybe the way she understood me, she conclude that is kill I want to kill the man. But that is not what I said."

It was enough for me. I agreed to find him. But deep inside me, what she said about him, about loving him, about being tied to him, that thing made me sick to my stomach. Not because I thought it was a sickness in her, but because I was jealous.

This was her flaw, and yet it was a flaw that pushed her further away from me. Right there, I wanted to find the man. Right there, I had a desire to do something evil to that man.

I could have started right away. In truth, I could have found that man in no time at all. But I have to say that after this lunch with her, I turned into a different man. I was behaving in ways that I knew was sinful and not right, but I walked into it same way, every step telling myself, man, you have to do better.

When we step out into the sunlight outside the restaurant, the woman selling orange just say casual, "Nice man, nice man. My Lord, buy the lady a orange, nuh. She look like she could eat a sweet orange."

Now, "My Lord" is what a man would normally call me, but some of them young girls start behave like man these days.

Cynthia smile. "My Lord," she say. "Buy me a orange, nuh."

And the way she say that, I know I was in trouble.

I pretend it was the glare making me rush for my shades. And when I walked that woman to the taxi place . . . imagining her naked body, sweating, moving over me, her breasts, her strong thighs, her batty—*Jesus* . . . Pushing through the crowd until I found one of my connections and give him some money, plus more, and tell him to take her to where she want to go as she protesting that she could just catch the bus, and all the noise around us, the traffic, the people chatting, the woman selling this and that, the bus and truck, the car horn, despite her protest, despite the world happening around me, all I could hear in my head was one thing: *I have to fuck you.*

For the next few days, all I did was scheme to do exactly that. Just to say it now fill me with such shame. I never used to talk about lovemaking like that. So why I was thinking that kinda language with her? Is not like say she was the kinda woman who use that kinda language. But I was entering a dark place, a place that was not really me.

I made a plan. A simple plan—make the search look like the hardest thing in the world, just like I used to do when a business hire me to steal information, and check in with her regular, and tell her things that was not really anything, not so much updates . . . that might not be the word . . . more like warnings . . . *I need to talk to you, off the cell phone, though . . . Best to talk in person . . . Hey, you don't know who might be watching you . . . I don't know . . . You can never tell . . . I know the drive long . . . With the toll on the causeway it should take me door-to-door a hour and mash.*

She lived out in Portmore, what was just beach and alligator swamp in the '70s when I was a boy. Quarter-million people out there now on the dump-up land looking over them shoulder for alligator—when it rain like is Florida them live.

She lived in one of the newer schemes out there in a regular hot two-bedroom flat prefab with a grill-round veranda add on.

At first that is where I'd give her the reports. She wouldn't really make me come inside. Maybe it was because the little girl was home on summer holiday. But that suit me fine because since the little girl couldn't hear, I could put forward some good arguments.

Now, they say self-praise is no recommendation, but when I think back I have to say that my argument them was good. Watch the ride: *I need some encouragement . . . My services are free, but a man could use a brawta now and then . . . I could search better if I could smell you on my lip all day . . . I wouldn't call it love, but all I know is you come in like you want to live inside my head all day . . . All I want is a little taste . . .*

So couple days of this went on, yes—at first I used to only go out there in the day time. I mean, Deloris wanted me to help Cynthia, but woman have instincts, and they get sharper when some suspicion give them the vague feeling you might want to be taking them for fool. So no vague feelings was going come from me to Deloris. So no regular nighttime visiting.

Until Deloris came to me in my office one afternoon looking kinda sad and say she sorry to give me short notice but she going to Miami to buy two new machine later on and she did mean to tell me before and she did mean to cook several meal for me that she could leave in the fridge, for she know me is a man who don't eat out a-road, and again she sorry for the short notice but could I cook for myself for one night while she gone . . .

As I'm saying this now is like I'm there . . . in Cynthia kitchen. Me and her face-to-face like we going dance a rent-a-tile tune. I can see everything like is right now . . . the two-burner stove, the pot of stew peas, the wall black up behind the stove . . . the Formica counter stain but clean-clean . . . the empty plate them on the table with a small slice of tomato still in mines . . . my belly full, the little girl sleeping.

Yeah man, everything was coming together nice, and so I time it good and put the argument to her. When I put it, this is what she said: "What, you don't believe me when I say I have AIDS?" And the way she say it, the serious way she say it, I knew right there that she was ready.

I wanted to say, *AIDS can't come between two people who love one another.* In my head she woulda took this as a joke, cause I woulda said it like a joke. I know how to do those things.

Be that as it may, I didn't joke it out though, I took it to her serious. I put my hand to her face and she flinch like she think I was going box her—reflexes, you know. And she lean against me heavy when my hand touch her skin, cause it touch her light-light. And when it touch her now she hug me up like she surprise, and is like her surprise make me feel my own kinda surprise. You know them kinda surprise there that make your hair lie down instead of stand up? Like say when you see a great cricketer make a late cut . . . pull back hard like him going rass a square cut through the gully, and when you expecting force now, him just take the hard-hard willow and feather-touch the ball through the slips. Or when a corporal in the off-key police band step forward in him white tunic and play one of them soft Latin tunes on him dull trombone.

Yeah man, certain kinda surprise make your hair lie down all over your body—at least that's how I feel it in my mind.

So no, I wasn't lying to anybody, least of all myself, when I brush my hand through Cynthia hair and say, "I believe you. And I know you done sort out how we can do it safe."

Cynthia didn't talk much while we was making love that night. Like most Jamaican woman she mostly moan and groan. Jamaica woman take sex serious—it's a thing I come to notice— sex and dancing, not too much laughy-laughy going on. Cynthia just moan. Anything more than that is one and two, "Uh-huh" and "Eeh-hee."

Cynthia talk loud with her body though. She drill me with it. Me, a man who think me know how to handle woman. Backside! Cynthia make me feel like a recruit. She handle me with efficiency and power, like she had to break me down and build me back up again to make me understand, in case I didn't understand before that I was her own.

Is only one time she talk. The whole time she talk only once. I was over her and she swing out her legs and wrap them around my back, and she put her two hands on my throat and put her mouth to one of my ears—that time her breath hot-hot—and say, "Men have done a lot of things for me, My Lord, but one thing"—her breath catch up, and her voice sink low—"one thing a man never do for me yet, My Lord. You know what it is?"

"No. What?"

"You know what it is?" This time her voice deep in her chest like she was shy. "No man ever kill for me yet, My Lord, no man. Oh Jesus!" Same time she grab me and start to tremble.

That was the seed. Plant like that. Simple, quiet. She never mention it again. But it take root inside me. Deep inside me.

Deloris till the soil and Cynthia do the planting. That's the truth. I've gone over this moment many times in my head and I understand it clear-clear now.

Be that as it may, fucking Cynthia didn't make me stop sleeping with Deloris. And a part of me feels like when she came back from Miami she must did know something happened because I was a different man. I picked her up at the airport and give it to her three times. And so it became every day after that, even in the office sometimes—just lock the front door and bend her over the sewing machine. I was really hungry for Cynthia but I couldn't have her. She kept telling me to wait. So Deloris got her share.

One morning as I was making love with Deloris in this same little cottage right here, she asked me if I find the man for Cynthia yet. And is like that question give me more strength. And it come in like she realize it or something, because after that, whenever she wanted me to put it on a certain way, she would mention Cynthia in my ears . . . like tell me that Cynthia call her to talk about the dress . . . or Cynthia call to ask her if she know anything about how the search for the husband going.

Did Deloris actually know? Like *know*? I don't really think so. The way I work it out is that she saw Cynthia as something damaged, and because I knew what that damage was, she was off limits to me. So thinking of Cynthia as damaged gave Deloris power over her. And if she have power over her, then it mean where Cynthia was concerned, she, Deloris, have power over me. And how she feel powerful now she start to get more confidence in herself and start to get out of order, even try one and two acrobatics in the bed. And when she start act like she want to rise up to me like this now, I felt I had to overpower her, break her down right back to where she was lower than me. And to do that I just had to imagine she was Cynthia. And this would get me murderous. And every push I push into Deloris was like I was giving her a stab.

One night, about a week of carrying on like this, I felt I had to tell Deloris I was in love. I just rolled over in the bed one morning and said it quiet and plain. No, it wasn't a week. It was more than that. About, say, nine days, because in truth I'd found out where the man was a few days before that.

Deloris get vex, of course, but what surprise me is when she never fight to keep me or nothing like that. No, sir. She just pack her things and leave. No, is lie. As she was closing her grip she say, "The woman out of your class, you know, Brownie? You is the biggest fool I know."

Yeah, that was kinda true.

Maybe, but I couldn't see that then cause here was my

thinking. Cynthia living with her daughter in that small dingy place in Portmore, and I know she made for better than that. I could see her comfortable in Constant Spring. Come up-town, live comfortable, me and she, put the girl in Immaculate, beautiful. Well Deloris had to leave for that to happen. And even though I never ask her to, well, to my mind she react perfect.

I wait to hear from Cynthia that Deloris call her or go by to fight her. But nothing like that happen.

So after a few days—a Thursday—I decide that it is time for me to seal the deal, as them say. I call Cynthia from the office and tell her I was going to find her husband over the weekend. I tell her I would come look for her Monday with all the information about him, and if she want I would take her to look for him on Tuesday. Then I tell her what I told Deloris. I was about to tell her that Deloris move out, but her reaction stop me. First I couldn't hear anything. Then she talk to me soft-soft.

"Why you do something like that, My Lord?"

"You know why."

"You shouldn't do that, My Lord."

"I had to . . ."

"You shouldn't do that," she say again. "No, you really shouldn't do that."

After that she never say a whole lot, so I promise her that she will understand and we will be all right. It wasn't the time to tell her how Deloris leave and how I already work out when she and the girl were going to move in. That would look too callous—like Deloris was disposable or something. I am not that kinda man at all. Now, if Deloris had started some foolishness, I would have to tell the woman, but Deloris, God bless her, deal with this thing with dignity, and the few times when I see her, is not vexation I see in her, but pity, a terrible kinda pity for me that was a new kinda punishment.

Be that as it may, at the time, I was in a zone. Love, man. Love. I hang up and start make plans.

Well, how did I find the man? Come on, that man wasn't difficult to find. Cynthia had done told me that he had family in St. Elizabeth. So all I had to do was to get to Santa Cruz, where she said his people was from, and the rest was easy.

I had some old police friends in the area. And when you're doing certain kinds of things you have to figure in the police. So I called my good squaddy One Drop one night and ask him to meet me at five the next morning in Santa. One Drop's name is really Wilson, but he's the kinda police that each time he has to draw his Glock, a man is going to fall.

So Drop met me outside a patty shop, in plainclothes as usual. Everything was closed. The place was still dark. But is country, so one or two goat and cow was loitering. We talked in the parking lot. Turns out he was looking for the husband too. It was one of the first things he said when the subject came up.

Some complaints had been coming in from prostitutes in Black River saying there was this man who was offering triple money for them to work without condom. Then when he was finished with them now, the man would just throw the thousand dollar on them belly and tell them to go get test for AIDS.

According to Drop, at least three of them come to him direct and tell him this personally. And when I say *personally*, just read between the lines and come to your own conclusion about what kinda relationship Drop as a police might be having with the prostitute them.

When Drop telling me about what the girls tell him, is like him start to laugh. When I ask him what was going on, him say that the idiot didn't know that most of the woman doing their business in Black River learn how to use female condom, so even though he thought him was getting a bareback ride, the woman them was well saddled.

Then Drop face change. Him look off toward the square, then down at him loafers, then look at me again.

Two of the younger girls, well, they was careless Ethiopians, and they never had the protection, and him blood really boil when they came to him.

Officially, if one of the girls test positive, the man was going get a murder charge. But between the two of us, Drop knew why the supe had put him on the case. Before that man dead him was going know what it was like to live without a cock or balls while rotting in prison for life.

So I laugh and told him how the man's wife hire me to find him because she was concerned about his health. I tell Drop that the way things look, maybe somebody was going to done the man before I could help him.

"Why you want to help a piece a shit like that?" Drop say.

"I work for pay. Woman hire me to save the man. So can't be helped."

And this is how you get police involve.

"Well, I going to find him before you, Brown," Drop said.

I laughed.

So who was going find him first? My skills is something that Drop respect. Five thousand Jamaican and a Chinese dinner. Wasn't no big bet.

The thing is, I knew I'd won already, because I knew where the fucker was, even how he was lying down, but Drop didn't need to know that.

You see, the day I went down to meet with One Drop was not the first time I'd gone down. I'd gone down there the day before, not to Santa Cruz up in the hills there, but way down south, even more south than Black River, down in a place name Treasure Beach. Down there is what you call real country. It don't even have a town. Is just red niggers, blue sea, and brown grass. The perfect place to get lost.

From what I had gathered through my intelligence, there was a routine to his days. Him would go out with the fishermen most mornings then spend the afternoons smoking weed on the beach till night. Then when night come now, him would catch a taxi down to Black River or even go as far as Montego Bay to do his work.

I ask a big-belly man with the smoothest skin you could ever see and some wild stick-up sea-salt rusty locks—fellow they call Boops, who used to be a serious fisherman but decide to use his boat for sightseeing for tourist and excursion up Black River from the sea—if he knew where the man was. He said the man was at the rocks this morning, but catch a ride with one of the tourist excursion up river and soon come back.

Well, I waited and when the boat come back the man was not in it, but the captain of the boat told me that he left the man by the shrimp dock a few miles up river. He said that the man sometimes just stay up there for the night because he had a woman there.

So I ask Boops to give me a run up the river, and I promise to pay for gas and a little something.

We move out as the sun dropping down behind the sea. We head out south like we going to Venezuela, then turn west and follow the coast until we come to the sweet-and-salt coolness of the river mouth. Boops push the boat toward the river mouth past where one of those flat-bottom tourist boat and a few fishing boat was dock.

A light mist take over the river when we motor past the white hanging roots of the mangrove that look like some gray dreadlocks. Long shadow and orange light everywhere you look. The ibises already crowd out the riverbank for the night.

In a bend in the river, I could make out a jetty, a rough-up cement-floor gazebo, and a narrow brick bungalow with about three little storefronts where they cook and serve the shrimps. Most days about five or six people cook and sell shrimp and bake crab from there. Only a fat woman cleaning up the place for the night was left.

And there he was—the man. Sitting under a almond tree smoking a cigarette and eating shrimp from some foil. Boops guide the boat against the jetty, and both of us climb up onto the concrete landing, and while I sat down on one of the wooden bench, Boops tie up the boat and walk behind the shop to piss.

I was watching the man who barely look around when we slide in. He was short. Red-skinned. The most ordinary, pimple-face man you would ever see. His hair was low-low on his head, and you could see the balding start already. He wasn't a fit man or anything. He was not the kinda man I did expect to see.

Boops walk around from the side and come sit beside me. The man watch Boops moving past like he really in a different world. It is then that he look at me like he want to ask what I was doing in his kingdom, and right away I know why my spirit never take to this man. Disdain. Like the man have disdain for everything around him. This one is not pride, self-assurance— them is good things. This one is disdain, like him is better than everybody else. I don't like those kinda people. And worse, when you red and disdainful, you have no basis but that you might a be a lucky sperm that make a move in a certain time in history. Nothing that you have done.

"Mr. Alvaranga?"

"Who asking?" He spit out a shrimp shell in his hand and throw it on the ground. "I say, who asking?"

"No problem, sir. You have answered my question."

As I start to walk back to the boat, hear him, "Who the rass is you, anyway?"

I turn my head sideways to talk behind me. "Nobody, boss-man. Not a damn soul. You know what? Call me Duppy."

Boops laugh out.

"Hey, Boops, who the rass is this man? Why you bring him out here for?"

"Take it easy, Alva. Him say him have a message from your wife." Boops look at me as if to say I must do what I said I was doing.

"She just want to know you living and healthy," I explained.

"Fuck the bitch!" he shouted. "Boops, don't do that again or I will fuck you up myself."

Boops laugh and start up the boat.

While we were going back down river toward the sea, Boops tell me that sometimes Alvaranga sleep in one of the shacks on the landing.

So, when I'd called One Drop to meet me in Santa Cruz, I was calling from Treasure Beach. Not Kingston. As I said, I already knew where the man was before I made the bet, even how he was lying down.

I called Cynthia with the news two days later. I needed time to clear my head. I was in Kingston, driving out to the airport to meet a rep for an airline that wanted to know when a rival was going to change its fares. The harbor was gray and choppy on my right and the hills dusty on the far side of it and the city, spreading and rising up and up killing itself one person at a time every two or so hours.

I didn't tell her anything about anything when she picked up. Just small talk. I wanted to give her the news in person, more like in her person. I wanted to be saying, *I did it for you, baby. I did it for you. Is you me done the fucker for*, as she made me come.

One Drop call me as I was waiting for my contact in a far

end of the parking lot. Hear him: "You owe me five thousand and a lo mein."

"For what?"

Him say, "How you mean?"

I turn down the radio. "So you arrest him?"

"Arrest him?"

"Yeah. You say you find him."

"The man dead, My Lord. Dead. One shot in the head."

"You too rass lie. So what you think, the AIDS fly up in him head or him conscience bite him and him commit suicide?"

"It don't look so—"

"So is you supposed to find that out or them bringing in a sense man from town?"

"Fuck you. Me know more than most of them little guys who call themself investigator. All them do is go on a little three-month course to England and come back like them is anything. Me learn more than them from *CSI* to bloodclaat."

And we laugh for bout two minute.

"So you feel is kill himself?"

"Yeah man. A man can't do that kinda fuckery and live with himself."

"So you can't get my money then. I catch you. You bugger you."

"You see how you stay?"

"Just cool, man. Your dinner safe with your money."

"Me no bet for lose, you know, Brownie." One Drop is a man like to boast sometimes. "Me no bet for lose."

"So how you find him?"

"One of my sources. You know how that go. Find him down by the shrimp place on Black River, few miles up from the coast. The body lay out on the ground like it was in a coffin, tidy, with a pillow under the head."

I went over the night in my mind: I came back by land.

Drove along the coast road then up into some hills then across some little dirt roads then walked down a track to the back of the jetty.

"So what about the next of kin and all that?" I asked, squeezing the button of the hand brake. "You wrap up in that too?"

"As a matter of fact, that is why I called you. Since you know her and she hire you, I thought you might want to tell her for me. Ease things a little. I can arrange for someone to call her later, but you going to see her, yes?"

"Yeah, I can tell her. But make sure the station call. Just to make it official."

I rang Cynthia with the news right after me and One Drop hung up. She sounded afraid—nervous. I asked her what happen, baby, and she said some policeman came by there and asked her about her husband. I asked her what she told him. She said she was afraid. I asked her where she was.

I could hear she was in her car so I tell her don't go home. Meet me. She said her daughter was at home so she had to go there. I asked if the child was there too when the police come, and she said yes, that the little girl was traumatized by all the guns.

How much of them was there? Did she remember any of the names? Was there a Wilson? She asked me where I was. I said out by the airport. I asked her if the police told her anything or if they just asked questions. She said just questions. When I asked for more information, she said we had to talk off the air, so I should come and meet her at home and drive fast-fast.

I called the airline rep and lied.

As I headed to Portmore, I kept thinking of how I felt when I went back to the jetty, the way the man sighed when he got the shot, and how it felt so indecent to leave him there like a cement bag, and how his body was still warm through the gloves when I moved his legs and arms and put the pillow under his shattered head in an attempt to fix him up.

My body was trembling as I was driving. By the time I got to the power station out by Rockfort I had to stop the car on the roadside.

I still remember the smell and taste of that vomit. A lump of it got stuck to the wall of my throat. I had to keep swallowing and swallowing to get it down.

Killing people is not a easy thing. I know I might be repeating myself. Is not a easy thing, sir. Who to tell? Maybe some people do it and sleep good at night. But not me. Killing has marked me for life.

Did I know I'd feel this when I went back to the jetty? I did. But sometimes you just have to do what you have to do, and when you finish doing it you fully consider the price. Otherwise you won't get it done.

I reached Portmore at around four o'clock, just when the traffic from Kingston start to get thick. It is strange how you can know when something wrong just by looking at a place. Or maybe this is something you tell yourself to feel wise when you looking back at a moment when you were clearly a fool.

There wasn't anybody in the place. I knew this right away. But it took maybe half a second to accept say Cynthia and her daughter never just gone down the road to the shop. The place vacate. The curtain them was gone. I knock on the grill with a stone.

Then I saw a envelope pushed between the bars. It had my name on it, and I couldn't miss her handwriting—just like a little child.

I opened it quick-quick. One sheet of paper. The note was short and simple:

Thank you, My Lord. I knew you would do this for us. I knew it when I asked you to help me, I knew it when you hold my body that you would do anything for me. So I don't

have to ask. I just have to say thank you. I am only telling
you that we left Jamaica and we're not coming back, so you
know we are fine. Thank you for everything. Take care.
Sincerely,
Cynthia

p.s. Your finder's fee is at Western Union.

Strange, to me at least, I didn't think of being abandoned
or that I'd messed up my life. What came to me was the first
time I'd seen Cynthia in my office. When she was standing just
inside the door and she noticed me looking at her, she gave me
a soft tired smile, and I could see the full white perfection of her
teeth, and a deep dimple in her right cheek.

That strong body. Those legs—long and firm and black and
shine with lotion. The dress hem up above her knee. Her shoe
heel was scrape down to almost nothing on one side though,
and the perm in her hair was soon going gone.

A lot of feelings come with this memory—some of it bitter-
bitter, some of it regretful, but the feeling that always wash over
me, despite everything else, is a sweetness. It is the kinda sweetness you keep in your pocket, and when things start to get bad,
you pull it out like a kerchief, and take a deep breath from it,
and it send you back to a place where, just for a little moment,
the world could never be sweeter. Nobody can't take that from
me, that is the truth.

My Lord . . .

THE WHITE GYAL WITH THE CAMERA

BY KEI MILLER

August Town

It was when the papers come out with the gyal's picture print big and broad on the front page that August Town people did find out her rightful name. Marilyn Fairweather. It sounded right. It sounded like a white woman's name. But for the six days she had been in August Town we had just called her "the white gyal with the camera." Or "the white gyal" for short.

She get the name because whatever Soft-Paw say we take it as gospel, and is Soft-Paw did send out word that if anybody see "the white gyal with the camera" we was not to trouble her; we was to leave her alone. But is like the white gyal with the camera never know or understand this—that she was living on grace—that if Soft-Paw never send out such a word she woulda dead from day one.

You had to give it to the white gyal though—is like she never have a coward bone in her body. She take a plane to Jamaica and in my books that alone count as bravery. Pretty blond girl on her own in the heart of Jamdown? Who ever hear of such a thing? But this white gyal take it further. Instead of staying at one of them hotels in New Kingston where she could order rum and Coke all day and listen to jazz in the gardens, or in a nice little apartment in Barbican or Liguanea, she did decide to rent a room right here in August Town.

It was one of them little rooms with its own kitchen and

everything. Miss Tina usually rent it out to university students, for UWI was just a ten-minute walk up the road. But it was July so the room was empty.

The white gyal did knock on Miss Tina gate after midnight, which of course did upset Miss Tina who was fast asleep, but she confess that she was glad for the chance to rent out the room, even for just a week, and seeing that the gyal was white, Miss Tina make sure to charge what she would usually charge for the whole month. You know how these things go. Still, Miss Tina tell the white gyal that August Town wasn't the safest place, but it come in like the white gyal with the camera wasn't interested in safety.

When Miss Tina fall back asleep, the white gyal take up her camera and walk straight into the baddest part of town. Imagine that—the time of night when we all have the doors close tight; the time of night when who don't come in yet not coming in at all; the time of night when we make sure to fall asleep on a low-low mattress because nobody want to sleep so high that a stray bullet could come inside and find us; the time of night when the only people walking on the street was gun-man or duppy—is that same time when the white gyal with the camera choose to go back out. They say a fool will walk where angels fear to trod, and the white gyal with the camera was such a fool as that.

Soft-Paw and the bwoy-dem was out there in the night, and to see them would make even a big man tremble, the way their trousers' pockets was big with guns. As to how I hear it, Soft-Paw and the bwoy-dem begin to notice when all of a sudden a light start to flash bout them. They think maybe it was lightning and they look up into the sky to see if rain was going to fall. But the sky was clear as glass and full of stars. The light start to flash bout them again and now they hear a clicking noise and they cannot believe they eyes when they turn round to see this bra-

zen white gyal lie down on her belly in the middle of the road
pointing her camera up at them like a solider with a gun.

Soft-Paw, being the leader, step away from the others and
start to walk to her slow and dangerous-like. The white gyal just
smile and get to her feet and brush down her skirt and start to
fiddle with the camera. Easy-easy, like she don't know she was
somewhere she not supposed to be. When Soft-Paw reach up to
her she turn the Nikon to him and show him the little screen
and she tell him, "Look!"

Now, Soft-Paw is not a kind of man you supposed to ever
give instructions to. Everybody know that. But he so surprised
by this situation, he so surprised by the whole night, that he
look. The white gyal start to flick through, going from picture
to picture, showing Soft-Paw the photos she had been taking.

Soft-Paw see photograph of himself lean up against the zinc
fence and talking to the bwoys, the angle making it seem that
the zinc was rising and rising forever. He see photograph of an
owl, pale and bright on the roof of Miss Inez house. He see photograph of the old car that was rusting for years just at the end
of the road. Soft-Paw face don't give away anything but I gather
now that he was thinking he never before see August Town in
the way that he was seeing it then—almost beautiful. And the
white gyal with the camera looking at him with a look that say
he was almost beautiful too. He smile at her, his teeth brown as
rust except for the one gold tooth glittering at the back. He ask
her, "What you doing here?"

And his question was soft. Usually when him ask this question, him ask it hard, like the night last year when they did see a
young fellow from the university on the road. Is like this fellow
did loss him way. Soft-Paw walk up and ask the same question,
"What you doing here?" and the boy did stammer and a circle
of piss did spread cross the front of his trousers. The bwoy-dem
did laugh. Soft-Paw face never change. Soft-Paw just flick out

a knife and push the blade into the young man's back, not so deep that it could kill him, but deep enough. The fellow bawl out loud. I remember the scream. But they say Soft-Paw never flinch and he run the knife down the back like he was opening a woman's dress. The fellow bawling like he give up all hope on life, but Soft-Paw tell him calmly, "Leave this bloodclaat place and never come back." You see what I trying to tell you? It is a dangerous thing to be where you not supposed to be.

So maybe the white gyal with the camera don't know that Soft-Paw's question could have been put to her in a hard and dangerous way. She never piss herself or nothing. She just say to him, "I am here for one week to take . . . photographs." She touch the camera when she say "photographs" as if she did need to touch it to remember the word. She had a funny way of talking, an accent none of us could place. She say to Soft-Paw, "I think you have a really, how do you say, lovely place here." And she lift up her head and look all around and smile a smile that would make you think she was standing in the middle of fucking paradise—and mind you, Jamaica can be paradise when it want, like those times when you standing on a white beach looking at the moon sinking below the coconut trees. But this white gyal wasn't on no beach. She was in August Town. She was in the heart of the ghetto, but she was smiling.

"You don't work for no police or nothing like that?" Soft-Paw ask.

She look at him with the most serious look she have all night. She touch herself on her chest. "I work for me. For myself alone. What I do is—it is art. I am not, how do you say, informer. No. That is not me."

Soft-Paw nod. "All right then," he say. "Do what you doing, but protection going to cost you. Hundred dollars a day. Hundred U.S. dollars. And a next thing: before you leave, you will have to show me all the pictures that you take. Is me who run this place. You understand? Me is the community leader, and I don't want you take no picture that we wouldn't like. You get me?"

She agree to this and so Soft-Paw send out word that if anybody see "the white gyal with the camera," they was not to trouble her. They was to leave her alone. The next morning when we get this word we all start to wonder: who the hell is this white gyal with this damn camera?

All day next day we was wondering so till we start to make joke that this so-called white gyal with her so-called camera must be some sort of vampire. What other kind of person would sleep during the entire day like she fraid of sun? Not a squeak nor a squawk from her during morning, midday, or afternoon.

In the evening when we all gather in the square as we always do, it was that time when Miss Tina tell us she actually set eyes on the white gyal with the camera, and that she was staying in the student room in her own yard. Miss Tina tell us how the white gyal did wake her up late the night before, and she herself couldn't believe that the white gyal did go out after that and meet up with Soft-Paw and the bwoy-dem.

One of the fellows start run joke and ask Miss Tina, "So you rent out you room to a vampire?"

Miss Tina, who at times could be a real jokified woman, smile and tell us that actually, just now as she was leaving the yard, she did in fact see a soft and unearthly light coming from under the door of the white gyal room.

Sister Doris, who go to the Bedward church, whisper, "Sweet Jesus!" when she hear that, though we who have more sense did know that it was probably just light from a computer. I would have said as much but when Miss Tina done her story, Bongo Collie arrive with another.

Bongo Collie report and say that just just now as him was

walking to the square, he walk by Miss Tina house and see the white gyal there himself! And that she did frighten him bad—big horse-steering rastaman though he was. He say at first he never see her sitting there on the veranda, she was so quiet, but then a small fire from nowhere light up her face. Poor Sister Doris almost faint that time.

Bongo Collie explain that this did make him nearly jump out of him skin, but he soon realize it was just a matches stick the white gyal did strike. She was lighting herself a cigarette. She look straight at Bongo Collie, and nod to him, very familiar-like, and he nod back but he say he couldn't help but think to himself—this white gyal is more than she appear.

And it was the kind of evening where you expect that as Bongo Collie done with him story, another story would arrive just like that. But even better than that. The white gyal herself did arrive. We get to see her with our own eyes. My dears, she just walk into the square like it was home, and like all of we and she was friend, and Sister Doris shake her head and make the sign of the cross.

But I have to tell you the truth. We all warm to the white gyal quick, for it turn out that she was a talkative and pleasant young lady. She even sit down with Miss Tina and Bongo Collie and Sister Doris, and she sit down with me as well, and it feel like we talk bout every godalmighty thing, though afterward I couldn't tell you what me or she did say.

Now and again she would lift up her camera to take a picture, but she would do it so quick and natural-like, without any announcement. And it was like the camera wasn't really there, and nobody feel the need to pose or model or be anything but themselves.

What make we know that this white gyal was really all right though was when she go over to the table where them old fellows was playing dominoes. The white gyal walk round in a slow circle from hand to hand, watching the game intense-like, like she trying to understand. The four fellows probably feel it was only polite to ask her if she wanted to play a round. They ask even though this white gyal had two things going against her— namely that she was white, and also that she was a gyal. A white gyal playing dominoes was even worse than a white gyal try- ing to shake her flat batty to Vybz Kartel or Beenie Man: them things wasn't normal; them things couldn't ever look right.

Well, the white gyal start to play and I tell you, I nearly fen- neh! What you think happen? In two twos this white gyal with the camera was slamming down tile like she really understand what she doing, and when Maas Delroy who was her pardy make a bad move, she cuss him blue from cross the table and ask him if he never read the game proper and see that is she have all the S them in her hand, and how he should have did play five-deuce and block the game from three moves back and how she woulda did win if him did only use him head and do that. And when she say all of that, everybody was quiet-quiet, and we all now thinking what Bongo Collie did think earlier— that this white gyal was more than she appear.

Make me be the first to confess it was a stupid thing to think. For what else we could expect? We did call her "the white gyal with the camera" but she had to be more than that. She had to have her own story, but is like it was a story no one did think to ask bout. For all the talk we did talk to her, we never get to know her. We only get curious after the bad thing happen—after she get her picture in the front page of the news- paper and we suddenly start call her Marilyn as if to say we did really know her all along.

Every night in August Town is a warm night, which is why we like to gather outside. But when it is coming on to midnight— the time when we know that Soft-Paw and the bwoy-dem will come out on the scene—we will begin to pack up from the square and go into our yards and close the doors tight and make sure to fall sleep on a low-low mattress, safe from stray bullets. For to see Soft-Paw during the day is one thing. In the daytime he is our neighbor. But to see him at night when him on the turf is another thing all together. The whole of August Town becomes his office, and you must never disturb a man from his work.

That first night when we saw the white gyal, we begin to leave at midnight as usual. We ask her if she wasn't turning in as well but she shake her head, a simple no, like she was quite happy to be out there by herself. More and more, she was lifting the damn camera to her eye, aiming at God-he-knows-what, snapping more and more pictures.

Miss Tina even ask her, "You ever go to sleep at all?"

The white gyal look on Miss Tina and tell her, "Not very much. I try to sleep during the day, but I am—how do you say it—light sleeper. I wake up at everything. But at nighttime like now, I am wide awake."

Hmph. That is the sound that Miss Tina did make as she walk off, and when Miss Tina did tell me this, I did make the same sound too. I tell you already, at a certain hours of night or morning, is only gunman and duppy supposed to be on the streets. We all know who the gunmen was. That was Soft-Paw and the bwoy-dem. So maybe the white gyal with the camera was practicing to be a duppy all along.

As to how the bwoy-dem tell it, for the six nights that the white gyal was here in August Town, there would always come a time, maybe at two or three o'clock, when they would see her before she did see them. Soft-Paw would walk up behind her, not making a sound. That is how he get his name. He would touch her suddenly, maybe on the back of her neck, and the bwoy-dem was always surprised to see that the white gyal never ever jump or look frighten or catch her breath. And they did even respect her a little too for this. But they notice something else—that she would seem to even relax at Soft-Paw's touch, like she was ready to lean back slow, if only him would press into her and hold her right there—something romantic like that. No romance did ever happen, but the bwoy-dem say it did always have that feeling.

Without turning round, the white gyal with the camera would reach into her pocket and take out a crisp green hundred-dollar bill and hold it up for Soft-Paw.

Soft-Paw would take the money and push it deep into his own pocket. Then he would ask her, "How tings?"

"Fine, yes. It is good. I am getting the pictures."

"Let me see?" And Soft-Paw was really asking. It wasn't his usual way of giving orders. It was like he was really interested.

She would turn the camera screen to his face then, and flick through the pictures. Soft-Paw see that she was getting everywhere in August Town. He see pictures that look like she was standing in the middle of the riverbed down by the part of town they call Angola, the moonlight showing how the houses on the bank was close to falling in the sand. He see pictures from outside Judgment Yard, the red and green and yellow flags flapping in the night as if it was a balmyard and a cure for deep sickness was inside. And he see pictures of the actual balmyard—Bedward's church. Bedward was that mad fellow who say he was going to fly. And then there was pictures of the plain and empty road, and pictures of the standpipe dripping water, and pictures of the old men in the square playing dominoes, and of Miss Tina standing under a streetlight looking at her red fingernails. And apparently Soft-Paw did sound almost sad when he tell the bwoy-dem that he had a feeling like he would love to always see August Town through the lens of the white gyal's camera, because he see things that he never see in all his twenty-nine years—a kind of loveliness in the people and in the place.

And I even understand there was more than one picture of me.

Every day and every night was the same until just like that, six of them pass and we know is only one more to go before the white gyal with the camera leave.

And all that week it seem that Soft-Paw wasn't himself, and every day him wasn't himself a little bit more. And maybe he just had a feeling growing inside him, a feeling he wasn't used to having, like he was bout to lose something, something more than the hundred U.S. the white gyal was giving him every night.

Well, on the sixth day everybody see that Soft-Paw was in a right foul mood. He was walking up and down August Town in the middle of the day like he on a rampage. When he see a mongrel dog, he kick it in its ribs. When he pass a clothesline with the just-washed clothes hang out to dry, he flash out his knife, cut the line, and make all the clothes drop back in the dirt. Soft-Paw must did know in himself that this kind of behavior is what you expect from some rude pickney—is not big-man behavior; is not even gunman behavior. Soft-Paw had to get control of himself, so he walk to the door of each of the bwoy-dem and knock loud-loud until they was all gathered together, rubbing their eyes, for they not used to seeing each other in the broad daylight.

The bwoy-dem ask him what was the matter so he tell them what I gather is the truth: "Is the white gyal with the camera!"

The bwoy-dem confused. They ask him, what bout the white gyal? And this time he tell them what seem to be a truth mix up with a lie, mix up with another truth, mix up with another lie. You couldn't separate one from the other. He tell them that though he had a good feeling about the white gyal, he never get to where he was, nor did he get away with all that he did get away with, by trusting people. He tell them he couldn't leave it to the white gyal to come to him later that night with all the pictures for him to inspect. He had to inspect the pictures before. It was important. For who to tell what kind of pictures she did really take. It could be bad things. Incriminating things. They had to get the camera from the white gyal before she had a chance to hide things.

Soft-Paw sound so convincing and passionate and like their whole world depend on this that the bwoy-dem nod yes and feel that nothing in this world more important than getting that camera. But Soft-Paw tell them to easy. Easy. He don't want to stir up anything just yet. All he want is the camera. And I think when Soft-Paw say that, him was telling the truth again. For sometimes you grow up in a place like August Town and you get so damn used to life being hard and everything being unfair and to seeing the worst in every situation, that when you see a spot of beauty, you just want to hang onto it, you just want to sit down with it and admire it, and that is why him was in a foul mood, because him never want to stop seeing the white gyal's pictures just yet.

The bwoy-dem nominate Ants to go and get the camera. They call this fellow Ants because of how he could walk up a wall and get inside a building as easy as any insect. If you show Ants a house that have no windows and no doors—just four walls and a ceiling—he would only need to walk round it one time before he figure out six or seven different ways to get inside. With Ants, tiefing wasn't a crime; it was a talent. They say Ants could tief the black from off your skin and you wouldn't feel a thing.

Remember the white gyal with the camera tell Miss Tina that she was a light sleeper? Well, Ants could tief lighter than the lightest sleep. Is like Ants don't need to hear snoring or deep breathing to know that somebody is dreaming; is like he could feel it and become part of the sleep and know how to walk round it and not disturb it. So Ants stay outside the white gyal room and when him feel her sleep and become part of it, it was then that he break the locks careful and let himself in.

The white gyal with the camera, he realize then, even sleep with the camera, her fingers tight round it. And she sleep naked too, her skin white as milk, and one heap of blond hair curl up round her pussy. On another day Ants might have done something bad, but he leave her alone. He take her fingers off the camera that he was going to give to Soft-Paw, and for himself and his troubles he take all the cash from out her wallet, and the phone from out her pocket.

Listen—it is not a nice thing for a woman to wake up one evening and to know that a man was in the same room as she and is not she did let him in. It is not a nice thing for a woman to know she was sleeping naked and that a man did stand up over her and she never know or feel his presence. It is not a nice thing for a woman to wake up and know that something bad could have did happen, and it don't matter if that bad thing don't happen—I telling you, it is not a nice feeling to know you was close to such a thing because you still get the taste of it.

I feel shame when I think bout it. Imagine, this white gyal with the camera come to Jamaica and maybe her friends did tell her not to go, but she come. And then this white gyal live with us for six days in a ghetto which not supposed to be safe, but she did feel safe. But all of a sudden she not feeling that no more. And this white gyal with the camera who did come to Kingston city and had seen something beautiful in all of us, all of a sudden everything was looking ugly. Is like the white gyal did just want to get out of that room. She stumble out the door and into the evening, and she don't stop to put on no clothes. The streetlight making her skin look even whiter than it was, like she was really a duppy, but none of it matter, none of it fucking matter no more. The white gyal out there in the streets of August Town, shaking and shaking, and then she scream, worse than how that boy from the university did scream last year. The white gyal scream.

Everybody hear it. Even Soft-Paw, from where he was, did hear it. And though for everyone else that scream did put a chill in our bones, for Soft-Paw it put a smile on his face. But listen—is not because he did take any pleasure in her distress, but because he was thinking he could make it all right. He seen the pictures now. He seen them slowly and carefully. And he realize that is all he wanted. He just wanted to look on August Town, look on how nice the place was, how it just had something to it, and how that something was in everybody. Now he could give the camera back to the white gyal, and he could tell her all was well. He could wish her safe travels. He could tell her to walk good, and walk with God.

We who was in the square and did hear the scream was walking toward Miss Tina house, and when we get there we see her—the white gyal without her camera, without any clothes or anything, standing in the middle of the road, under the streetlight that make her look like a duppy. She did see us coming, all of August Town, and the look on her face say that she never see a set of people so ugly in all her life. I did feel sick to see the look she give we. And maybe she wonder to herself if it was only now, after six days, that she was seeing the truth—seeing the place for what it was. Seeing us for who we really was. And maybe she thinking she been in Jamaica for six days, but is only now that she really arrive.

The white gyal was crying now. "Stay away from me! Stay away!" And she fanning us off and shouting and shaking, and we was thinking, Lord have mercy! The white gyal gone crazy! She gone stark raving mad. We form a circle round her not knowing whether to advance or to stay back. We was just watching her, and she was just watching us. Sister Doris start to pray, and then she start to sing, and some of the other women join in, but the white gyal just keep shaking and crying and looking at us like we was the devil.

And then Soft-Paw come. The crowd part for him. Soft-Paw have the white gyal camera in his hands and he holding it up for her to see. He smiling like as if to say he was Jesus come to save her. And it was another warm night in August Town. The sky was clear, and the stars was like glass, and we could hear the low river eating away at the banks of Angola. And Sister Doris with her eyes close tight was humming the tune, *The word of the Lord is a strong tower, the mighty run into it and they are saved.* Soft-Paw walking toward the white-gyal now, but she looking at him terrified-like, and her eyes say that she was finally seeing the man that most people see—a man with a hard face, a man with teeth as brown as rust except for the one gold tooth glittering at the back, a man who was more dangerous than most. And the streetlight shining on her was making her look not just white, but transparent, like a piece of tissue. And the blond hairs curl up round her pussy look white as well. And it come to me that I never see before that she was such a small thing.

Soft-Paw smiling and he ask her, "What wrong wid you, white gyal? Why you going on so for? Nothing to worry bout. See your camera here. You can have it back."

The white gyal shout at Soft-Paw, "Stay back! Don't touch me!"

Soft-Paw laugh a strange laugh and he step forward.

"NO!" the white gyal shout at him. "I say stay back!"

She was crying now. Crying hard like when little pickney can't find them mommy. This small gyal with her skin like tissue. And then she was looking up at this bigger black man, like him was the ugliest man in the world, and Soft-Paw must have seen it too. He have to see that something did gone from her eyes, and I wonder if he know that is he who take it from her.

Soft-Paw now raising his voice and saying, "Calm down, white gyal! Calm down." He make another step toward her. "See your camera here." He try to hand it over. "Just take the bloodclaat camera and stop the cowbawling!"

The white gyal in a awful state now. A awful, awful state. She box the camera out of Soft-Paw's hand. It fall on the ground and break. It make a sound like it was the only sound in August Town that night. Like even the river did stop. And those who was praying stop praying. And those who was singing stop singing. And I don't know why, but we all did jump back when the camera break—and then we look down on all its pieces like we was looking at a dead body.

The white-gyal staring up at Soft-Paw. She trembling. And my dears, who to tell why she do it, but she box him in him face. Box him, right there in front of all of we. And you could suddenly hear the river again. And I believe, for a small while, we could even hear the stars. And all of we was just standing there, holding our breaths.

TOMCAT BERETTA

BY PATRICIA POWELL

New Kingston

Mita landed in Kingston at three and instructed the cabby to take her to the Courtleigh . . . Knutsford Boulevard . . . New Kingston.

A slip of paper with the addresses and names was getting damp in her bra. She gazed out the window at the glittering sea, trying hard to relax, but it was impossible. The sea hugged the side of the flat smooth road for miles until it cut away from the sea altogether and became narrow and rutted and cars swerved dangerously past the meager little houses leaning shoulder to shoulder. Soon they were in the heart of midtown in slow-moving traffic, the sidewalks overflowing with people, and floors and floors of office windows climbing to the sky.

At the hotel, she paid cash up front for a week, hung out the *Do Not Disturb* sign, and slipped into bed.

It was night when she woke. The room was dark and her throat was dry. She sat up, lowered her feet to the floor, unsure of how much time had passed, unsure of where she was. Her toes were tense. They'd become used to concrete. They cringed against the carpet, then relaxed. Fuck. How long had she been asleep?

She showered, oiled her scalp until it shone—the head was still shaven—slipped into a shimmering black dress that hugged her curves, and gashed her lips with burgundy.

Downstairs in the lobby there was a band of old timers playing ska. Couples danced close by the pool. Around the corner was the bar. People were laughing and talking loud and smoking and drinking there. Dense clouds of smoke hung heavily around their heads. She elbowed her way up to the counter, ordered two shots of Appleton back to back, swallowed them down swiftly, and nursed the third while studying the bartenders. There were three of them, all wearing sparkling white shirts and black trousers. She was looking for the one named Ralph. She'd been told he had a runaway eye. When she spotted him, she waved him over, ordered a plate of cow foot stew.

This Ralph did not look anything like his uncle Gracie, she thought. He wore a big badge of a mustache and he was attractive and flirtatious and when he smiled he showed all his teeth and they were big and magnificent and bright. She paid him in cash and when he handed back her change, she clamped his hand with hers. She eased her mouth to his ear. I need a gun right away, she said. Fear creamed from the pores on his hot cheek. She could smell it. His hand stirred, shivered. She held it down. He dragged it. She let go. He straightened up and glowered. The runaway eye began to roam along the wall behind her. The other one fixed her like a nail.

Who the fuck you is? he said, without moving his lips. The ridiculous little badge over his mouth trembled.

I'm Gracie's friend, she said, taking care to sound and look at ease. Gracie in San Francisco. He sent me to you. He said you'd . . . know . . .

Gracie, he said, looking her up and down. His face was tense. You know Gracie? Gracie no dead?

He's in prison, she said.

His cheeks bagged a little.

I need it right away, she said, sliding an envelope toward him. Tomorrow morning first thing. Her voice was low and hard. Room 211. She did not look at him again. She slipped off the stool and stepped out, her shoulder blades drawn tight.

A man in a dark shirt who had been eyeing her eased up from his seat at the bar, laid out a few dollars on the counter, and trailed her outside into the courtyard.

The night was black and there was neither moon nor stars in the sky, just the unbearable heat settling down heavily on her face and bare arms and blotching her dress at once.

When the man appeared beside her she said nothing to him, and he said nothing to her. But she could feel his gentle presence right away and her shoulders that had edged themselves up near her ears softened. She sighed long and deep into the night. He was tall. But that's all she could make out. He was little more than a shadow softened even more by smoke. The eye of his cigarette winked each time he sucked in. She spoke only after he had crushed the butt into the concrete.

I'd love a cigarette, she said, facing him.

Smoke was still trailing from the corner of his mouth.

She narrowed her eyes to see him more clearly in the weak wash of light from the bar and the street. He cocked his head as if thinking, fumbled in his pocket, brought out a crumpled pack of Benson & Hedges. When he struck the match, she could see the shape and color of his eyes, the scattering of moles on his face, and she could tell he was a man who was content with his own company, neither happy nor sad, but good to the core. No, he wouldn't need anything from her . . . didn't need much from anybody, maybe now and then a little closeness, but that's all. The shirt hung loosely off his square shoulders.

Music from the band skittered toward them and they stood silent together and smoked. She could smell Old Spice on him and the Dragon stout he'd been drinking. Out on the roadway the lights of passing cars flashed, their engines revving and whining. From somewhere distant came the tap-tap of pistols. She thought briefly of the bartender, Ralph. She knew she had frightened him. That's how things get done down there, Gracie had said. Act like a badass. She shook her head slowly. Gracie was in for life. Probably wouldn't see his country again. She sucked deeply on the cigarette and breathed out heavily from way down deep inside. Was really a miracle how she got out. A fucking miracle. But that was another story altogether. In the sky she saw an airplane's winking lights. And every now and again the wind would shift and bring the smell of gas, of exhaust, and, although they were miles from the sea, of kelp.

Mita and the man in the black shirt and cream pants stayed together smoking in silence till the pack was done. By then an understanding had formed between them. He turned to leave and she followed him. She wanted company tonight and she liked his quiet, his calm.

He had a suite on the highest floor and he took her through the tall glass doors that led out to the balcony. Red and silver lights were sparkling and shaking and slurring for miles into the distance. The breeze was just as hot as it was downstairs but had more flutter. Toy cars zigzagged ten floors below, the sound of them stretching and shortening, fading and growing, then melting away in waves.

What can I get you? he said when they were back inside. The room had a pair of matching couches. The flat screen on the wall was on, but silent. Soccer. She stood in front of it, watching but not really seeing, marking time, with drinks.

Suddenly his breath was warm on her neck. Was this even what she wanted? She turned into him. Now they were too close. His long, mole-sprinkled face was narrow and kind. He reminded her of a horse. She stepped away. What could he get her? What did she want? A bath, she said.

And it surprised her to hear her need jump out so fierce in front of this man she'd met less than an hour before.

A bath coming up, he said, and disappeared.

Inside the bedroom there was a suitcase open on the bed and she rummaged through it quickly without disturbing the neatly folded trousers, the striped shirts with stiff collars, his white briefs. She couldn't tell if he was going or coming. Back in the living room, she switched the channel to tennis. Serena was playing Wimbledon. She turned it off and poured herself a glass of water.

She still hadn't decided yet if she would sleep with him. She had not been with anyone, man or woman, in years. He wasn't exactly her type though she had no earthly idea what that was anymore. For a minute, her ex-husband had been her type, and then the woman she'd lived with for seven years before had been her type. She couldn't say that about the transients in between . . . and this man now . . . he didn't look like he could hold her, he didn't look strong, but then again she could relax with him. Wasn't easy to relax after six years. Would've been twenty without early release. But she wanted to learn how to rest again and start her life over.

The man called out to her, and as she approached the bathroom she could see that he had turned out the lights and arranged candles in a row on the edge of the tub. Their flames gave off a soft moon glow. The water was perfumed with ylangylang and scattered with rose petals he'd gotten from the bouquet on the nightstand.

He did not hover. He was respectful. He stepped out while she undressed and returned only after she had slipped in. He was down to his boxers and his dick inside them was hard, but his movements over her body were languid. He sponged her back and her neck and her breasts and her clavicles. He sponged her feet; he sponged her polished toes. There was desire in his touch, patience in his movements. But he asked nothing of her. For this she was grateful. Right now she only wanted care and she liked that he could sense this. She closed her eyes. She let her face soften.

She must've dozed off, for when she woke again she was naked in his bed under his sheets and she could hear him snoring on the couch in the living room. She put a hand to her eyes. The sun was bright through the half-turned blinds.

She let herself out without looking at him. She left him as a sound.

Mita returned to her room to find a plastic bag wrapped in duct tape on the chair near the window. She edged up to it, a tiny smile breaking the corners of her lips. So, things were working then, she thought. The boy had come through. She sat on the bed in her black dress from the night before and turned the package over slowly.

It was small, less than half a pound, and flat . . . no roundness or grooves, so no barrel. She imagined a semiautomatic. Something that could fit easily in her purse, like the one she used to take with her to work at the lot.

It was wrapped in a dense wad of tape and plastic and newspaper. It took forever to tear through the layers.

That fucker! she cried when all the unwrapping was done. The metal chinked the concrete wall and thunked on the carpet when she flung it.

An L-joint piece of copper pipe.

She grabbed the piece of plumbing and tore downstairs to the bar to deal with that fucking boy. She could see through the glass wall that the lights were off. The chairs turned down. The place was closed. She pounded on the wooden door. Tried the lock. Leaned in with her shoulder. That fucker!

A watchman in a uniform appeared. He looked about twenty or so.

Bar not open yet, miss, not until this evening, bout five.

What about Ralph? she said.

Ralph, miss?

I'm going to kill him, she said. As there is a God. He took two hundred of my good, good money.

The watchman started to grin and then he stopped himself and straightened up his face.

Ralph is a sweet boy, miss. Women grab onto him. You have to watch yourself. He make plenty woman cry.

She looked at the watchman for a second. Finally she caught on. She put the pipe behind her.

When is he working again? You know?

Thursday, miss.

It was now Monday. Three whole fucking days she had to wait. Three! Who had that kind of money to waste on a hotel? Who had that kind of time? She kissed her teeth sharply and hurried back upstairs. She had to think quick.

She brewed coffee in the one-cup maker on top of the mini-bar. She brewed it bitter and strong and drank it quick, standing by the window, curtains smothering the light from outside. Then she made a second cup. And while this one cooled she carved out a new plan. When she began to drink again, she was calmer and she slurped noisily from the cup.

After she'd gotten out of prison, the first thing Mita did was to track down her ex-husband Errol. This had taken her nearly six weeks. When she finally got hold of his number, she called him. By then he'd already moved back to Jamaica with Moira, their only child.

I'm coming to get her, she'd said. For that was all she wanted: to see her girl. I haven't seen her in six years, she said, and six years is a damn long time.

He'd paused for so long she thought he'd hung up.

Finally he'd said to her, Over my dead body.

She couldn't believe her ears. After all she'd gone through. After all that fucker had done to her. Then it will be over your dead body, asshole, she'd said in return, and hung up.

It had taken her a month to gather up the money to make the trip.

After she was finished with her second cup, Mita showered, changed her clothes, put the pipe inside her purse. She went downstairs and got a cab.

Valentine Castle Avenue, she told the driver.

You mean off Red Hills Road? His eyes searched her face in the rearview mirror.

She glared at him. Yes, she said softly. How the hell was she to know?

The drive was slow in the white Corolla, bumper-to-bumper. This was never the way she thought she'd visit her husband's country. But this was life. She listened to the horns blare incessantly around her and watched as the dust from the construction sites pillowed up over the whole world turning it white. On the radio, callers were complaining to a man named Mr. Thwaites.

Last time she'd seen her daughter she was four. Long skinny legs like her father, big shiny forehead like her. What would she look like now, at ten years old? Would she even recognize her? That thought brought a pain to her stomach. But it didn't matter. They'd come to know each other. In time.

Just up from the big clock tower, at a traffic light in Half Way Tree, a swarm of vendors mobbed the car, rattling the door handles, pressing their faces against the glass. Mita drew her arms tight against her sides. Double-checked that she'd locked the doors.

The driver gestured roughly at the crowd. Shouted. Cursed. Ordered them to move, but they didn't care. A boy no more than seven had already started to wash and scrub the wind-shield. She locked eyes with him for a second then turned away. What if she couldn't get her girl? What if this whole trip was a waste of time? What if she didn't even get a chance to see her child?

Thirty minutes later she was easing out of the taxi by the bus stop in front of a bakery flanked by a row of shops, and for a while she just walked, noting her surroundings. A sign told her she was on Red Hills Road.

The sun was high and hot and she sweated inside her sleeveless white dress and white pumps. Even the mangy dogs roaming the empty streets seemed stunned by the heat. Four men played dominoes on a table under a tree.

Empress! One of them called.

She hurried on.

The address was on a side street, more residential. The houses were long and rectangular and they all had the same red clay roofs and glimmering white walls and sprinklers spinning madly in the yards, which had rosebushes and fruit trees growing be-hind the wrought-iron gates. She found number ten. A Bombay mango tree stood beside the gate and she rested underneath its branches for a while watching the croaking lizards as they stuck out their yellow tongues at her and nodded.

She smoked two cigarettes while an hour passed and still she saw and heard no one except for the rhythmic thwacking of a machete trimming grass two or so houses away. It was mid-morning. Inside her chest a mix of feelings battered against her heart. The red mailbox latched to the gate had two airmail en-velopes. She stuffed them in her purse. Then she scaled the fence, one eye turned over her shoulder in case there was a dog—she had the piece of old pipe ready—and tiptoed around the barred windows. The heavy drapes were drawn. She could not see in.

In the backyard there was a playpen and a swing. She noticed shoes under a coconut tree . . . red sneakers good for climbing . . . the size of about ten-year-old feet. She brought them to her nose and that was when she heard the growl.

Before she could turn, a dark gray blur had turned solid and heavy against her chest. The shoes and her purse flew from her hands. The pipe fell out and slid across the grass. She rolled clumsily toward it. The dog pranced forward, pawing her as it barked. It wanted to play but she couldn't really tell. Its eyes were small and hard and dark and otherworldly. Its nails were ripping at her dress. She was on her back but still turning when she felt the metal in her hand. She swung. The dog, its hot mouth near her neck, yelped and flopped down shivering. There was blood on its face but not much. She could tell from its eyes it was stunned.

She went back the next day and the day afterward. She went at all hours of the day and night peering through the barred windows, walking by the gate and pretending not to look though she had the corners of her eyes peeled. The dog kept his distance. If he came close, even looked like he was going to bark, she just raised her arm and glared at him.

Hullo, can I help you?

She spun at the sound of the voice. It was early evening. Shadows creeping in.

I notice you come by all the time. The woman wiped her hands on her apron and extended them. You looking for the people next door? Mr. Errol and them?

She swallowed at the sound of her ex-husband's name.

Them on vacation. Coming back tomorrow. She paused. Boy, you favor the little girl, bad.

Moira, you mean?

Yes, you must be relation. You have the same eyes, the same cheeks. I think the mother dead, not so? She shook her head slowly.

Mita started to answer.

Anyway, my name is Winsome, if you need anything. They'll be back tomorrow. Is summertime now and they travel often, especially with the children out of school and everything. But my name is Winsome. All right. She smiled big and bright and sashayed back inside the house.

Mita stalked down the road.

So she was dead. That's what the fucker who had sent her to prison and stolen her child was telling people. She was dead. That's probably what he'd told her daughter too.

Well, she was going to show him dead. She was going to fucking show him.

That night her friend, or was it her lover—she wasn't sure how to think of him—drew the bath and lit the candles. It was becoming ritual for them now, except that tonight she wanted to scream. She paced the two small rooms, moving from the couch to the bed to the couch again, her breath shallow, her eyes wide, the TV on the wall mute and brilliant with pictures.

Will you just stay still? he cried out finally.

She looked at him, turned away, fell into one of the couches, drew her knees to her breasts, balled her fists, and wailed.

He stood and watched her for a while. He didn't ask her a word. That was the understanding between them. After she'd wept until she'd emptied, he moved behind the couch and she sat up and he massaged her neck and shoulders till she fell asleep. He brought her to his bed and undressed her, closed the door behind him, and went to sleep on the couch.

* * *

When Mita returned to Valentine Castle Avenue the next day, the front yard was filled with bands of children—children shrieking, children crying, children shouting and jumping and tugging and fighting and spitting and doubled over laughing.

Was it some kind of birthday party? She didn't want to draw attention to herself, so she walked by without stopping, glancing every now and then as she passed the long line of cars parked against the curb. On the veranda she saw people who walked and talked and looked like her ex-husband. But she did not see him. And she did not see her girl.

She walked by the house a second time and paused in the shade of a mango tree. She would snatch her if she saw her, just so. She would take her girl. Bring her back to California. Find work again. Make her a home. The piece of pipe was in her bag. Just in case. What was good for his dog would be good for him. A gun would be better. Just to scare him. But she had no gun. That fucker had fooled her.

She lit a cigarette and imagined Errol's face as she last saw it. Saw the gun pressed to his Adam's apple. Saw his eyes big and wild with fear. If push came to shove she'd use it, she told herself. She would. She wouldn't back down. She'd go back to prison if it came to that. At least it would be for something she'd actually done.

Then she saw her.

Moira was standing by herself under a tree off to the side. Tall and straight. It had been many years, and the girl was at a distance, but Mita knew in her heart it was her. And the cigarette slipped from her fingers and lay smoldering in the grass.

She watched her daughter talking to herself. She couldn't hear what she was saying, but from twenty yards away she could tell that her voice was high and thin.

Moira, she called out, careful not to speak too loudly, not to draw attention. She didn't want the other children to see, but some were already looking and pointing. She moved closer to the white concrete fence, and called again over the hedge: My love, is that you?

She held her breath. The girl turned. Her face was framed by two long plaits that fell halfway down her chest. Her eyes were big and wise, an old woman already.

Just that morning, Mita had gone to the store and bought her a polka dot dress with spaghetti straps. Just that morning, she had bought her a pair of barrettes for her hair, colored clips. She had bought her a set of six panties with assorted stripes.

Moira? she called again, as the girl eyed her with interest.

Who are you? said the girl.

I am Mita.

Mita, the girl said, moving closer. So close Mita could smell the castor oil in her hair.

The little girl pulled back. My mother's name is also Mita, she said.

Yes? Mita said. Hope filling her voice. And where's your mother?

Dead. Dead like a door post. And whatever light had been in Moira's face was blown out now. She cocked her head then cackled for a long time. My mother is dead, she told Mita again.

And it was like a knife in Mita's belly. Who told you that? she cried. She was trying not to scream.

She went to sleep one night and did not wake the next morning. My dad woke to find her dead beside him.

Who told you that?

For me to know and you to find out.

If it's your father, he lied to you. If it's anybody, they lied to you.

My daddy is not a liar. My daddy is good to me. He loves me.

Look at me good, Moira. Come closer. Can't you see it's me? It's me, Mita. Your mother. Don't you remember?

You are crazy, Moira said, taking several backward steps. She began to glance toward the veranda at the adults. Her voice turned cold and flat.

My mother is dead, she said. And whoever you are, Miss Mita, you are crazy with a capital C.

She spun away after that. Mita watched her trot across the grass, ignoring the other children, and disappear inside the house.

From a place outside herself Mita could see the children in the yard watching her and pointing. She could see their lips open and close. But heard no sound at all.

That night, she took off her clothes and called Wallace into the bedroom. She had no sensations at all in her limbs.

Fuck me, she said to him.

Not like this, he said, sitting on the bed next to her in the dark. It's like you've seen a ghost. He ran his hand across her face. Her eyes didn't register. You're not even here, he said.

There was the sound of water running in the tub, there was the scent of ylang-ylang perfuming the air. There were the candles already turning to grease.

She couldn't feel herself. She wanted to feel herself. You're a faggot, she hissed.

He laughed.

Come he said, reaching out his arms to her.

But she pulled away, got dressed in the living room, grabbed her purse, and shunted out. She could not stand still. The elevator took more than ten seconds to come. She walked the ten floors down to the bar, where she demanded a double scotch.

It was a slow night. The place was almost empty. She began to look around for Ralph. Three men sat studying their amber drinks at a table in a corner. Smooth jazz piped in from tiny speakers in the walls. As she ordered her second drink she made out that there was a woman eating by herself at another table. A plump, fair-skinned woman digging into something meaty.

Then she saw him. Ralph. He was sitting at a table in a far corner talking with a man whose back was turned to her. Still, she recognized the steeply sloping shoulders right away. It was Errol. The ex-husband. Errol.

Her breath grew shallow. She turned her lips inside her mouth to wet them. He had grown large and bald. From the width of him, she could see he'd grown a gut.

But there he was throwing back his head and laughing, a sound she would recognize anywhere, the hearty roar of it. He had his feet perched on the rung of the chair. He still wore brown loafers with the penny in the groove. And there was Ralph. That fucking little rat. It was obvious now they were friends.

As if they could feel her eyes, the two of them turned in her direction at once. A flicker of smile crossed the ex-husband's face. Ralph, though, looked terribly unhappy.

Everything that happened afterward happened quickly.

She woke up in Wallace's room. And when she saw his face swollen and bruised, she started to cry. Every bone in her body hurt. Every muscle in her body hurt. He had put ointment on all her wounds and bandaged her up.

It's not so bad, he said. He had stretched her out next to him on the couch, her head cradled in his lap.

If we had fucked, she said, this wouldn't have happened. She meant it as a joke and she tried to laugh, but her lips were so swollen, they didn't move at all.

He had a bowl of ice; he put a cube on her lips and another on his. Just rest yourself, he said.

I won't rest till I finish what I started down there tonight.

People who can't fight mustn't fight, he said. If you step to a man with a piece of pipe and a Red Stripe bottle like that, what you think the man going do? It wasn't right for him to man-handle you like that and box-box you up, but still . . . Is not just a defense thing, you know. Is a pride thing. A man thing. From the way he was box-boxing you up, I can tell it was about pride. That was a man defending pride.

He nursed her in his room for two days, and on the third day he asked her, What the hell is this about?

By this time all the swelling had gone down.

It's a long story, she said.

They were in the tub, facing each other. They were like an old married couple. Naked with soft nipples. Familiar.

When she tried to blow him off, he said, We have time.

She hated to have to go back to those years. Travel down those memories. But there were his eyes, hard and steady on her.

Moira was about four, she said. And the marriage was pretty much done. We'd fight over everything. And sometimes it'd get so bad I'd leave and go and live with my sister. Then weeks would pass and he'd call and say we should try again and then we'd get back and the same shit would happen again.

And then his cousin came to live with us for a while and it was like evil had stepped through the door. She paused. She took a sip of the local rotgut rum Wallace liked. We couldn't stop fucking, she said heavily. And all this time he was stealing from Errol. Errol had a used car business that was doing pretty good. And the two of them were always quarreling over money, and the accountant, Mr. Sams, was always complaining to Er-rol. And this cousin said it was money Errol owed him.

She stopped to drain the glass of overproof and then to pour a fresh shot from the bottle and to put in more ice from the bucket on the floor. She turned on more hot water as well, and when the temperature in the tub was just right she turned off the tap and continued.

I couldn't stop it with this guy. It was like an addiction. And then one day Errol found out. After that, I took Moira and left for good. He tried to throw out the cousin, but he'd just come out of prison, he didn't have anywhere to go. Week after I moved, the cousin called me. We met up in a hotel room. As usual we fucked. And before I even got back to my sister's, the police picked me up. There was all this money he'd put in my purse, Errol's money, and the gun, the gun that bastard used to shoot Mr. Sams with.

So Errol got the kid and you went to prison.

She said nothing at first. Then: Don't even know what happen to that bastard Carlton.

Carlton who? He has a last name?

Yes, but what does that have to do with anything?

Please.

Lewis, she said. Carlton Lewis.

He described Carlton from head to toe. She shifted uneasily in the water.

Dead, he said. Big news in the papers. Police shootout some years back. Drugs. They kill him.

Jesus.

So what the hell is really going on with you?

I came so I could see my kid, she said. That's all. Just to see her face again, talk to her, touch her hands, listen to her breath. She looks like my mother. Exact stamp of her.

Wallace looked up at the ceiling. I can get you the kid, he said.

Really? She stared at the long strong neck and the circles of hair around his nipples.

That easy to arrange. When you want her—today? Tomorrow?

He kept his eyes on the ceiling as they talked.

Just so? she said. Her stomach felt suddenly queasy. Who exactly was this man?

He reached over the edge of the tub for a glass of rum, took a sip. Looked in her direction but not in her eyes, just a bit above them, somewhere between her hairline and her brows. When he stopped sipping, his Adam's apple kept moving up and down.

I think I need to talk to him first, she said.

He looked her in the eye now.

I can't just take her like that. He's holding her hostage. There's something he wants from me.

He's punishing you, he said, for fucking his cousin. As I said, what happened the other night was a pride thing.

I know, she said. But there's something else. I have to figure out what will make him let her go. I have to give him something.

He started to speak and she raised her hand. Let me just think, Wallace, please. They were quiet for several moments. And for the first time, she was afraid. Genuinely afraid. Who was this man? And then she poured herself half a tumbler of rum and downed it quickly. She started to bathe him. Just so she could think, buy time. She soaped the wrinkles and folds of his skin speckled with moles and he brought his eyelids together and moaned. It was soft, his skin, and it hung loosely on the heavy bones of his slim body. For a while there was only the breath between them, loud and raggedy in the room, and the flickering candles making shadows on their faces. She wanted to just relax again, she wanted the innocence again, but all that was gone now. When the water grew cool again, they stepped out and towel dried.

I'm going over there, she said.

He looked at her. You want me close by, just in case? His voice was soft and it unnerved her.

She laughed. And it was a reckless laugh. I don't think so, she said.

I wouldn't play with that man, not after those blows he gave you.

I know, she said. But I'm putting down my weapon. I just going same as you see me.

That's noble and all, he said. But let me come with you. I'll park a little ways off so you can have your privacy.

She arrived just as the sun was sinking. The sky was a fiery red. Wallace dropped her off near the bus stop. And she walked. She had a gun. A Tomcat Beretta, semiautomatic, Wallace wouldn't let up until she'd taken it. It was a nice gun, as guns go, small, light, easy to handle. She'd owned one before when she lived with Errol and they had the used car business. It gave her a little boost, though, the gun. She could feel it in her girth, the way she moved down the road, as if this earth belonged to her. She waved to the men playing dominoes under the tree. She stopped in a shop to buy tamarind balls and the *Star*.

She saw Errol before he could see her and she watched him for a long time. He was in the front garden, about ten paces from the fence. His brown face was wrapped in white gauze and he was there pruning a wild rosebush. As she got up closer, she could actually hear him. He was singing under his breath.

He jerked up suddenly, perhaps sensing her, and a vein as big as a pipe throbbed in his neck.

I know you know I didn't shoot Mr. Sams or take your money, she said, her voice low. I know you put me away because of what happened with Carlton. What had happened to our marriage. I know you wanted to punish me. You wanted me gone. You wanted somebody to pay. And I paid, Errol, six years of prison time. Longer than anybody should have to pay for a little fuck. And maybe it's my time to see her now, to raise her now. Maybe it's my time now.

He'd been listening and studying her, but now he sucked

his teeth, now he muttered something caustic underneath his breath and turned away from her, now he went back to his pruning, and he gave her his back.

She thought to pull out the gun and whack him hard across his face. Whack him until it was mush. She was talking to him. She was fucking talking to him. She at least deserved his attention.

But as she reached into her purse, she noticed the glistening lines on his cheeks. She noticed his slow-moving lips. How you could shame me like that? he muttered. How you could bring me so low?

Look, I had no business doing what I did with Carlton. It was wrong. Damn wrong, she said. And I know it cut you up. But prison, Wallace. Prison? You think I deserved to go to prison for that? Now you tell me. Six whole years I sat up in that hellhole. Because you feel shame. Because I bring you down low. Because of your pride. Your manhood. What if right now I should punish you for what you did to me? Cause I could very well do that to you right now. I could crush you right now, Errol. But I am not going to do that. I just want to be with Moira. That's all. I just want to feel her close again. And so everything is up to you now. Everything is up to you. And I would advise you to make the right choice this time. I would advise you to act right.

She watched his shoulders heaving. She glanced at her watch. Ten minutes had passed. Wallace would be driving by soon. He would do so only once, he'd said. If she missed him she'd be on her own.

Errol still had not turned to face her, still had not said anything, but she knew him. He was listening; he was turning things over. His shoulders had grown slack.

She took her hand from her purse, backed away from the gate, and began walking in reverse. As she stepped away, she thought she caught the movement of a curtain. She stopped. Looked.

Errol threw down the shears and hurried inside. Should she wait? She continued her slow retreat, hoping to hear Errol or Moira's voice, continuing to hope when it made no sense to think she'd be able to hear them from so far.

When she got to the main road she continued walking backward, stumbling at times, but her hand still in her purse, holding the gun.

Wallace was sitting in his Mercedes SUV at the bus stop.

Half an hour of driving elapsed before she spoke. She didn't even recognize her own voice. You know what, Wallace? Turn round this damn vehicle right now. I can't go home. I have to get my girl. I have to get her now.

A GRAVE UNDERTAKING
BY IAN THOMSON
Downtown Kingston

How my father came to die in Kingston, the unfortunate circumstances of his death there, remains unclear. Was it an accident? Nothing is known for sure. But this much I do know: my parents had gone to Jamaica for a winter vacation, which ended in a mortuary. Air-freighting my father's body home to New York was an ordeal: few of us expect to die while abroad.

What can I tell you about him?

As a child I had been in awe of my father; daughters often are. His complexion was smooth and pink, his small, near-sighted eyes shone beadily behind horn-rimmed glasses. There was nothing tangible to dislike him for; Jimmy Ruff was my dad. He reviewed books for a living, and I guess he was doing fairly well at it, well enough, at any rate, to make a discreet name for himself at the *New York Times*. His forte was the savage put-down; any author he considered overrated (or who had simply won a literary prize) was tossed and gored. It took me awhile to work out that my father was not a writer after all, but a hack, though you might make it sound more important by calling him a literary critic.

My mother is the well-known food writer Fanny L'Estrange. By the time she met my father in 1984, she was the most infamously successful purveyor in New York of gaudy cookbook writing. "I want to bring out the *beast* in shy carnivores, and spur tenderloin-holics to tattoo *Fanny L'Estrange* on their rump roasts."

I honestly believe that the worst writing in the entire world is to be found in my mother's cookbooks. She, of course, does not know this (nor, one hopes, do her readers). But that was the first reason for her marvelous success as a food writer— her dismal taste. Mom had married young and she was even younger (sixteen, maybe seventeen) when she hung out with the Warhol crowd at The Factory in midtown. For all her outward propriety, she belonged to the age of New York punk and Patti Smith. This, despite (or perhaps because of) the fact that she had grown up on a pig farm in Ohio.

In my teens, distressingly for me, I had been handed a diagnosis of anxiety disorder. The diagnosis gave my mother the shock of her life. "Why can't you be like other people?" The diagnosis was unmistakably accurate. I am prone to attacks of panic-fear and made easily depressed. At my high school in Brooklyn the feelings of social isolation—of mental *discomposure*—intensified. I was in a minority of white kids anyway, but my anxiety made me feel like a Martian in the classroom. Even now, at the age of twenty-seven, I have few close friends. I am unmarried, and am likely to remain that way.

I am not wealthy (I have no private means), yet I manage to sublet a studio apartment off Sackett Street in Brooklyn, between Hoyt and Bond. For years I have struggled to survive there as an artist. Awhile back I conceived and executed a mural on a wall in downtown Brooklyn, which won plaudits locally in the press (*How observant she is. She seems to notice everything*). The mural was followed by *Born Free*, a study of lions and other animals in the Prospect Park zoo; then, in close succession, by *Hereafters* and *Through the Void*, paintings on the theme of death and dying in general.

The recession has knocked the bottom out of the art market; I scrape by on a pittance. Sometimes I feel an itch of regret at not having tried my hand at accounting (I am good with numbers). But who would have had me? The smallest things distress me. The physical and mental effort it has cost me to write this story alone has been considerable.

Like I say, all my mother wanted was to ignore my diagnosis; she would not even discuss it with my father. If she was unhappy in her marriage, my father's drinking did not help. It began tentatively, I believe, like going to a forbidden cookie jar; then it got worse. Bottle after bottle of bourbon. As their disenchantment deepened, my parents began to lose all affection in each other's company; they became a mystery to each other. To my shame, Mom started to behave wildly, taking up with anyone who would have her. Her affairs came mostly in serial form. All that she required of her men was that they be young, good-looking, and less drunk than Dad.

One night I turned up unexpectedly (I forget exactly why) at my parents' place three or four neighborhoods away in Williamsburg. I unlocked the door, stepped inside, shut it. It was way after eleven; a dim light came from the ceiling lamp in the hall. Everything looked neat and tidy; the cleaner must have been in that day. I glanced at the walls hung with the familiar Hollywood film posters—*The Big Steal, Where the Sidewalk Ends*—and the Warhol silk screen of my mother aged about seventeen. The Siamese cat, Decca, lay on the chaise longue, her fur matted and eyes unseeing (Decca had been blind these past five years). I picked her up gently in my arms and tickled under her chin. She began to purr. At that moment I thought I heard a murmur of voices down the hall. I soft-footed down the trail of sound. What I found shocked me.

Mom was on the kitchen floor with another man.

"You!" she shrieked. "What the fuck are you doing here?" Her face was twisted and red with shame. I had never seen her in such a rage. The man looked at me and it seemed his eyes stayed on me an instant too long. I clenched my fists; a terrible anguish took hold. I fled the apartment in tears and contemplated throwing myself in the East River. For weeks afterward Mom behaved in my presence with a painful naturalness, as if nothing had happened. I was furious with her. Fortunately (for her), she had a holy belief in the restorative power of religion, and in her despair she turned to the spiritualist credence of her Ohio farmer ancestors. Spiritualism made her feel less alone, she said; her own dear departed could get in touch through mediums and rapping noises. ("Knock twice if you can hear me, Mother.") She was deadly serious about it.

My father, meanwhile, did the same as any man does whose wife walks out on him: he started to eat more, drink more, and chase after women. In just under a month, he put on fifteen pounds. The added weight made him look ungainly; his face took on a tumid, pouchy look; to conceal his swelling jowls (or maybe offset his creeping baldness) he grew a goatee, which I disliked.

Before long, his doctor recommended that he take a vacation. It was important to find somewhere to get away from it all. Had he ever thought of the Caribbean? Jamaica, maybe? The visit to the doctor proved to be an unexpected success; afterward, as occasionally happened, Dad had a good idea: he determined to cut back on the alcohol.

With his drinking diminished and my mother's affairs now less numerous, my parents resolved to make up their differences and together booked a round-trip flight to Jamaica. It seemed like a good idea. Travel abroad in search of new foodstuffs had been my mother's passion; my father used to join her whenever he could. This time, however, they were going to a place whose laws and culture they did not know. My own knowledge of Jamaica was limited to the island's music and a couple of travel books. Jamaican deejay styles of "toasting" (scatting and talking over records) had influenced hip-hop. And Jamaican dub reggae, with its slowed-down, marijuana-heavy beat, offers me a kind of solace in times of anxiety.

To help finance the trip, Dad persuaded *National Geographic* to commission him to write an article on Afro-Caribbean funerary customs. Pleased, he began to read all he could on Jamaican countryside burial cults and Revival-inspired wakes. Mom's own interest in spiritualism (an insidious form of necromancy, if you ask me) complemented the subject. "And it really is fascinating," Dad told me on the phone the day before he left. In Jamaica, he explained, relatives may gather at a dead person's house for a wake that can last as long as nine days. "And get this," he went on, unstoppably, "the house becomes known for the duration as *the dead yard*. What a name! These dead yard funerals, they're often ecstatic, like they're a reggae version of a New Orleans jazz funeral. People dance! As if possessed by ghosts." Right. What did he know about reggae or jazz funerals? He was talking through his hat—again.

A week later, my parents flew Air Jamaica to Kingston. It was snowing in New York when they left and in the snow everything looked curiously still and quiet. At first it seems the vacation was a success. No sexual infidelity. No heavy drinking. My father phoned to say that he was busy reading about Caribbean mortuary customs at the Institute of Jamaica library. It seems he had become an object of interest on the streets of downtown Kingston, probably because he walked everywhere. A white man without a car in Jamaica has either lost his mind or his place in society. (I read that in a book.) Mom, predictably, enthused to me about the hotel breakfasts of callaloo and salt fish. They had booked themselves into the four-star Jamaica Pegasus on Knutsford Boulevard.

All this, what I've been telling you, happened last winter, a couple of weeks before Christmas. I was staying at my parents' place at the time: they thought it would make a change from the "gloom" (as they called it) of my Sackett Street studio. In reality, the studio represented everything that was comprehensible and reassuring to me. Nevertheless, I thought I could relax in Williamsburg. The apartment walls had big red geometric designs painted on them, which I found oddly soothing. All I had to do, apart from take the garbage out on Tuesdays, was feed the cat.

It was a chill December weekend, I remember, and the windows were wide open to the late afternoon. Decca stirred slightly and purred. I went to the kitchen to fetch her a tin of Happy Heart chopped liver. Duke Ellington's "Jump for Joy" was playing on the kitchen radio when the phone rang.

"Baby?" It was my mother. "Oh my *God*—baby—hi . . . I almost lost you—*Jesus*—listen." Her voice sounded drawly, inebriated, maybe.

"Mom?"

"Are you alone?" she asked.

"Yes. Why?"

"Something has happened. Your father—he's had a heart attack."

"Heart? Attack how? He's not *dead*?" I stared at the red-colored designs on the wall.

"Not dead. But—"

"Was it bad?" I asked.

"Pretty bad. He's had a bypass. The doctors say he may not live until Wednesday."

My stomach turned over.

"But today's Saturday. This is serious!"

"Serious? I don't know about *serious*. It's certainly Saturday." My mother sounded angry: something about another woman.

"Calm down," I said, more to myself. (I could feel a familiar anxiety creeping in.) "So when was the last time you saw

Dad, actually? To talk to. Please. As much detail as you can remember."

Mom took a moment to reply. "We were in a restaurant in Kingston for lunch and we'd ordered this stunning, peony pink wine—"

"Okay, spare me the particulars."

"*Okay.* Suddenly we had a row—the worst ever." According to Mom, the wine bottle had gone over first; then the plates had slid toward her as Dad yanked at the tablecloth and buried the lower part of her body in a confusion of china, rosé wine, glassware, and warm food.

"He stormed out of the restaurant, your father did, leaving *me* to pick up the check. Can you believe it?"

(I could: it was part of his insecurity.)

"And then?"

"And then I did something crazy. I took a taxi to the airport and flew—to Montego Bay!"

"Are you joking?"

"Joking? No."

"You must be. Or you must be crazy. Montego Bay? That's on the other side of Jamaica."

"I'm not crazy, and I'm not joking."

"Where are you? *Where are you?*"

"I'm in Montego Bay."

"Jesus Kee-rist!" The vehemence of my voice surprised me; I was feeling really quite tense.

Mom mumbled something to herself—I was unable to make out what—before she continued in a shaky voice. "How *could* he?"

How could he *what?*

But I was no longer thinking. I looked out the kitchen window; a light snow was falling against the darkness.

If I understood, my father had gone back to the Pegasus

Hotel and started to drink. By midnight the liquor must have gotten him well and truly licked; early the next morning they found him seminaked on the bedroom floor in a cold sweat and deathly pale. A girl in a "gold ankle chain and blond wig" (according to one witness) was seen running off after alerting the desk downstairs to what had happened. It seems the girl had gone earlier to my parents' room—508—after receiving a call. So that was it. In a moment of impetuosity fueled by alcohol, my father had phoned for a hooker. What happened next is not so hard to imagine. His heart had stopped beating during intercourse. Or maybe the girl had tried to rob him? Filled with horror, she had run off, and with her disappearance, with my father's cardiac arrest, with my parents' marriage now in tatters, it seemed there was nothing left.

"I don't hate your father," my mother was saying. "I hate that bitch. She got to sleep with him, instead of me."

"*Mom!*" I felt a rush of resentment against her. She had neglected me shamelessly as a mother. What was she doing in Montego Bay?

She went on talking, but I did not hear her. "You still there?" she said after a moment.

"Yes."

The hotel had dialed for an ambulance, apparently, which arrived promptly at the address on Knutsford Boulevard. A paramedic injected my father with insulin as he lay incoherent on the carpet. Within the hour, a surgeon had phoned my mother in Montego Bay; the surgeon informed her that her husband was a very sick man but there was a chance of saving his life if he went under the knife. Mom had told the surgeon to go ahead and operate.

To me she said: "Drop everything, baby—book a flight to Jamaica. Now."

"I'm so sorry, Mom," I said. "This is awful."

I hung up and began to pace from one end of the kitchen to the other. Then I tried to shut my eyes to let the darkness in, but when I opened them everything was as frightening and unpredictable as before. My father's heart attack was going to force me to confront long-buried feelings of resentment and anger. I felt an undefined need to examine all the suppressed fears and anxieties I had ever entertained. Of course I slept fitfully that night; my mind felt weighted down with a nameless dread and the sense of my own life as a dead weight.

Next day as I left for the airport, a chill wind was blowing up in gusts from the East River. The bright tropic warmth of Jamaica seemed light years away; but it was appropriate weather, I thought, for an unplanned farewell, should Dad die now. And I was sure he would die. Why else had I begun to see the world divided into those who have fathers and those who do not?

I saw very little from the plane, but the journey went on for such a long time that I grew anxious. We did not seem to be moving, but standing still. My anxiety dissolved as the plane banked down toward a landscape of alien lushness. Way below me I could make out the thin brown ribbon of a river winding through a valley. In the Taino Indian language, Jamaica—*Xamaica*—had meant a country abounding in springs and emerald uplands. What could I expect to find there? I got off the plane with only one thought in mind—to see my father alive for maybe the last time. It was December 8, a Sunday.

The Pegasus, a high-rise hotel in the heart of Kingston's financial district, had a gelid, marble-floored vestibule with piped Marley reggae, a polo lounge, and a pool bar. I walked on past the lobby to the elevator and rode up to the fifth floor. I got out of the elevator. A Christmas tree with winking lights stood at one end of the corridor. I approached room 508 with a rapidly increasing sense of dread (though a moment before I had not been conscious of any at all). I knocked, waited, knocked again. Mom opened the door: she looked haggard, depleted. "I feel funny inside," she told me, and made as if to hug me.

"Here, hold on to me. Are you okay?" (Me—asking Mom if she was okay!)

"I think so. It comes over you, and then it goes." Her voice sounded blurred and throaty; she had been crying. She said she had flown in from Montego Bay that morning. Room 508, when she got there, showed evidence of the previous night's turmoil: spent insulin ampoules, the bedsheets rumpled. A book on Jamaica, *The Dead Yard*, lay open on the floor by the bed.

I stared at Mom, then dropped into a chair. It was about eleven o'clock in the morning and most of the blinds were still down. She was wearing a bathrobe over her clothes and, as usual, a mass of jangly jewelry. In her black-frame glasses she looked like Velma Dinkley in *Scooby-Doo*. Her long, black plastic earrings made a really irritating clacking noise (and her bathrobe was an unbecoming shade of purple).

Dabbing her eyes, she said: "Tomorrow morning, what we do is visit your father in the hospital. It's been arranged."

For a moment I felt an intense loneliness.

"Drink, Mom?"

"That would be nice."

Over glasses of scotch—neat for me, soda for Mom—I tried to lighten the mood with talk of Jamaican cuisine. Jerk chicken. Salt fish. But, try as I might, the conversation kept coming back to funerals.

Thoughtlessly I asked out loud: "Who was it that said the living are the dead on vacation?"

"How should I know?" Mom made an irritated motion with her glass. "All I know is, Kingston could well be your father's *last* vacation." She gave me a look. "No matter how hard you try to prepare for these tragic moments, you never know when they're going to happen."

"But Dad isn't dead yet," I said, crossing the carpeted room to get some ice from the minibar. "We have to hope. Like they say in Jamaica: *No call man dead till you bury him*" (the expression came from the Jamaican phrase book I had been reading on the plane).

Mom looked doubtful. Had I misinterpreted something she said? Slowly, painfully, she got to her feet, went to the minibar, and poured herself another drink.

"You know, sometimes I'm sorry I ever met your father. I don't like to say a thing like that, but it's true."

"True?"

"Oh, I don't know," she said, sitting down again. "Things *could* have been different. He could have been a proper writer, your father could." Dad's newspaper reviews had an occasionally effective belligerent tone, all right, Mom conceded, but probably that was sour grapes. In all his years as a critic he had produced just one book, *Lick Me*, a collection of "vintage" ice-cream and lollipop ads which had impressed him as a boy growing up in North Carolina. Whatever his standing as a critic, as a writer Dad had some way to go. He was one of those people who had failed to find life attractive or interesting, and so took it out on others. Why else did he domineer so unpleasantly on the books pages of the *New York Times*? Why else did he glut himself daily on causing injury to others?

For all Dad's assertiveness, though, Mom was the one who held the whip hand. Ever since they had met at a disco in Manhattan some thirty years ago, she had wanted to know how and exactly *where* he spent his evenings. In the end Dad had looked elsewhere for his pleasures; and Mom had retaliated with infidelities of her own. For much of their married life they showed each other a terrible disloyalty. The memory of finding my mother with another man on the kitchen floor, along with others less lurid, continued to distress me.

Mom took a swallow of her drink, sighed, and raised her eyebrows expressively. "You know the police have interviewed that woman? The one with the ankle chain? Turns out she works at a nightclub—The Gemini or someplace—on Half Way Tree Road, I think they said." She added with bitter indignation: "Can you imagine? A *prostitute*? A common prostitute?" Foul play had been ruled out. Dad had not been unduly prevailed upon, lured, or in any way been the victim of a trap. Heart attack remained the likely verdict.

I sipped my scotch. (It was good enough to sip.) How long had we been talking for? Daylight was beginning to fade from the room.

"I feel like death myself, you know," Mom said.

What she needed was a good long, uninterrupted nap. "You ought to be asleep," I told her. "You need your sleep." Bleary-eyed, she got up and threw herself on the bed next door and lay awhile staring at the ceiling. Before long she was snoring faintly. I took half an antidepressant (trademark Celexa), got undressed, and lay down alongside her. In a strange way, my mother had become more of an individual now that Dad was so ill; I almost felt sorry for her.

Early the next morning, bewildered by the turn of events, we took a cab to Kingston Public Hospital. I knew that Jamaica was going to be hot: I'd had a sense of the heat when I arrived yesterday afternoon. The strong hot breath of Kingston had seemed to rub against my skin and make the air positively hum. But I had not imagined this sort of heat: solid, soupy, without a breeze. Amid the hazy mass of traffic on Knutsford Boulevard we crawled agonizingly along. Kingston during rush hour was a hectic interchange of cars and buses. The heat was blistering, with exhaust fumes coming in.

Downtown, near the intersection of North Street with Orange Street, we stalled in a four-lane tangle; I could feel the sweat running warm between my shoulder blades. Rastafarians sped enviably past us on their bone-shakers (they at least had the right idea). Mom raised her head doglike in the backseat and sniffed. "What's that smell?" It was the bonfire whiff of burning collie weed. Surely she knew that?

"The traffic really is awful," I said, avoiding her question.

"You don't know what Kingston traffic is," she laughed uneasily.

But my mind was elsewhere; the fact kept repeating itself to me: *Dad might die. Dad might die.*

An hour later, from the gasoline-fumed depths of the morning gridlock, we came to a five-story ochre building with blue-painted balconies: Kingston Public Hospital.

The lobby was filled with people waiting, leaning against walls, tired of waiting, tired of life. (Tired, I thought, just tired.) In post-cardiac intensive care it was awhile before anyone turned up to see us. "The surgeon soon come," a nurse kept telling us. *Soon come.* I had read about this expression in my phrase book. It is, they say, an expression which "haunts" Jamaican life and, to outsiders, "epitomizes" the Jamaican soul. You can fuss and fume all you like, but *soon come* usually means a very long time indeed.

At long last, a man of about forty with high cheekbones and skin the color of cork came to introduce himself: "I'm Dr. Kong—the cardiac surgeon."

His face did not seem to bear a very hopeful expression.

"These are critical days," he said. "Mr. Ruff has survived the bypass and may regain consciousness, but I'm afraid his kidneys have gone into shock and are not dealing sufficiently with the body's toxins."

Saying this, he showed us into the cramped ward where my father lay, artificially vitalized, on a ventilator. It was very hot when we came in. Most of the windows were shut and the blinds were down. A faint ammonia tang of urine mingled with disinfectant pervaded the air. Patients lay motionless on their wheeled beds; surgical polyethylene bags full of urine hung like udders below their beds. An occasional beep sounded from a heart monitor.

Though Dad was the only white man in the ward, I could barely recognize him. Drips were hooked to his right arm and a tube protruded from his mouth. He was sedated and his eyes were closed. He had the battered look of someone just arrived from a bad journey; he looked like a damned vagrant.

Dr. Kong gestured Mom to a bedside chair; she sat down on it and leaned toward Dad. "Hello, Jimmy, dear heart. It's Fanny. You're in good hands here." She took his left hand in her right. "A good rest will fix you up fine. Yes, things will be right again." Already my mother was picking up bad habits of hope: Dad looked *beyond* hope, even I could see that. Today was December 9, a Monday; Dad had been dead to the world, effectively, for two days. His condition was critical; we were just waiting for the chandelier to fall.

From time to time the door opened and a nurse walked in behind a trolley-load of rattling serum bottles. No noise could wake my father and I wondered what thoughts pulsed in his head. "He may or may not be aware of your presence," a nurse offered gently, "but there's some weak electrical activity in the brain. So, please, you can try to talk to him."

I put my face close to Dad's. His chin, doubled and unshaven, still had that goatee, and his breath reeked. "Dad? You've got yourself in a nice fix. But you're not really dying, are you? We won't let you die." No answer. I may as well have been talking to the dead. The sedative—some sort of anaesthetic—had left him stupid in his sheets. Did he not hear my words to him through his hospital sleep? The question was like a challenge to life itself.

For a few hopeful days we trusted that things might get better and waited anxiously in the Pegasus for the phone to ring. Outside, the sun was burning hot and the sky a bright burning blue, yet each time we visited my father he was less recognizably himself. Downtown Kingston, meanwhile, had begun to confuse and frustrate me; crowded, infernally noisy, it left me jittery with unaccountable bad moods and loss of appetite. The moods were a part of my anxiety, but they were a part, too, of the senseless, contrary place I found myself in. If Kingston was going to affect me in this way, I had better get used to it.

On December 13, a Friday, came distressing news that my father's blood pressure had dropped so low that cardiac massage had to be administered. *Down, down, the compass needle pointing dead on death.* Dreadfully, late on the evening of the next day, he died. Cause of death: *Acute myocardial infarction.* The autopsy revealed diabetes, kidney stones, and an "occluded" artery to the heart. So my father had been going down the long slide to death for years. He was fifty-four and I had assumed he would live to a grand old age. But his wretched heart just would not let him live.

All that night at the Pegasus, my mother kept thinking that Dad was in the next room or moving down the corridor. But the nurses were no longer watching him; he was in a mortuary. "Oh, but he's not *really* dead," Mom insisted one night. "He's passed to spirit, what others call heaven." She said she wanted to get in touch with Dad through a spiritualist medium she had located in Kingston. "Don't worry, we'll have him back on board." *Back on board?* What did that mean? This talk of mediums and moonshine was beginning to fray my nerves.

As far as I was concerned, the dead were dead and they could stay that way.

With Kingston basking in a hot bright light the next morning, I pulled on my clothes and brushed my teeth. Mom emerged from the shower in a towel-turban and stood before the mirror. She did not look at me. She had never showed more than a polite interest in my life. Why should she now? This morning we had work to do. We had to collect Dad's belongings from the hospital.

On the way there, I took in the bombardment of impressions. Dancehall music, a numbingly insistent rap, blared from the shops along North Street, as the cab jounced drunkenly over potholes. At one point we were overtaken by a hearse; it was big, black, and expensive, and it honked loudly as it surged (or tried to surge) through the traffic. I felt ready to drop from fatigue.

On the second floor, Dr. Kong touched my mother's arm. "Please accept my condolences." Had her husband survived, he went on solemnly, he would have been an invalid "drifting in and out of consciousness" on a kidney machine. So it seemed this was a merciful death. "Look after your mother," the surgeon told me as a parting shot. Now at last I understood where my place was: with the fatherless.

Presently a porter arrived with a tagged black plastic bag for us to inspect. The bag disclosed bright red underwear (very risqué), a key ring, and a sum of Jamaican currency. These little things tugged at me, but my father's wrist watch made me gasp. The mechanism relied on the wearer's wrist movement but, locked away, the hands had stopped ticking at 12:46 a.m. on December 9, two days after the heart attack. Now, as I tapped the watch, the hands began to move again as if propelled to do so by a ghost. Mom said it might indicate a message from the

Beyond. "You don't know what nonsense you're talking," I said. I had already forgiven her so much.

Later that awful day, back in room 508, I struggled to make sense of Kingston and what had happened. The onslaught of bright lights, harsh colors, and unrelenting noise made me want to retreat into myself and shut down. I continued to take Celexa and tried to listen to Jamaican music on my iPod (King Tubby. Yabby You: old-school dub). The reggae echoed soothingly through the darkness of the hotel room. Still, I sometimes had the sensation that I was living, but without being alive. The paperwork involved in getting my father's body home was oppressive enough. Certificates had to be rubber-stamped and tied in metaphorical red tape. Pathologists, notaries, and coroners: all were to be involved.

Meanwhile, my father's death certificate was due for collection from the hospital mortuary. This time we decided to go to the hospital on foot. Apparently, tourists rarely venture downtown unaccompanied. ("People are very grudgeful down there," the hotel reception clerk had warned us. "You have to know what you're doing.") Yet, so far, we had found only friendliness downtown and, in Kingston Public Hospital anyway, a sociable atmosphere. The problem was the heat; the heat was stovelike in its ferocity.

It was midmorning when we got to the hospital. A heat haze hung over the building in gauzy, thinning clouds, with the morning sun breaking in. Groups of dogs, cowed-looking, slunk through a roadside litter of plastic bottles and discarded KFC boxes. Amid the heat and narrow lanes round the hospital, rap, ragga, and reggae boomed from giant loudspeaker cabinets.

The mortuary was situated in the same drab complex as the hospital on North Road. Outside the mortuary office, a couple of mandrill-faced youths were speaking into their cell phones.

("We do a nice bashy package deal on your dead," I overheard one of them say.) Later I understood who they were; they were among the "dead hustlers" or unlicensed morticians of Kingston, who make a killing out of the unsuspecting bereaved. Few of them own a hearse or even a cold room; cynically they fleece the poor. A hardness about their eyes suggested a difficult home life (or no home life at all).

We gave them a wide berth and knocked on the door which had MANAGEMENT lettered on a glass panel. Within sat a middle-aged woman in a white blouse and black skirt. "Don't talk to those dutty bad youth outside," she said to us, as she rose from her chair and gave a little bob of greeting. "Respecters of nothing." The office was stuffy, and in the sticky air mosquitoes began to whine thinly and bite us. I looked up at a picture on the wall of Jesus walking on the water. *At least He looks cool.*

Professionally doleful, the woman started by asking Mom whether she would like her husband "dressed up" and explained that relatives often prefer to see their loved ones returned to a semblance of life before they "vanish forever." This was the Jamaican manner, I thought. We must follow the ritual. To my surprise (and I must say relief), Mom objected that fussing over a corpse in this way was "uncivilized." She said she did not want her man "done up like Lenin or James Brown" in a suit and tie. A plain white shroud would do, thank you very much. The woman narrowed her eyes a little at this. Then she said she understood.

With infinite care, she began to draft a preliminary death certificate. The certificate, on its completion, was stamped with the hopeful Jamaican motto: *Out of Many, One People.* I again felt an acute need to clear my mind of the fog of doubts and fears that had been plaguing me since I left New York. The consequences of Dad's death seemed to drag bewilderingly on.

As we left, the woman told us where we could buy a coffin:

the House of Comfort Funeral Home Ltd. at 162 Hagley Park Road. "They stock a wide range of casket merchandise, and"—she looked at us sympathetically—"they should satisfy all your mortuary requirements."

Kingston continued to confound and amaze me. The beep and brake of the traffic outside our hotel was deafening. Market women yelled like harridans from their shack-shanty stalls downtown. At times the noise grew so loud that I had an impulse to cover my ears. Certain types of fabric had begun to make my nerves jump and my skin itch. I could no longer wear my jeans. It was not just the heat. It was my anxious disposition at work.

In all this difficulty, Mom was no help to me at all. While the paperwork swelled, all she did was sit by the pool drinking tumblers of white rum and Coke, apparently indifferent to my distress and to what had happened to us. In the mornings she gave off a flowery, powerful chemical smell of the hairdresser. She was what she was: self-absorbed.

Though I am not usually given to analyzing my states of mind, certain things had become clear. Dad's death had not only brought me to the edge of a new period of my life, it had opened up an unexplored territory in myself through which I was going to have to pass. Mom, though, seemed to display no such understanding (let alone self-analysis). She was not even entertainingly self-absorbed; she was a blank.

As I have mentioned, our relationship had never been an intimate one. My mother would not even come with me to oversee diplomatic formalities at the American embassy. I had to go there on my own as she was off researching a *Marie Claire* feature on Jamaican cuisine (at a time like this?).

Security was strict at the fortresslike embassy on Old Hope Road. "Excuse me. Is that a camera in your pocket?" The U.S.

Marine spoke to me from a cubicle of bulletproof glass. All I could see of him was a pair of squinty eyes beneath a peaked white cap. I was glad that I did not have to make eye contact with him.

"No camera," I declared.

"Please surrender your passport."

Afterward I was met by a rather effete, silky-looking junior diplomat named Donald Katz, who was responsible for other red tape involved in air-freighting Dad home. "I'm so sorry to hear about your loss," he said, putting on a face. (I could not tell if it was the *right* face; his eyes seemed to hold a friendly expression but without really having any expression at all.) He was a medium-sized blond man with white eyebrows and a tight, worried face. Not my type at all.

"Take a seat, won't you?" We sat at either end of a sofa opposite a large framed photograph on the wall of Barack Obama. "Can I get you a coffee?"

As I sipped from the coffee mug Mr. Katz said he required a doctor's note to show that my father's body contained no "infective substances or tissues"; I had a copy for him and he thanked me for that. Then he said: "You know, we get very few American deaths here in Kingston. In Montego Bay it's different. Nationals die there of alcohol, drugs, all-night partying." He spoke as if this kind of thing happened every day. Maybe it did. (There was the case, only last month, of two elderly Americans who had gone to a Montego Bay nightclub called X-Tatic Moods, drank a whole lot, and were later found washed up on the beach, drowned.) Each year, Mr. Katz went on, hundreds of Americans are "repatriated" from all corners of the world; they die of electrocutions, traffic accidents, suicide. Airport cargo-handlers refer to human remains as HUM.

"Most international flights have a couple of 'hummers' in the hold," Mr. Katz let me know, adding: "I'm afraid that's the way of it with repatriations. It's not pleasant. But the bodies are there, you can't just close your eyes and pretend they aren't."

What he said seemed logical, but it made no sense to me. Why should we *not* close our eyes to such horror? But then nothing in this story is plain as day. (I mean, previously, I had thought that Hummer was the make of an automobile, not a deceased human being.)

Mr. Katz got to his feet and said gravely: "Your father's coffin will have to have a drop-in zinc liner and will be hermetically sealed." (The zinc, he explained, was to guard against sepsis and other infections.) "Regrettably, we have to conform to airline and consular specifications." He showed me to the door, and, taking my hand in his, said: "It's been nice meeting you. It isn't often that I get to talk about the things that matter."

He smiled and made (I thought) an ambivalent gesture. I said goodbye to him and headed off in the direction of the funeral parlor we had been recommended. As I hurried toward Hagley Park Road, the sun was high and intense, sucking the color out of the sky. By the time I got to the bus stop on Parade, my brain was swarming with the beginnings of thoughts fastened onto the beginnings of other thoughts. Receiving so many thoughts took all my attention. I was preoccupied, above all, with the thought of how I might broach the subject of my father's death with the undertaker. Dad as a living person seemed impossibly distant now; how to make him even remotely real?

It was nearly one o'clock when I reached Hagley Park Road. There, amid the secondhand Japanese car dealers and past the Ethiopia Repatriation record shop (the reggae bass reverberating heavy in my stomach), I found myself on a narrow strip of asphalt lined with shacks and barren yards. My face felt as if it was dissolving in the heat. I stopped at a bar for ten minutes and had a cooling Ting at the counter. Opposite the bar, the House of Comfort Funeral Home Ltd. radiated a suitably dismal air. Through dark-tinted windows I could make out a floral tribute to *Mom* next to another, to *Pop*.

After a long wait, I braced myself to enter. Inside, as well as plastic wreaths, hung a pungent smell which I could not place. Formaldehyde? At the far end of the parlor, a dark-suited man was sitting at a desk beneath a huge TV screen up on the wall advertising, *Limousine Service. Import & Export of Human Remains. Embalming.* He appeared to ignore me while I looked around. On one wall, in big gold plastic lettering, was a quotation (or misquotation) from Corinthians, 15:55: *Oh death, where is thy Ting?*

The man finally got up and moved toward me. "I'm Derek Maunder," he said, maybe a little wary. "The director."

"Hello."

"You look like a stranger."

"I *am* a stranger."

"So where you from, may I ask? From distant parts?" He stared at me so searchingly that I had to focus my gaze on his eyebrows.

"I'm from New York. Brooklyn."

"New York?" His eyebrows quirked. "I've got a cousin in Brooklyn, or maybe it's the Bronx." There was a pause. "So how may I be of assistance?"

"Well, it's sort of hard. I don't quite know how to tell you. It's a little delicate . . ."

"Delicate, you say?" Mr. Maunder held up a palm like a traffic signal to stop. "I must put my hand on my heart. Here at Comfort Ltd. we respect all delicacies. You know, service is more than just a word with us." He gave a slight bow at this. "For those who require it, we even offer a session of free grief counseling." To judge by the keening plaster angel on his desk, Mr. Maunder also offered eternal salvation as part of his undertaking package.

I explained my business.

"Repatriation?" He pondered this awhile. "I trust you don't mean to Africa."

"Africa? No, to New York. Why Africa?"

"I was just thinking. Here in Jamaica, *repatriation* is mostly a back-to-Africa thing. Haile Selassie. Ethiopia. That class of thing." He looked at me quizzically. "You are not of the Rastafari faith?"

"Jah. Do I look like it?"

The director smiled slightly and got to the point. "So your father has died. Here in Kingston."

"Yes. At the Pegasus Hotel."

"My condolences." His face seemed to express sympathy— or was it consternation?

"It could happen to any of us," I said, not meaning to sound sarcastic.

"Touch wood it won't." On the word *wood*, with its suggestion of coffin, Mr. Maunder had tactfully lowered his voice. He was making a favorable impression on me.

"Have you been in Kingston long?"

"About a week now."

Neither of us said anything for a couple of seconds. Then Mr. Maunder went to his desk and twitched an important-looking pile of paperwork. "May I ask if your father died of natural causes? We have to be sure. If your father did not die of natural causes, there will need to be an inquest. It's the Jamaican law."

"No, my father's death was natural, all too natural."

Actually, I was not so sure. Manslaughter? Accident? If a crime *was* committed, the motive remained uncertain: nothing, it seemed, had been stolen from room 508. Heart attack still seemed to be the sole plausible explanation.

Mr. Maunder pressed the heels of his hands together. "For health and safety reasons," he said very softly, "your father will have to be embalmed. Embalming is a legal requirement for most repatriations." He added that embalming had become *de rigueur* ("if you'll pardon my French") in the U.S. during the Civil War, when young men died so far from home.

"If you like," he went on after a genuinely funereal silence, "we can perform the embalming here." Saying which, he led me to a small, white-walled chamber at the back of the parlor. Three metal trolleys there stood against one wall; a large, hospital-type sink with elbow-operated taps stood in a far corner. "We use an up-to-date alcohol injection method," said Mr. Maunder. Dad would have liked that. For all his business savvy, the director said he believed passionately in caring for the dead. The meaning of life is everywhere connected to what it means to die, he insisted.

We went into the showroom adjacent to a makeshift-looking chapel, where I had to choose a coffin from among the many models on display. "We have baroque, gothic, or jazzy styles," Mr. Maunder said in a patiently reassuring tone. "I would suggest a Sea Mist polished finish. Or maybe a Lilac Bloom."

On a trestle table in the chapel, disconcertingly, lay an open casket surrounded by a quietly grieving family. Embarrassed by their grief, I tried to select a coffin for Dad. The lighting was poor—just a couple of spots in the ceiling—but I managed to choose a casket of ash-blond wood; it was the plainest yet most expensive model in the showroom.

"That's the Colonial Classic," said Mr. Maunder (I think approvingly). Other models were gold-encrusted, with glass lids and frilly pink linings; even death wears bling.

But now a new thought struck terror to my heart. What if Dad was not in fact dead? Death is the final insensibility, they say, but still we have to make sure a person actually is dead, do we not?

"Not dead?" The director stared at me with great seriousness (like the doctor who had arrived at my diagnosis all those years ago). "Either a person is dead—or a person is not dead." Dead or not dead. I took comfort in those stark oppositions, and I thought to myself: I have made no mistakes so far; why should anything go wrong now?

For such a grave undertaking, my visit to the funeral parlor had filled me with a curious energy. I popped another antidepressant and telephoned the mortician in Brooklyn who was to oversee transfer of my father's corpse from JFK airport.

"Door to door, our basic repatriation fee is $2,500," he told me, adding reassuringly: "We offer a bespoke service." I arranged a site for Dad's grave and began notifying relatives.

Exhausted by the effort, I lay down on the bed in room 508 and looked at my wristwatch. It was past nine thirty. Mom was dining downstairs in the Columbus Restaurant (*Dress Code Observed*; she was wearing a floral-print bikini combination under her purple bathrobe). I got up and stood by the window, and watched the moon riding, careering through the night clouds. Kingston had turned into an adventure for me, one in which my father was the detonating factor. Yet almost all of the adventure was taking place in his absence. I found the thought unsettling. Abruptly, a great sob tore though my body, and I wept uncontrollably. *Oh fuck.* Tomorrow I would have to steel myself for the worst task of all: I would have to "positively identify" my father's body. It was a U.S. embassy stipulation. The wrong body might otherwise be flown home, or the *right* coffin put on the *wrong* aircraft. And that would be awkward.

Dawn was breaking when I got up the next day, went to the window, and pulled up the blinds. As usual the Kingston day had come up hot and still. Mom was in her bed snoring faintly. How long had we been in Jamaica for? Five days? Ten days?

The time sequence was beginning to confuse me. I sat on the edge of my bed, and thought: through all these days of trial and uncertainty, only a numbness registered my shock at what had happened. When would it lift, this numbness? I put on my clothes—my mind was functioning—and took a cab downtown toward the worst horror of all.

Taking a breath, I walked into the refrigerated room on my own. My father's body had been brought up to me in a lift from underground storage and now it lay in unremitting stillness beneath its white shroud. This freezing place, with its hum of refrigerators, galvanized buckets, and bare, carbolic-scrubbed walls had been my father's habitation for the five days (it was definitely five days) since he died. I stepped close, looked at the placid, yellowish face. The eyes were half open and stared incuriously at the ceiling; they had a strange, flat glitter in them. I could not believe that this was my real father, in a real hospital mortuary. Who would have thought that his world would end here? I guess it was the closest he would ever get to a Jamaican dead yard ritual.

It seemed as if my whole life had been leading to this one awful moment.

Overcome with sadness, I put the palm of my hand to his forehead: it was cold as snow. I smoothed the forehead, and let my hand run softly over his hair. After a brief hesitation, and with a feeling maybe of guilt, I eased back the shroud to reveal his chest: a tangle of wiry white hairs, the nipples a livid gray-blue. An autopsy scar showed jagged down the chest like a railway track. Derek Maunder, with his corny undertaker's trick of making things look new, had tried to make the corpse appear untainted by decay. Yet death is unfakeable. All the light had gone out of my father's face; bruising showed blue around his lips from the ventilator tube. But what scared me most was the shape his open mouth made with the teeth bared. Was it a grimace? A smile? I decided it was a snarl. It was as though Dad was still reviewing books for the *New York Times*.

I stood very still. There it was again. The noise. I thought I could hear a noise. It was quite loud now. Three loud raps. In apprehension I waited for it to stop; but it got louder. I caught my breath and listened.

"Going someplace?"

To my astonishment it was my father speaking.

"Me?"

"Uh-huh."

"I'm going back to the hotel."

"That's too bad. It's so cold here. I don't want to live in the cold."

"I'm sorry—about the cold."

A voice from the past warned me: *Don't trust Dad.* And then I suddenly saw my younger self talking to him in New York sometime back in the 1990s.

"Dad, will you be nice to that new novel?"

"Me, *nice?* Over my dead body." There was a silence. "So you're on your way back to the hotel?"

"Yes. I'm going to leave this town. I'm not going to hang around."

"So long, then."

My father was going to saddle up and ride off into the sunset, was he? I felt he was amusing himself at my expense. Hardhearted and mocking to the end: that, sadly, was the dad I had come to know.

On our last day in Kingston, if against my will, we called on the psychic medium whom my mother had heard about from the hotel masseuse. The Reverend Dr. Mavis Campbell Grimstick (apparently her real name) lived in the cool, rhododendron-rich heights above Kingston in a suburb called Stony Hill. She boasted an ability to hear the dead—"clairaudience"—and advertised herself (humorously, I guess) as the "top-ranking conduit from the Beyond." As we set off, I resisted making a joke about striking a happy medium.

Twenty minutes later, we rang the bell to a house signposted *Bon Accord* and waited. By now the sun was well up; children's voices were raised in playful chatter somewhere.

The door opened and an elderly black woman said to us in a poised contralto voice: "I am the Reverend Dr. Mavis Campbell Grimstick, whom nothing does baffle," adding (I think with a smile): "You are cordially welcome." She had neatly set gray hair and not much of it.

We went into her lounge and sat down on a sofa.

"You have a nice place," said Mom.

"Thank you."

In fact the room was small, mean, and tawdry. The drapes at the single window were torn; marks had been left on a wall from swatted flies. Here, too, Christmas was on its way. A cluster of colored balls dangled over a cocktail cabinet; fairy lights on a small silver tree enhanced the festive cheer.

I noticed that my mother was pointing to a picture on the wall; after a hesitation she asked the medium: "Is that what I think it is?"

The medium smiled mysteriously, and said, "It is." The picture (Mom later told me) showed the Fox sisters' house in Hydesville, New York, which in 1848 had unaccountably produced a series of "rapping noises" and given birth, they say, to the modern spiritualist movement.

The session was a snip at U.S. $150.

"Have you been meditating of late?" the Reverend Grimstick asked my mother outright. "No? Because I'm getting a lovely pinkish light off of you, oh *yes*, man. Nuff-nuff light I'm getting—and you will be bathed in this light until the time you get cured." The medium fluttered her hands. "Yes, I like the psychic aura that you have, Mrs. Ruff, but I do want you to drink more milk. Oh, I know it can be fattening, but you could do with healing, my dear."

I broke in quietly: "Mom doesn't drink milk. Scotch, yes; milk, never."

"I see," said the medium. "Spirits should be taken in moderation—above all, rum." Her accent sounded a little too strenuously clipped, like a fake Queen's English; though some-times it was more Jamaican in its lilt. Beaming ambiguously, the medium continued: "Now why do I see Stonehenge? You are familiar with Stonehenge, Fanny? I may call you Fanny? Are you the sort that reaches out for the ancient understanding, I wonder?"

"As a matter of fact, I do. Reach out for it."

"That's lovely." The medium gave Mom a distant look, and went on: "All right now. Does the name Willie mean anything to you? Because I'm linking up with a Willie Ruff here from New York. And as I link up with this Ruff or Roff or Ralph, I'm getting a lot of tension in my abdominal zones, like he ate too much when he was on the earth plane. Do you understand me?"

"I do understand you," said Mom.

If memory served, Willie Ruff was a jazz musician who played alongside Miles Davis back in the 1960s. Why had a jazzman beamed into the room? Was he even dead? Willie Ruff, disconcertingly, was a homonymous near-miss to Jimmy Ruff, my father's name. Were the two related? I felt a chill down my neck.

The medium wiped her face with a hand towel, threw back her head to the ceiling, and began to speak in a deep low voice that sounded eerily like Dad's. "How are you, Fanny? Me? I am sitting in God's house in comfort, since you ask. That's right, you've guessed it. *I am no longer alive.* Sure, I would have liked to have lived a bit longer. But, since God has willed otherwise, do not grieve too much. After all, being dead's not so bad once you've gotten the knack of it, is it, Fanny?"

The voice stopped as abruptly as it had started.

Far from showing delight at this speech from the Beyond, Mom remonstrated angrily with the medium: "I didn't want my husband on earth, and I don't want him now. Take him back!" The unexpected self-disclosure even after all the disdain she had showed for Dad came as a shock.

"Mom!"

"Don't *Mom* me!"

"Relax yourself, Mrs. Ruff." The Reverend Grimstick looked quite affronted.

"Relax myself? How can I? You must tell me. Was that really my husband? Was that Jimmy Ruff talking?" Jimmy Ruff *resurrectus*: I almost laughed at the image the idea evoked.

The medium seemed mildly surprised at Mom's insistence. Unfortunately, the roar of an airplane coming in to land over Kingston muted what she had to say. She was silent now; even her face said nothing.

"It's no good, my dear," she said eventually, now with a heavier Jamaican accent. "When I was a likkle child in Kingston, we didn't have all these low-flying aircraft come roaring over us, nuh? It make it very hard to concentrate." She went on to say that she was lonely. All her relatives had "gone home" (meaning they had died?). "Yes, all of them dead out. I don't even have my grandsons here now, all of them done away with and dead out."

The medium was possibly mad as well as, surely, a mountebank. Yet when she accurately divined not only the date of Mom's birth but her mother's maiden name, I was not so sure.

We had no intention of hanging round for her offer of "mortuary information": namely, the dates of our deaths. So we left the Reverend Dr. Mavis Campbell Grimstick to her spook-dabbling, and returned to the Pegasus Hotel, even more confused than before.

At last, on the afternoon of December 23, my father was flown "HUM" in the cargo hold of Air Jamaica flight JA285. Documents signed by the U.S. vice-consul in Kingston confirmed that *only the remains of Mr. Jimmy Ruff and nothing else*" were contained in the coffin; no cocaine, no Kalashnikov rifles. Dressed in his white shroud, Dad arrived punctually at JFK at nine thirty p.m. local time and passed swiftly through immigration (the dead have no need of passports). My father's long supine journey home was finally at an end. Or so I thought.

Dreadfully, *unbelievably*, the wrong body had been repatriated. The body belonged to a vacationing American named Coleman Goodman. "Coleman *who?*" my mother asked in disbelief from the kitchen. (She had just sent out the invites for Dad's funeral.) "Coleman Goodman," I repeated, numb with shock. Apparently, a carelessness in cargo stowage was to blame. Trust Dad's rotten luck. Trust *our* rotten luck.

A week has gone by, and still no sign of my father. Wherever he is now, an abyss separates me from him; yes, we move in very different circles these days, my father and I. Maybe Dad did get repatriated to Africa after all. Maybe he has become a duppy, and is making mischief now among the living, just as he did in life. Foul play? Oh, we have talked about the possibility of foul play, my mother and I. It is now the New Year. I have just turned twenty-eight. Decca stirs slightly and begins to purr. I open a tin of Happy Heart cat food for her. Then I look out over the East River. There is no sun at the windows. Everything is more complicated and more serious than we had supposed.

PART II

Is This Love?

PART II

IMMACULATE

BY MARLON JAMES

Constant Spring

Man, look at Kingston, it so pretty from here, all them light right out to the sea.

1

This is what Ruth Stenton was wearing when she went to the Central Police Station/Criminal Intelligence Branch on East Queen Street in downtown Kingston: a sapphire halter top that pulled her breasts up from her chest but exposed sagging fat ripples on her back; white Dolce & Gabbana jeans with the logo slashed across the backside in red; a white Fendi bag that she wore like an afterthought, constantly pulling it up on her shoulder after it slipped down her arm.

The big station was busy with squaddies rushing in and out, sometimes with boys in handcuffs, papers shuffling up and down, the click-click of one-finger typing, the laughter of tired constables, and the thick cloud of cigarette smoke.

At reception, a policeman pointed left to a glass door with words printed in reverse. She stepped in and waited by the door until a uniformed constable called her over with his finger. He had just dripped ketchup on his shirt and was scowling into a box of fries from Burger King.

—Can I help you, ma'am? he said, looking from his snack to his calendar, where *Friday, October 22* jumped out in bold type.

—You don't have air-conditioning in here? she said.

—Can I help you, ma'am?

—Me is here to report a missing.

—A missing what? Cow, donkey, or goat?

—Don't get fresh with somebody who could be your mother.

—My mother don't look like she work New Kingston every night.

—But you fresh!

—What you want to report, ma'am?

—A missing. A missing girl. Me did call and somebody tell me to come in and make a statement.

—When you call?

—This morning. Boy, me could use a Rothmans.

—This look like Chiney shop? How long the girl missing?

—From Wednesday.

—Friday October 22, young girl reported missing. Who the girl?

—Janet Stenton.

—Relationship.

—What? Me look like no sodomite? A—

—Mother? Daughter? Church Sister?

—Oh, she is me daughter. Born 1979.

—Your daughter missing three day and you just coming to report it?

—She always a take off like she name kite. But never for so long. Plus she take me two good ears-ring. Not thiefing that? Grand larceny you call it.

—Then you is here to report a larceny or a missing?

—A larceny *and* a missing. Me ears-ring missing and she larcen it. That gal just buss 'way like kite. She is a little dutty gyal, that one. Never take no instruction from her mother. From she born, me say, this little one, this little one going turn slut like her auntie. Sometime me wonder if is fi her own or fi me. Anyway, she gone from Wednesday morning. Leave out before the sun even rise and is not the first time neither. But this time she take me ears-ring and me Julia of Paris shoes. Me no business bout the shoes. Imagine, she take off to go school from four in the morning? I mean to say, who love school so much that they leave four hour early? Me can smoke in here?

—No. Where you think she gone?

—How you mean? Where else schoolgirl going if she leave her house too early by herself? You no know the song? *Send the gal Nicky go a school, Nicky gone turn and gone a man yard*—

—No singing in here, ma'am.

—Me did hear things bout this new teacher. Him pants did too tight so me did think him was a battyman. But is so the devil deceive, praise Jesus. Anyway, you need to find that damn girl so me can discipline her.

—Discipline her, eeh?

—You going discipline her youself? Make sure take out me ears-ring cause is three hundred dollar that cost. She just like her father. One minute she here, next minute . . . That damn gyal a take man, you hear me? You going to the school to check bout the teacher?

—Which school?

—Immaculate.

This is how buses used to run in downtown Kingston in 1993. Because public buses were shut down by the government in the late '80s, Japanese sixteen-seaters with names like *Terminator 2* and *Smooth Operator* painted on the sides hit the road by five in the morning, sometimes already overstuffed with students feeling up each others' parts on their way to classes that began at seven thirty or eight.

The girls all loved one bus, *Prince Machoperi*, because the driver played Buju Banton, Snow, and Mariah Carey, and the conductor really knew how to balance on the door ledge off the heaving, swerving HiAce like he was practicing to surf.

At six thirty on the morning Ruth Stenton went to Central, *Machoperi* was bustling north from downtown toward Constant Spring, like a runaway carnival float with all those uniforms flashing by. Gray and red for Queens. Blue and cream for Holy Childhood. White for Immaculate Conception High.

As it neared Dunrobin Avenue, five miles north of downtown, the conductor, a boy barely eighteen, dressed in baggy pants, four gold-plated rings, and a T-shirt saying *Damn Yankees World Tour '91*, asked a Queens girl when last she saw Jacqueline.

—Who?

—The Immaculate girl?

—Not since Tuesday. Don't she take this bus every day? Nuh she always up front with the driver?

This is what a gaggle of Immaculate girls were doing at the school gate at 7:50 on the Friday morning that the 'ductor asked the Queens girl about Jacqueline, and Ruth Stenton was going to Central to make a missing persons report.

—Anna-Kaye Frater daddy drop her off in him jalopy yet?

—But Anna-Kaye always walk down from Manor Park.

—No, idiot. Mr. Frater drop her off in Manor Park. She walk down so that nobody would see her come out of a Ford Escort. My boyfriend Patrick say that is what his Hortense drive.

—Hortense?

—The helper, ninny.

—Jennifer Innis father driving a new Volvo.

—That's not the only thing him driving. And another . . . Oh my God, Kenisha, how you sneak that hairdo into this school? It ah take life.

—Yes, my girl, it is the lick.

—Well, all you need is a crimping iron and you set.

—You see Jennifer Innis father playing golf last week? He

always standing by the fence like him searching for a ball.

—The way him old, that's not the only ball him have to search for.

—Oh my God, *Prince Machoperi* coming up the street! Wave, girls.

—Me don't wave at lower-class boy in minibus.

—Rashid Shatani take that bus.

—Lie you lie. Rashid Shatani have three car.

—You can't drive and feel up girl at the same time. You going to House Arrest 2? Ambassador Disco spinning.

—All I get at House Arrest 1 was feel up.

—Buy you own drinks and stop take drinks from boys, that is the lesson deh so.

—Anyway, they change the venue from Tavistock Terrace to Morgan's Harbour.

—We going to Miami next week. I got Daddy to buy tickets to go see Whitney Houston. *I'm every woman, it's all in meeeeeeee.*

—Me hungry. Anybody see Irie Bruce?

—Maybe the Sisters drive him away again.

—But me hungry.

—Gal, everybody know you going vomit it up before lunch break, so this way you stomach already empty.

—Shut you shit, gal.

—Wait, wait. Volvo. Shelly Jordan driving up.

—But Shelly take the bus.

—Not on a Friday, fool.

—Is near eight o'clock, wipe that lipstick off.

—Is not me using shoe polish in me eyebrow.

—Is not me put on maxipad the wrong way and have to go to nurse.

—Look. Is who that?

—Look like Jacqueline Stenton friend. You know, Miss Goody-Goody, Melissa Leo.

—Which part o' she good if she run with Jacqueline? She only going on like . . .

—Why she running like that?

—Long way from downtown m'love.

—No, Kenisha, you can see anything? Open the gate wider!

—Is him. Is him. Him driving beside her.

—Car horn honking all the way down the street

—Him don't care.

—Last week him tell me that my pussy look like it would need two finger. Like me fraid of boy that drive car. So me just play like them dumb girl that boy like and say, *But how you mean?*

—*What-what-what-what? How me mean? Did I utter, mutter, or stutter* . . .

—Jesus Christ, Kenisha, you say it just like him. Mind me get goose pimple at the gate.

—Come inna me car now and deal with me buddy, *Did I utter, mutter, or stutter* . . .

—My gal, then you hear say the other day Sister Mary Agatha had to come out and tell him to drive off the premises after the nasty rass park him red car in front of the grade ten for one whole hour.

—Yeah, but is a Saab though.

—Listen to me, if I don't drape up that boy by him little balls one day my name is not Alicia Mowatt. Watch him, rolling down on Goody-Goody like him is cat and she is mouse. Little stumpy fat boy think him is man because him drive a car with a name him can't even spell. Speaking of Goody-Goody, where is the Jeckle to her Heckle? Anybody see Jacqueline from morning?

—Not since Tuesday.

—She sick again? I have words to give that damn girl.

* * *

Why you don't tell him to leave me alone? No, it not funny, people at school seeing him taking step with me like me is something to him.

2

This is when they found her: Monday morning, October 25, 1993. This is where they found her: South Parade, below St. William Grant Park in downtown Kingston, a place where morning roosters crowed like it was country, giving the wake-up call for madmen and whores to shuffle away and the starting signal for higglers to cart their fruit, vegetables, and chingum to the nearby market grounds, where minibuses ran a ring around the collar of the old colonial square, and Syrian haberdasheries stayed closed until nine.

This is how they found her. Faceup, legs wide in a death swing to spread-eagle. White skirt up, salmon panties down on one leg, pubic hair pulled up and roughed up. Under a minibus that had not parked there overnight.

The driver, dumpling fat and squeezing into a Michael Jackson *Dangerous* tour T-shirt shouted to the police that him don't know how dead gal get under the bus. At first people thought he was lying, that he mowed her down and did not stop, not knowing the bus was dragging her along like road kill.

But she was lying beside a patterned burgundy rug as if she was rolled out of it, one hand slung cross her chest, and her school uniform was clean, immaculate like the name of her school.

Her straightened hair was parted in two, but strands had slipped out of the loosened plaits. Some hair stuck to her face, heart-shaped with wild brows, a line below her forehead. Her lips, smudged with lipstick, were parted as if to kiss, and she stared at the sky, the whites of her eyes now light blue. Maybe somebody beat her, a higgler said. You think them rape her? What schoolgirl doing out so early by herself? School don't start till eight.

* * *

This is what the police took down for a statement: *Date: Monday, October 25, 1993, 8:45 a.m. Victim, a schoolgirl from Immaculate Conception High School, was discovered under Number 35 minibus, licence plate PP 0898. Aforementioned vehicle arrived into South Parade, in the vicinity of downtown Kingston, at 5:45 a.m. Witnesses who claim to have been in South Parade from 5:00 a.m. remember little to moderate traffic. No evidence of crime having been commited or perpetrators on the scene. Witnesses claim that terminus was clear and empty before the bus came. Nobody saw a body. At some time between the bus coming to the terminus and the bus driving off, somebody killed the high school girl and put her dead body under the bus without managing to be witnessed. There also may be evidence of unlawful carnal knowledge.*

Here are seven (7) things the police did not know about Janet Stenton:

1. Under her fingernails is one man. Sprinkled and spattered between her legs are more.

2. Periwinkle is not her favorite color, but she wore periwinkle panties every Thursday she left home early, four in the morning for school at eight o'clock.

3. When she left her mother's house in Trench Town, and walked two miles to a bus stop where nobody would recognize her, it was on a Wednesday morning, not Thursday.

4. Her favorite TV show was *MacGyver*. She had watched *MacGyver* every Thursday morning on videotape for the past three weeks. The school had a note signed by her mother asking that her daughter be excused from the first three hours of school for the next five Thursdays to take her aunt to the clinic for her dialysis treatment. Dialysis was not her idea.

5. She had already broken her hymen with two fingers.

6. Her chest smelled of Jergens talcum powder and her vagina smelled like a clean floor.

7. The panties on her left leg were not hers.

This is what Alicia Mowatt, student fifteen years old of Immaculate Conception High School, said while squeezing a ball from the nine-hole course next door after a few minutes of listening to a nun telling her class of Jacqueline Stenton's horrible tragedy that same morning:

—What, you sure is she? Downtown? But she not supposed to be downtown. I mean, she don't go to school downtown.

Alicia thought of flinging the ball at Sister Rose Maria just to get her to shut the bullshit about praying to God for discernment in this matter. She was no friend of Jacqueline Stenton. Damn girl acted too innocent, when she most certainly was not—*that* she found out only a few days ago. This was the damn Sisters' fault, leaving him there to just park his red Saab outside the grade twelve block and watch the girls.

—Fucking monster.

—Alicia Mowatt! No Immaculate student should ever speak in such a manner, no matter the occasion! Oh Mary, mother of God! Intercede blessed Virgin. Show us the true meaning of the heavenly Father, show us the meaning.

Alicia hissed. But then she looked around and saw that another girl was missing and went outside. Fifty feet away, clutching her backpack instead of wearing it, and walking fast, was Melissa Leo.

—Goody-Goody Leo! Where the fuck you think you going?

—Alicia Mowatt, don't bother with me this morning. Don't bother with me.

—Where you going?

—Don't bother with me.

—Where you going?

—You know where me going. Me going home. You uptown people can go to—

—You think is him. Not even him could—

Melissa Leo stopped.

—I don't know what you talking bout, she said.

—I saw her. I know where she was going.

—Go bout your business, Alicia Mowatt.

—You know where she was going too.

—I say I don't know what you bloodclaat talking bout.

—You girls come up from Cross Roads like you know how uptown run. If you knew how uptown run, you would know who run it.

—You can keep your bloodclaat uptown then. Me gone.

I tell you a secret. Is not Jacqueline alone I name. I hate the name Janet, you see.

This is what Ruth Stenton was wearing when the crew from JBC TV came to her house at twelve noon, thirty-five minutes after the police had left: a pink halter top and a plaid tennis skirt.

The crew got to her house in Trench Town, a city ghetto six miles west of where the body was found, having just left Immaculate Conception High School where in asking for reactions from the girls, the girls first learned that Jacqueline Stenton was murdered. Ruth was outside her house—blue, yellow, and small with a rusty zinc roof and packed tight beside the others flanking it. The reporter had stepped through the picket fence gate, pausing when she thought of dogs.

—Me don't believe no police. No sah, not me daughter. After them never show me no picture. Them say me have to come identify the girl, but me nah go nowhere fi go look pon dead body. And now TV camera in me house. You couldn't make me fix up the whatnot and breakfront little bit? Is just like she fi do this. Damn gal probably in some house somewhere a laugh bout how so many people a talk bout her. What a damn gal love when people take notice. Her father she get it from. After she, me just say no more pickney.

—Ma'am, the police are saying—

—Oi, camera man, you can see me from this side? Under the tree no have too much shadow? Are we on the air?

—It's not live, Miss Stenton.

—Wah? Then me can go put on me other outfit?

—Ma'am, what do you remember most about your daughter Jacqueline?

—Who?

—Jacqueline?

—Me daughter don't name no Jacqueline. She name Janet. Same thing me tell the damn police, that me daughter don't name no Jacqueline. Is who playing poppy show with me?

—Ma'am, are you saying this is not your daughter?

The reporter whipped out a photo she stole from the police headquarters. Ruth Stenton fainted.

This is how Grace McDonald made morning coffee. She scooped one more teaspoon than usual into the filter and set it in the coffeemaker. She waited, hummed with the machine, and turned on the TV.

Outside, if she looked hard enough, beyond her second-floor balcony, beyond the trees in the front yard that made her town home look like country to the road, rush hour traffic was already starting up. Across the road was a wedding center that played Celine Dion all the time, especially Saturday nights, making her cringe. That was it, fucking Celine Dion. At work, the nurse would play her at the reception desk, even the hard-core sky juice vendor with his cart by the hospital gate would be humming that shit song from *Beauty and the Beast*.

On the morning news, in between Miss Jamaica heading off to Miss World and the rise in gas prices at the pump, was a breaking story about a dead girl from Immaculate Conception High School found at South Parade underneath a bus. Name withheld until the family had been contacted.

What Grace really wanted was a cigarette, cancer in the titty could kiss her rass if it ever showed up. She thought about combing her hair, making herself nice for the man who was going to show up like *poof!* as her mother liked to say. Her mother also said her black nail polish made her look like a lesbian.

Nothing wrong with jeans, even if the button was getting harder to button, she thought. And she had on an honest-to-goodness floral top this morning, the tip of the neck was even lace. Thank God her lab coat would hide the rest of it, for she already felt like an idiot.

She did agree with her mother to wear lipstick, though, just because of how her mother talked about it like it was the new thing, the lick. Isn't that what you young people say? The lick?

Dead girl arranged on a blanket underneath a bus in broad daylight. Maybe this going be the lick now in this goddamn place. Pretty but so scrupulously violent. When she was in med school at Georgetown she used to joke with her friends that if they really wanted to be trauma surgeons they should do their internship in Kingston, at Dutty Public—the (un)popular name for Kingston Public Hopsital.

The phone rang. It was the director of public prosecutions, Michael "Barracuda" Barracat.

—McDonald, you see this business on the news?

—What business, Mr. Barracat?

—Come, girl, I'm in the middle of bush and hear about it before you?

—Sir?

—The Immaculate girl. My own mother just called me about it. Damn woman bawl so much she almost short circuit her phone. Ole girl went to Immaculate too, you know. Pull!

—Sir?

—Shit.

—Excuse me, sir, I don't get—

—One second, McDonald . . . How you mean, *Busha?* Your eyes in the back of your head or the front of your backside? You totally launch that at the wrong angle, you damn ass . . . Then *you* go and find it while I shoot the next one . . . Pull! Ha . . . yes . . . McDonald. Sorry about that. Some people think they can cheat at clay pigeon just because they name Sanguinetti.

—Are we back now?

—Yes. Sorry. So, my girl . . .

—You talking to me?

—Yes, McDonald, back to you. I swear these new mobile phones are nothing but grief. Try holding one with your shoulder and shooting. Impossible. Simply impossible. Don't get one, McDonald. Anyway, I need you to work on that girl today, you hear me? I already getting calls out here that this case need to move fast. Very fast. What nasty business, eh? Murdering an Immaculate girl. Almost make me wish it was Merl Grove girl, but that's a terrible thing to say, don't it? What school you went to, by the way?

—Wolmer's.

—Good enough. I hope to Jesus she's not from uptown. Otherwise this thing could get sticky.

You make me pack big bag and leave my mother house. Stop calling me little girl.

This is what Ruth Stenton was wearing when she went to the

morgue on North Street, two miles northeast of where they found her daughter's body: a cream satin dress with ruffles round the neck and lace down the sleeves. The hem flounced several inches topside her knee.

Her Jheri curl wet look was still damp. She dabbed her neck-back with bath tissue.

Ruth Stenton had fainted at the sight of her daughter in the police photo but still didn't believe it. She was going to know once and for all that very day. First she went to her sister in Rose Town to ask her to identify the body because she couldn't take any stress from people who were bound to start talking about the loose mother who send her daughter out at four o'clock in the morning when school don't start till eight o'clock.

No, the Sister said. If is she then is you why the girl dead, bitch, move you bomboclaat from me gate.

She took a bus right to the morgue but turned away from the entrance three times when she got there. That girl was somewhere at some man yard taking cocky and laughing at her mother, she just knew it. That photo didn't even show her face too good. She was sure now, plus that was not even Janet's school uniform. A higgler across the street was blasting her boombox from a hand-built stall—Nelson Mandela has won the peace prize, the newscaster just said. Ruth went inside.

Outside the cold chamber, Ruth turned to the policewoman standing beside her.

—Me sick of people telling me that me never want me daughter. If me didn't want me daughter she would have never born.

The policewoman looked at Ruth Stenton as if to say something, but pointed at the door. When Ruth had the urge to slap a woman, usually she slapped the bitch, but the policewoman had a club and a gun.

—Ma'am, you not the only person who have a viewing today, the policewoman said. The room was dark and cold with the *whup whup whup* of the fan above. Three bodies were laid down on slabs. Two were draped. One, an old man with dried blood below his nostrils, lay exposed.

—What kinda place this? Ruth Stenton said.

A fat man with thick glasses, a white coat, and a large yellow notepad came in. He looked like a doctor at the door, but as he passed Ruth with his hurried shuffle he looked like a butcher. He said nothing and yanked the gray sheet off the head, stopping at the neck.

—Lord Jesus Christ, Lord Jesus Christ, Lord Jesus Christ, Ruth Stenton said. The man had pulled the cloth to the shoulder, but Ruth pulled it down further.

—When them find her?

—She was found in the morning hours, the man in the white coat said. Early-morning hours.

—Is stiff she stiff?

—The process of rigor mortis is almost completely gone, ma'am.

—What that mean? The news reporter say them just murder her.

—No ma'am, they just found her. We still don't know exact time of death.

—You mean they never kill her in downtown?

—You're going to have to ask the police further questions, ma'am.

—Oh. Her breast them just stand up so in this blouse. Is rape them rape her?

—You're going to have to ask the police, ma'am.

—Then you never see things on her that not supposed to be there?

—You shall have to ask the police, ma'am.

—You must did see something when she come in here?

—She's still in her school uniform, ma'am. That is how they found her.

Ruth pulled the cover down further.

—That is not her school uniform. The girl only in grade ten, this is a senior girl uniform.

—Ma'am?

—She didn't have no ears-ring? On her, I mean.

—Whatever is there is what she had, ma'am.

—It worth three hundred dollars.

—As I said, ma'am.

—Uh-huh. You not saying much.

—Maybe whoever is the perpetrator took what you're looking for, ma'am. You'll have to identify the bag at the front desk, since they found it far away from the body.

—Where them find it?

—Let me see. Norbrook Crescent. That's off Norbrook Drive.

—What the bag doing up in Norbrook? After the school not in Norbrook.

—Norbrook on the way if you drive down from the hills, ma'am.

—She look like she drive? What she would be doing going to school from Norbrook? She come from Trench Town.

—Ma'am?

—Stop call me *ma'am*, me no look like no rassclaat old woman.

—Don't bother with the ghetto behavior in here, lady, the policewoman said.

—A who you ah call . . . I mean, excuse my French, officer.

—Ahem, are you saying these are not her clothes, ma'am? the man said.

—Since ah me is the mother who buy the school uniform, that is what me telling you.

—That's what the victim was wearing—I mean your daughter, that is what she was wearing.

—Why my daughter would wear them things? She didn't even like school too good.

—Ma'am, she was wearing those clothes and a pink underwear.

—Them make a man check little girl panty? Is what kinda slackness this?

—Look here, lady, I already tell you don't give this man any trouble, the policewoman said.

—Make me see this yah panty.

—Ma'am, you can't just—

—But this is not me daughter clothes. Officer, you of all people must know say is old-time panty this? And why me daughter in this uniform? Why nobody telling me that?

—Your daughter was not a student of Immaculate Conception High School?

—Yeah, but she not in grade twelve. She not even sixteen yet. No that me just say? Lawd a massy, is what deh pon me now, Father? You talk to that teacher yet?

These are three of the five questions that the autopsy specialist had about the girl but did not ask her mother. The other two he forgot after he received a telephone call:

1. Why was her uniform clean when her face, hands, and legs appeared to have all sorts of marks and bruises?

2. Was she alive downtown for any length of time or was she brought to the scene post mortem?

3. In what manner was she placed underneath the bus? How long after filing a report will the police try to forget about it?

3

*You going to get me in trouble, you know. Is bad enough you have me
leaving out on Thursday, now you have me doing Wednesday too.*

The next day, Tuesday, October 26, the *Star* newspaper carried
as its headline, *IMMACULATE GIRL BODY FOUND UN-
DER BUS.* The story had no statement from the police. Her
mother said she was a good girl who liked school and was even
going to become Catholic, and she doesn't know which demon
out there would kill her daughter. The director of public prosecution, the Right Honorable Mr. Michael Barracat, promised
a speedy resolution to the case.

The article also quoted the head of the Jamaica Council of
Churches, who said Jamaica must be going to hell when even
decent little girls whose countenance would never ask for rape,
get raped and murdered.

Two schoolgirls said they saw Janet being followed by a red
Saab twice, the last time on Wednesday, October 19, five days
before the discovery of her body. The same Saab has been seen
on the school grounds more than once in the past few weeks.

One of her teachers, whose name is being withheld as the
police proceed with their investigation, said she was a fine student, about to do well in the GCE O levels. On Wednesday,
the *Star* had as its second-page headline, *THE SEARCH FOR
THE SAAB.*

On Thursday, on the third page, in the top right col-
umn, the headline read, *STREET VENDOR WANTED IN
QUESTIONING.*

This is what the police knew about Irie Bruce, sky juice vendor
who parked his push cart every day outside Immaculate's front
gate. He said he wasn't running when they caught him. Him
was chilling with him queen when man knock pon him door,

and in the ghetto when a man knock hard pon a man door it either mean gunman or judgment. No, him never hear no police say, *Police! Open Up!* Everybody know that police don't make no sound when them pounce, them just sneak in like Nicodemus, a thief in the night. He said he didn't have no reason why he didn't sell outside the school on that day or the days after that. Him was just chilling with him queen when Babylon knock pon him door. *You is a nasty rapist who fuck little girl pussy then kill them, that's what you is,* a policeman said. Twenty-four hours in the lock-up at Central Police Station, his left eye had swollen shut and he was so dizzy that he nearly shit himself.

Forty-eight hours later his two legs were swollen and he screamed at odd times that them shocking him with current up him balls. A white man, belly pushing out of his gray suit, showed up at the lock-up seventy-two hours after Irie Bruce was detained, asking if he was being arrested for anything other than not selling sky juice on the day Janet Stenton was murdered. He had an American accent. *You come too late, him already confess,* the policeman on guard said.

What going on? You don't sound like you when you say that. I don't know. You don't sound like you.

These are the specifications of a Saab 900 Ruby:
Width: 70.9 in.
Height: 57.1 in.
Length: 182.9 in.
Ground clearance: 5.9 in.
Front track: 60.0 in.
Rear track: 59.3 in.
Wheel base: 105.3 in.
Cargo capacity, all seats in place: 15.0 cu.ft.
Maximum cargo capacity: 15.0 cu.ft.

EPA interior volume: 108.4 cu.ft.

The Saab 900 Ruby is only available in the UK. The lining of the trunk is gray carpet and not resistant to stains.

This is how you administer the Electric Boogie. Brandish an electric cord, ripped from an old appliance such as a blender, toaster, or table lamp, but preferably an extension cord, which is longer. Cut along the seam to separate the two electric wires and trim rubber from the exposed ends. Wire on left is the fixed electrode, wire on the right is the movable electrode. Have a man in the appliance repair shop across the street attach a box so that it can be switched on and off. Subdue the perpetrator and remove all clothing. Insert dishrag in the perpetrator's mouth to prevent talking. Suspect's own T-shirt can also be used. Approach table large enough to hold suspect but keep hands and feet hanging off table. Employ three or four personnel to restrict movement of limbs, and cuff wrists and ankles to table legs. Pull back the foreskin and wrap the fixed wire around the glans of the penis. Insert plug in electrical outlet. Blindfold the perpetrator. Apply second wire to feet, mouth, nipples, anus, and testicles in random sequence. The closer the movable electrode to the fixed electrode, the greater the shock.

This is the transcript of Irie Bruce's confession after the return to his jail cell: Me did was going to the school like me always do every day of the week. Me did was pushing me cart from the ice factory after me pick up crush ice for the day. Me did was walking from the ice factory down by Tower Street then pushing the cart west, then north until me reach South Parade Circle. That is when me did see the victim waiting at the bus stop for a bus. The place did still dark and streetlight still a glow. Me wonder why a girl all by herself out waiting for the bus when no bus was running yet. Cause me did know that no bus was coming for a long time, me allow lust to full up me heart. And it did full of wicked thoughts. Why me did full of wicked thoughts is cause me was a wicked person. Me walk up to her from behind and didn't raise no alarm cause me want to perpetrate the act quiet. Nobody was there when me grab her and take her to water lane which did dark. The lane did was like fifty yard from South Parade—no, thirty yard; no, sixty yard. South. Me grab her neck with one hand and cover her mouth with the other one and pull her backaway, bout fifty, sixty step till we reach the lane. She struggle and elbow me, which is why me have bruise all over me rib cage and toe and ankle and cheek. And the side of me head. And the cut above me eye. All them cut and bruise is what she do when me dragging her. And when me beat her up. Me did ready and push her down and take out me cocky, but she kick after me and the foot catch me balls which is why me balls also bruise up. And me cocky. And why me little finger break. She do it, she do all of it. And cause me never get to use me cocky, me kill her. She make me mad, madder than woman ever make me mad. And me grab her and knock her and squeeze her throat with me hand. Them say me strangle her—yes, me strangle her. And she break me finger. She do it.

Wait . . . wait. You hear that? You hear that? Sound like more than one car. You never tell me he was coming back.

This is the medical transcription report that the autopsy specialist at Kingston Public Hospital, the short, fat man with thick glasses who showed Ruth Stenton her daughter's body, took upstairs to the government pathologist for her approval.

It was Tuesday, October 26, the day after Ruth identified her daughter. The government pathologist, Grace McDonald, a woman, thirty-two years old, in a blue floral blouse and a doctor's white coat, with gold-rimmed glasses, shoulder-length black hair, and a hard-to-quit smoking habit, was packing her things to leave for the day.

—One more for you, McDonald.

—The Immaculate girl?

—Yeah.

—Shit, I might as well read this before the *Gleaner* come bothering me again, I don't know how them always find me, she said.

DESCRIPTION, AUTOPSY:
Asphyxia due to strangulation.

EXTERNAL EXAMINATION

The autopsy began at 8:30 a.m. on October 26, 1993. The body is presented in a black body bag. The victim is wearing a royal-blue jacket, a white frilled skirt, both the uniform of a senior student of Immaculate Conception High School for girls, pink panties, white brassiere. Jewelry includes two smooth-textured silver hoop pierced earrings in her top left pocket, and one silver ring on her left index finger.

The body is that of a normally developed young negroid female measuring 61 inches and weighing 92 pounds, and appearing generally consistent with the stated age of 14 years. The body is cold and unembalmed. Lividity is fixed in the distal portions of the limbs. The eyes are open. The irises are brown and corneas are cloudy. Petechial hemorrhaging is present in the conjunctival surfaces of the eyes. The hair is black and woolly.

Removal of jacket revealed two abrasions (known throughout this report as Abrasions A and B) on both sides of the neck below the mandible. Abrasion A is approximately 1.5 inches wide and 1 inch long and is on the left side of the neck. Abrasion B is 2.7 inches wide and 5 inches long with three spaces in between, leaving the conclusion that they were left by fingers. The skin of the neck above and below the abrasions showing petechial hemorrhaging indicates these injuries to be cause of death. There is a bruise with bleeding on the left cheek.

Upon removal of the victim's clothing, a pine disinfectant odor was detected. Areas of the body were swabbed and submitted for detection of pine oil and other cleaning agents. Following removal of the jacket, a ligature mark (Ligature A) was observed above victim's breasts with an abrasion above her left nipple indicative of a bite mark. Four scratch marks are on her left thigh to the front and three on the right. Skin is broken in three of the marks. A second ligature (Ligature B) encircles the waist, and is not consistent with what caused Abrasions A and B. The absence of abrasions associated with the ligatures, along with the variations in the width of the ligature mark, are consistent with a soft ligature, such as a length of fabric. No trace evidence was recovered from Ligature B that might assist in identification of the ligature used.

The genitalia are that of an adolescent female. Limbs are equal, symmetrically developed, and show no evidence of injury. The fingernails are medium length and fingernail beds are blue. There is a residual scar on the right knee.

INTERNAL EXAMINATION

HEAD—CENTRAL NERVOUS SYSTEM: Subsequent autopsy shows a broken hyoid bone. Hemorrhaging from Abrasions A and B penetrate the skin and subdermal tissues of the neck.

SKELETAL SYSTEM: *The hyoid bone is fractured.*

RESPIRATORY SYSTEM—THROAT STRUCTURES:
The oral cavity shows no lesions. Petechial hemorrhaging is present in the mucosa of the lips and the interior of the mouth. Otherwise, the mucosa is intact and there are no injuries to the lips, teeth, or gums. There is no obstruction of the airway. The mucosa of the epiglottis, glottis, piriform sinuses, trachea, and major bronchi are anatomic. No injuries are seen and there are no mucosal lesions. The hyoid bone, the thyroid, and the cricoid cartilages are fractured.

Grace flipped back to the first page, then looked down at her desk.

—Richardson, the printer cartridge run out of ink again? she said.

—Huh? What? No, I don't think so. The printer woulda make some noise. The page not clear?

—The page very clear, but the report missing one or two.

—What on the last page?

—The cricoid cartilages are fractured.

—No, that is it. Cause of death: strangulation by hand.

—And that's it?

—That's it.

—Oh.

—Where you heading off to? Date tonight with that man of yours? That you people from America call it? A date?

—Jamaican just like you Richardson. You fishing for something?

—Ha, ha. I thought you were leaving.

—Soon, but me forget something.

—Well, me gone, my girl. See you tomorrow.

—Later, Richardson.

She couldn't stand when the four-eyed, fat son of a bitch called her *girl*. He'd been calling her girl ever since the hospital promoted her over him, and that was nearly a year ago. He'd said it to a coworker, who then told her that he said it was only because she got her medical degree in fucking foreign that they promoted her. That, and because she was clearly fucking the Right Honourable Mr. Mark Barracat, the director of public prosecution, you should see how them close, he call her every morning, you know? She is also a lesbian.

Grace kept glancing at her watch until twenty minutes were gone. The lazy fucker had left by now. Richardson was always lazy. There weren't many doctors trained to perform autopsies these days, so she was stuck with him. But he always preferred to stop the autopsy as soon as the first credible cause of death jumped out into the open and exposed itself. This wouldn't be the first time she went back downstairs to finish the job he started, and it was not as if he would check back to find that his reports were filed twice as long. Besides, his conclusions were right, just lacking in detail. But this was the worst, with a full half of the report incomplete. No toxicology request, no blood work, no contents of the stomach, no lung investigation—and for a high school girl found murdered with her panties half off, no investigation of the genitalia or anus. There was enough negligence here to acquit a criminal caught on video. She buttoned her coat and went downstairs.

She pulled out the slab with Janet Stenton's body. Other than a direct light over the corpse, the room was dark. She checked the neck herself and saw all that Richardson mentioned in the report. She saw the bite mark above the girl's nipple and the scratch marks on her thighs, everything almost making a V to her center that screamed, *Look at me, read me, read the final page!* His report had mentioned a scar on her right knee, but it was a bruise, not a scar, and in the harsh fluorescent light it looked green. She grabbed a tweezer and a magnifying glass.

—Fucking idiot. Fucking fool. Either that or this man clearly never see more than one or two vagina in him life.

Grass. Recently fertilized, a lawn where people bothered to fertilize grass. Grass also stuck out from under toenails, so plainly green that she wondered if Richardson had looked anywhere below Janet Stenton's knee. Grass in her toenails and in a fresh bruise on her knee. She was running, probably in a garden recently watered, and fell. Her fingernails had no dirt or grass but somebody had scrubbed them down with an abrasive, scouring pad maybe. They smelled of Pinesol. The marks on her thighs looked like fingernail scratches, and unless Janet Stenton had a truly disgusting habit, tufts of pubic hair were ripped out by someone else. Grace went over to the door and switched on the overhead lamp. She grabbed the phone on the wall.

—Hey, you have a rape kit upstairs there? . . . Yeah, yeah, yeah, I know. Look, I've been trying to leave from five. . . Right, like you don't know why me down here when I already have a man doing autopsy. Anyway, you have a rape kit?

Grace began to work.

Petechial hemmorhage in the conjunctiva confirmed that she was strangled, but sperm in her vagina, along with Pinesol, meant she was raped and the perpetrator tried to wash away himself post mortem with household cleaner. Or themselves. She took swabs for analysis. She had been raped, more than once, by more than three men, some more forceful than others. The girl was damaged, inside and out. Her chest was still white from baby powder. Grace combed through her arm and pubic hair and collected loose strands for the microscope in the lab right next to hers. Several hairs appeared to match but several did not. Grace took swabs for analysis. She put the hairs in rape kit packets. She made smears of Janet's body and sealed those in packets as well. She clipped her nails and cut locks of hair. Grace would have to send everything off for DNA testing, a process that still took too long.

She was just about to return to the locker, but a new smell bothered her. No, not new, it had come in faint waves which she'd assumed to be something that Richardson left behind, maybe in the waste paper basket, by the door. Peanut, maybe some shells that he tossed, or a peanut butter sandwich he gave up on. He had a way of eating in the lab that made her sick if she thought about it too long. Grace had almost forgotten about it again when she turned Janet Stenton over.

—Jesus Christ, sweet girl. Sweet Jesus.

Me not going run again me not going run again me not going run yes me like Ketel One no not straight not straight me throat burning not straight not straight yes yes yes no no no no no no no no no me want me mother me want me mother me want me mother. Me want me mother.

This is what Ruth Stenton wore on the way to the post office on the same day that Grace McDonald said *Sweet Jesus* like she believed in God: white leather string slippers that wrapped three times around her ankles and exposed her dark purple nail polish. A black skirt that crested right above the knee but itched, and made scratchy sounds whenever her hands brushed the black velvet stripes. Her sister, the one working for that old woman in New York, had sent it down through Federal Express for the funeral. Ruth had told her not to send nothing through that rassclaat post office because them mangy-foot bitch will thief just bout everything that send from foreign except for book. She hissed, seeing herself in the glass door as she stepped inside.

—Me have this pink slip for a letter, she said to the first clerk in the window.

—There is a line, ma'am.

—Oh, excuse me, please.

Ruth went to the back of the line convinced that everybody was now watching her. Damn woman embarrass her so. And look pon the bitch too. She can't even spend little bit of her pay to style her hair, and her red blouse soon pink because she don't know how to wash. This was the kind of woman that don't care bout no man because she can't get one. But then maybe she be the one who better off. Only one thing turn a girl from a good girl who love her mother to a backtalking, whoring slut in just one summer, and that was man.

This was not what Ruth had planned. Janet was supposed to go after man, yes, and a man from uptown too. But she was to make sure she get something before she give up the punani. She, Ruth, taught her that from she was eleven. No matter how broke you be or how ugly God make you, you have something that all man in Jamaica want, even the battymen, when them trying to throw the battyboy stink off themself. But first you ask for some Kentucky and Canei before him take you home. Then a box to take home for your family. Then money for just one thing at the supermarket, like cereal, then start to rub you wrist or you finger like you missing something (but not the ring finger cause that going scare them), rub it until he buy you a nice little bracelet, then tell him how you fraid that somebody going see it and rob you and kill you so you going keep it somewhere safe and special, special like him, then you take it to jewelry store and sell it to them Syrian people and give the money to your mother.

But the damn girl never do any such thing. Keeping all the money for herself, saying that she working herself out of this fucking ghetto and nobody going stop her, least of all some damn woman who want to whore out her own daughter, like that was true. The plan was never to whore her out but for her to use the little thing she got to get what she want, and once she get it, don't ignore the woman who still work hard, with no man to help her to send you to good school, you dutty stinking ungrateful little bitch.

She searched all over the house for that girl's money, under her dresser, in that shoe box from the shoes she bought her seven years ago. Her school bag, the perfume boxes that she kept under her bed. She knew all the places, checking as she did every few months for ganja or some nasty book, or a love letter from some man, maybe the new teacher. Between the mattress and the divan, every one of her shoes, including the high heels that this man buy for her. Maybe it wasn't the school teacher since everybody knew that teacher didn't make no money. Maybe it was a man that she didn't want to know that she come from the ghetto and who would want that anyway, since once he see that she was a ghetto girl all he would want was the ghetto slam in exchange for two-meal deal at Burger King. Stupid girl, thinking that man was going take her out of something. You had to use the man to take *yourself* out, something she herself could have done when she had the chance but she made that chance go stale and that man was now in New York since 1979. By 1984 he stopped promising to send for her and the pickney. By 1987 he stopped sending money every other month, and by 1990 all letters and telegrams to his address in New York returned to sender. And after all that, the dutty stinking little bitch, that woman—no, that child, that girl, my girl, my girly girl girl, oh God—

—Ma'am, we don't have all day and people behind you.

—W-What? Oh, sorry. Sorry. Me have this pink slip for a parcel.

—Let me see it. Is not a parcel, is a registered letter.

—What that mean?

—Means it's registered. Wait here, please.

Ruth waited until she returned home to open the envelope. It was bigger than she expected, the size of Janet's composition book, and brown. The weight in her hand felt strange, not like a letter or a Christmas card. She ripped it open and money scattered around the bedroom. She counted it four times, each time disbelieving it more and more. She checked the envelope for return address but there was none. She panicked, wondering if she was being watched, and stooped down to the floor to count the rest of it. Her other children would be home in a few hours. She counted thirteen thousand dollars.

This is the exact account of the phone call between Grace and Mr. Barracat, the dee pee pee, the day after Grace said *Sweet Jesus* like she believed in God and Ruth Stenton counted out thirteen thousand dollars—November 2—over a week after Janet's body was found.

—Good afternoon, Mr. Barracat.

—How you knew it was me?

—Well, nobody else calls me before my morning coffee, sir.

—Hell hath no fury like a McDonald? Anyway, what is this big folder business you leave on my desk?

—What? You mean the autopsy? I'm still waiting on toxicology. And a positive ID on further things found inside her. Don't even start to talk bout DNA.

—I don't know why you even bothered. We got a confession from last week.

—A confession?

—Baby, even the *Star* and the *Gleaner* know about it, and as usual, you don't. You know, McDonald, they call it having a life. Take your backside out of work every now and then.

—What you mean by confession, sir? Who confessed?

—The sky juice vendor who use to sell outside Immaculate High School gate. He strangled her.

—Him and who else?

—What you mean?

—He said he strangled her?

—Yeah man. Grab her from behind then carry her into Water Lane to rape her, but she put up a fight and he strangled her.

—He raped her?

—No.

—No?

—Well, of course the son of a bitch tried to, but she kicked him in the balls. God bless the poor girl.

—Mr. Barracat, you read my report?

—Grace, you know how many sons of bitches I have today that claiming they innocent? I have one who film himself and the four schoolboys he invite into his minibus to rape a school-girl and he pleaded not guilty anyway. Thank God for one who finds himself guilty before I have to tell him.

—This girl was not murdered in Water Lane. And she was raped.

—Maybe she was going home from a night orgy.

—Sir, I don't think that's funny. Please read my report. The only thing in the man's confession that matches the report is the strangulation. And she was raped.

—Fine. He raped her. Shouldn't be a problem getting him to confess to that too, but who fucking cares? We got the son of a bitch on murder anyway.

—There is no way he acted alone, sir. Not unless he raped her multiple times—

—So him rape her multiple times. The brethren can stan pon it long, as the ghetto people say.

—Each time with a different penis? And unless grass grow-ing in Water Lane now, she was never there. And for God's sake, this sky juice man kill a girl, then somehow find a brand-new Moroccan rug, not some hire purchase layaway rug, Mr. Barracat, a real Moroccan rug from fucking Morocco, and wrap her in it? You know that rug cost more than my year's rent?

—No, but I do know I don't much care for that tone.

—Sorry, sir.

—He stole it. Like a murderer stealing something going to shock anybody.

—And then he leave her under a bus like she's a damn tableau?

—Don't understand French.

—Sir, they didn't even bother to take the damn thing out of her behind. They didn't even bother.

—Fine, I'll ask him who he's protecting when I put him on the stand. You happy now?

—You not going to ask me about her behind?

—Surely he's not going to take this fall himself if he had company.

—I want to see his statement.

—Then go to the station and knock yourself out.

—Sir, please read my report.

These are the four things that were on Grace McDonald's desk two hours later when she received a call from Toxicology: a pack of Matterhorn's, cold coffee in a University of the West Indies—Mary Seacole Hall mug, a pencil chewed out of its original yellow, and a new file, opened before she released Janet Stenton's body for burial.

Her office had one window which gazed over to another window right across. Between the two windows the hospital had a way of feeling like a prison, especially five floors up. She would get up and pry open the window, keeping it that way for a few minutes to an hour listening for traffic or that sky juice vendor playing Celine Dion, until the hospital smell came through.

Sometimes she felt that she took the smell home and couldn't wash it off. The phone rang.

—Yeah?

—Grace, I have some of the lab work.

—Already? You nah joke.

—Barracat know you doing this?

—You don't worry about Barracat. What you have for me?

—First thing first, you establish time of death?

—Yeah, Sunday, October 24. They discovered the body on the 25th.

—Saturday.

—Saturday?

—Yeah, I did a histology on one of the samples you sent me. She was murdered Saturday.

—They kept the body an entire day?

—Yeah. Somebody who know a butcher or somebody who have a refrigerated room. Also, I checked the hairs you sent me.

—You got all of them? The black one and the other two, which look white? I just couldn't tell the rest, and then there are the ones on her bottom.

—All the ones from her buttocks come from the same source and they match a few from her front. But the reason why you couldn't identify the other hairs is that they weren't hairs.

—Oh?

—No, not hair. Two of them are wool, like from a rug or something.

—Ah, the rug they wrap her up in.

—Maybe, but the others, Grace.

—Yeah?

—Fur.

—What you just say?

—Fur.

—No.

—Yeah.

—They couldn't . . . they just couldn't.

—It might just be that the person was a dog lover and had just played with his pets.

—Can you tell which dog?

—No. A big black one, though. One that don't shed much. Grace, I'm going to tell you something. You don't have dogs so you don't know. That thing you found up her rectum, you know, the rubber thing?

—Yeah?

—I assume you know what it is.

—No, I don't. I just know it doesn't belong there.

—It's a Stuff n' Chew dog toy. A dog treat holder. You fill it with peanut butter and throw it to your dog. Takes them hours to figure it out. I use it when I just can't be bothered to play with Boxer. Me always busy so that's pretty much all the time . . . Grace? Grace? You there? Grace?

—You get anything on the grass?

—Yeah, industrial fertilizer. You can't buy it at the hardware just so. Probably a gardening service.

—Gardening service in Jamaica? A who rich so?

—You can check Glidden's. They the only one I know.

This is what the woman who answered the phone at Glidden's Tools and Gardening said when Grace called her immediately:

—We don't release that kind of information, ma'am.

—Confidentiality? Really? What, you have confessional booth behind the Miracle-Gro? I'm asking if your staff use this fertilizer anytime in the past two weeks and where.

—I can't really help you, ma'am.

—Put your supervisor on the phone.

—She stepped out.

—When is she coming back?

—Me no know, ma'am.

—Anway, I'm sure you have record somewhere, so please save me the trouble of coming down there.

—Can't do that, ma'am.

—You know what? That's fine, you're being a good employee. Now just hope that when me and the six policeman come down there, and turn everything upside down, that you have enough time to fix up the place before your boss come back.

—You can't do that.

—Really? You going to see me do it in less than thirty minutes. And by the way, tell your boss that in a month she will be audited too.

—Hold on. Hold on.

—Hello? Who is this?

—No, the question is who is *you?* I'm going to guess that you're the manager. Had a good walk? Good. Now, listen to what you going do for me right now.

Me want me mother me want me mother me want me mother. Me want me mother.

This is the magazine that Ruth Stenton carried in her hand at the same time Grace McDonald got a call from Toxicology: *Elle.*

Ruth was on her way to the dressmaker she knew. She had browsed a bookshop only hours before and leafed through *Vogue, Vogue Patterns, Redbook,* and *Harper's Bazaar* before she found it, a black dress that she wanted for the funeral now that she had twice worn the skirt her sister sent her. The small card lodged at the bottom of the envelope had said, *For Jacqueline,* and it was for her, but a good dress for the funeral was for her too. That, and a gray hearse and a pink coffin with light gray silk trim. The funeral home had shown her a small box covered in purple velvet like fabric at first, and she cursed them out shouting bout if them think is cause she come from ghetto that she can't get decent coffin for her big daughter. The funeral home director offered her a discount when he recognized Janet Stenton's name from the newpaper and TV reports, which she took, saying there is no situation so bad that you can't appreciate a good bargain, right?

After that, she took the magazine to the dressmaker, a stout woman whose dresses always had lace trim and who lived in Riverton City, a zinc-shack ghetto five miles west of Trench Town. Ruth stuffed herself into a packed taxi that ran the Spanish Town Road highway west and came off by the garbage dump that surrounded Riverton City. The garbage rose as high as hills and boys and women picked through, looking for things that they stuffed in black plastic bags. The slow-burning stink worked its way into everything, so complete that the smell vanished for all but those who visited.

—Boy, me know things tough with you, Miss Ruth, but me can't give you no more dress pon credit.

—But what a way you facety. See it deh, me have money. Me have plenty money. You done now? How much me owe you? Me will pay you. Now, me want this frock.

—White more for wedding than funeral, Miss Ruth.

—Huh? Not that one, the purple one beside it. And me want it in black.

—But that is not no funeral dress.

—Is that me want.

—It don't have no sleeve.

—Is that me want.

—Sequin not cheap, Miss Ruth.

—Me say me have money.

—You want the split too?

—Yes, me want the split.

—You leaving the funeral to go to party or something?

—You know what me tired of? You know what me tired of, lady? People who think they can judge me. Everybody who walk past me think they should leave word like me is bank and what them think is deposit. You know what? You don't know nothing bout me and you don't know how you can do everything you think you can do, and people just do what they want anyway because man tell them to.

—Me never did say nothing.

—You say everything. You a damn Jamaican who think you can talk by looking. Well, me tired of it from people who think them better than me. You is just some little seamstress who can't even get work at the free zone and you should be glad me spending money with you.

—Look here.

—No, you look here. Shut you rassclaat mouth and make me a damn dress.

—Sorry, ma'am. But at least you must be happy them catch the killer?

—No, me not happy. How any of this to make me happy? Me not happy at all.

Crabgrass is a weed, though some Jamaicans think it is grass. This is one of the things that Grace McDonald was thinking as she drove around Norbrook for hours, turn after turn, avenue after avenue, crescent after crescent, mews after mews, weaving in and out, somehow always looping round again on Norbrook Drive, which cuts the community in half.

She should have taken a map. What the fuck was she thinking? Going out with just the list from Glidden's. Four people had bought their special crabgrass formulation and service in the last three months. For most people, crabgrass in the lawn was fine as long as everything was mowed level. It was like having a head with different grades of hair.

The first house she found, thank God, seemed empty. A beige one-floor bungalow. Spanish-tiled roof. Glass sliding windows and doors.

She parked on the street and went inside, thinking all the time what to say if someone asked what the hell she was doing on their property picking grass.

Must a good thing to be so rich that you don't need to worry about thief, she thought. Open gate? Glass windows and doors?

This lawn had neither crabgrass nor the smell of the weed killer, the thing that her nose couldn't place when she'd inspected the corpse of Janet.

The second house had the weed in the lawn but not the smell.

The third house was like the first—tile roof as well—but two floors. As she moved toward the five-foot iron gate, two barking rottweilers swerved into view. Time stopped. They raced. Time moved again. And they were on their hind legs with their front paws flat on the top of the gate, nails out.

Grace backstepped into her car.

She shook her head. They had a suspect who confessed to the crime and she was a doctor, not a detective. Maybe she had watched too many damn episodes of *Quincy* on TV Land when she lived in D.C. It's his fault that she switched from pediatrics to forensics, him and his punk rock episode (*punk rock is killing the kids!*). She laughed knowing that nobody at the hospital would have gotten the reference, not even the Indians. But this case had a stink that would not go away. She kept thinking of how settled her life would have been, how much more satisfying it would have been to just smoke the day away had she not turned the poor girl over.

Raping a girl was one thing. Killing her was another. But this was just a different level, a defiance, some man or men saying, *Bitch I'm going to keep on disrespecting you, even as a corpse.*

Even a madman killer leave a corpse alone, even he can see that the damage is already done, leave some bit of respect now. But not this man, and it wasn't a group that do that, come to think of it, it was one man—that kind of shit doesn't happen by consensus, it happens by ego. That kind of shit comes from a man who want to make it public that the girl was in the palm of his hand, and watch now, Jamaica, watch now, world, while I make a fist.

She was halfway across the lawn before she smelled it.

This is what Alicia Mowatt saw on the day Janet went missing. She was slouching up Norbrook Road at around four p.m. after her Wednesday tennis practice.

Forty or so yards ahead was Stenton, not in school uniform, but a T-shirt and jeans, and wobbling in high heels as she continued uphill. Her hair was parted in two as it usually was, but the halves were loose. She was trying to pull it out and walk at the same time.

Alicia thought to call her name, but they were not friends and she could not think of a single thing to talk about all the way to the top of Norbrook Road. They could always talk about how Spanish turn so boring since grade ten, or it must be something to not need to look good because Sister Mary Clarice would have shaved her moustache by now, or how it long overdue that Georgina stop crimping her hair because 1989 gone and it not coming back, or if she has a boyfriend yet and has the boyfriend touched her breast, or shared a cigarette, or made her listen to Shabba Ranks.

But then a white Land Rover sped past her so fast that she jumped back, even though she was on the sidewalk. The vehicle slowed down a few feet behind Stenton, crawling, then speeding up, then braking fast to draw level.

Stenton was stomping, the wobbly clunk in her heels loud

enough for Alicia to hear. As she stopped, the Land Rover stopped. As she started walking, the Rover rolled. She stopped again, looking down, turning full around so that Alicia jumped back behind a bougainvillea hedge. Her heart was pumping furious. She knew the Land Rover.

Stenton paused again, the Land Rover pausing with her. Stenton leaned toward the door and began to gesture, at one point throwing her arms in the air and just letting them flop down. Then she stepped back and crossed her arms and looked down at her shoes and up at the sky. The door eased open from inside. Stenton shook her head and seemed to smile—it was hard to see—and climbed in.

The big white vehicle drove off but not as fast as before. A hundred yards later it made a left turn and pulled into a driveway through an open gate.

Alicia waited. She had forgotten her Seiko so she counted to sixty, seven times, before she began to walk again. She couldn't care less about Jacqueline Stenton but had hoped so hard that she even whispered it: not that house, not that damn house.

Alicia continued counting as she made her way up the grade. When she got to the house she slowed down and looked, not out of the corner of her eye, although this was what she'd intended. She turned her whole head and stared. Cause she wanted to see what that Stenton was up to in this house she knew. You need details when you take back gossip to the girls. Right, that was it. Nothing to to do with her—besides, Stenton could clearly take care of herself if she was running with this type of crew.

But . . .

There was a but here, a big one that she couldn't leave at the gate. Dig one grave here, you going end up digging two, she thought. The driveway was empty, she noticed. Like the Land Rover was parked in the back.

She was about fifty yards past the gate when she heard a screech ahead of her and saw the red Saab slide out of a side road like it was in a rally, wheels turned one way and back-skidding the next, before it straightened up and came onrushing down the grade. She looked away when it flew past, partly out of shame and partly from the grit it kicked up in her eyes.

She found herself in two places at the same time. On her feet on the side of Norbrook Road, and in an upstairs bedroom inside that house, that house where she knew the car would stop and turn in.

It hurt the first time, she told him. And he wouldn't stop. It hurt the second time. And the third time too, when she felt like she walked right into it. But it was cause she did too tight and fool, he said, so she went home and used her finger in the shower to get looser. She didn't know what to do with her mouth either so he suggested a banana and laughed at her when she told him she tried it. If she rubbed her cheek just right she would remember what it felt like, the backhand, the ring from Daddy, balancing the smart of the pain against knowing she had a real boyfriend who would tell her to never disrespect him. Three years ago. Twelve years old. There's a difference between knowing when to leave and being kicked out. The whole time he made him watch.

4

Why you don't tell your brother to leave me alone? No, it not funny, people at school seeing him taking step with me like me is something to him.

I love how you did handle him when him did come by earlier. You bad him up for real. Me never know say is so you can going bad? But truthfully, you don't think him did trail me? Come on. So how as soon as I reach him reach then?

Anyway, I like how you went out and put him in him place, but still. How long that going last? No, I don't think him badder than you. Easy, baby.

Then tell him again, cause him getting ruder and ruder. You sure him right in the head? And you know say him going after my friend Melissa now. You know why I think him vex? Is cause me choose you instead?

No, I not fraid for him. But is you supposed to handle him because is your brother. And you don't know what him do out at the school . . .

Beg your pardon?

Yes, is your brother . . . Wha? You think only uptown people care bout family? Don't bring me mother into this . . . You don't even know me mother.

Lawd . . . you no tired yet? You going to get me in trouble, you know. Is bad enough you have me leaving out on Thursday, now you have me doing Wednesday too.

No, do it this way. Slow down, where you rushing to? After this we going to pick up the visa?

We can close the window over there. That one looking out the road. I don't know, it feel weird. Like somebody watching. No, is you the one with guilt conscience.

Me can't just laugh like that. Somebody have to give me a joke. Give me a joke then, nuh?

No, you come over here. This couch bigger and it nearer to the TV. Shut up, I do more things than watch TV.

You not closing the windows? Them so big you must get a whole heap of mosquito. Oh, mosquito fraid of uptown. Ha ha.

Rass. I can't believe how time fly. Night already. Man, look at Kingston, it so pretty from here, all them light right out to the sea. I would want my bedroom right here and with only glass so I can see the view all the time.

You know how hard it was walking up your rich people hill? You was supposed to pick me up at the bottom, not the middle. Imagine, *have me walking up like some household helper. In these shoes. You like me shoes? You really like it?*

Make we use the pool, nuh. You no say your parents gone for the whole weekend. Thank God your brother gone.

So you like me shoes? Tell me again.

So when you carry me to Miami you going buy one even better than this for me. You wretch you, I catch you. You think I forgot.

So when we going?

When we going . . . What? Me can't remember what me was going say now. You sure you brother gone? All right, is nothing. Maybe I just remembering what him say, why me feel like he's . . .

So you would do that to me?

When we going to Miami? No, me never want to get married. You want me do what? Is which little girl you using that with?

You think me is a fool?

My mother still good for teaching one or two thing bout man. What she don't teach me, me learn from her all the same.

No, my mother didn't go to Immaculate.

G'way, I don't talk too much. You talk too much.

Well, if you want me talk less, stop giving me screwdrivers.

Wait . . . wait. You hear that? You hear that? Sound like the Saab. But is not it alone. Hear there. Is more than one car. I putting on my fucking clothes.

Go deal with him. Go. You don't hear him calling you? Go. Tell him I not here. Tell him I gone already.

I don't know. Just tell him that.

How you mean you can't hear me? I don't want him to know I'm here. What you want me do? Bawl it out? Sometimes you just go on like you don't have no fucking sense.

Don't lick me. Leggo off o' me. You see, is only me you have strength for. You no have no strength for your brother, though.

Them coming upstairs. Them coming upstairs. Sorry. Sorry. Go lock the door. Go lock the door. Let me go. Let me go. You no bloodclaat hear me bomboclaat say leggo me pussyclaat, boy.

Me naah make no man rape me! Me naah make no man rape me! Go suck you mother.

Do . . . beg you . . .

Look what me come to, dear Jesus. Look how you make the man them come open the door. The Lord is my shepherd. The Lord is my shepherd. The Lord is my shepherd.

Mewantmemothermewantmemothermewantmemother.

5

This is the phone call Grace McDonald received at one a.m. on Wednesday, November 3, hours after going up to Norbrook Road searching for a smell.

—Grace.

—Somebody better be pregnant or dead.

—First thing you should learn is some manners.

—Who the *fuck* is this?

—Richardson.

—Well, it sounds like you, but it couldn't be you at this time of the night. Plus, what the fuck is this attitude about? Listen, it's way too early for me to tell you I'm tired of you and your shit. And I way too sleepy to tell you to stop going on like say I owe you something or I do you something.

—You done talk, my girl?

—You know what? Me tired of every fucking man in this profession thinking me is his girl.

—Tell it to somebody who care, sweetheart, cause me no give a rass. Two thing this phone call bout, you listening? First thing: learn some manners. Second thing: leave things that too big for you.

—Richardson? Don't take any step with me.

—You already take enough step for the both of we. What a fucking idiot. You blind or you fool?

—I'm hanging up right now.

—Why you mess with my report?

—You call that a report? And what you mean *mess with?* It was incompetent. It was fucking incomplete. You don't just come across a dead girl with her panties half off and don't check for anything. Is so UWI teach forensics?

—You think you know everything, don't it? You go to your little poppy-show med school in America feel say you is any big thing. Well, everybody know that if it wasn't for your DPP boyfriend who promote you, you wouldn't have position over me. Who the fuck are you to go behind my back and check up and change up what I do? Did I ask your fucking opinion? Did anybody ask your fucking opinion?

—Do your job.

—Who the fuck you think you talking to, girl? I *am* doing my job. Which country you live in? Cause is sure not this one. Me no understand how the fuck you get promotion and don't know shit about how this world work.

—Your report stopped at the part where it shouldn't have stopped.

—No fool. It end where it should end. There's a big difference between stop and end. You figure it out.

—You know they set a dog on her?

—What you want me to do with that information?

—You know I figured out who did it?

—Yes, little girl. And him already know you know. Why you think me calling you at one in the morning, cause me want to swap recipe? They know, Grace. What the fuck you think you doing? Why you think it come back to me? The fuckers called me three times, Grace. Three fucking times. The last call came ten minutes ago. The bloodclaat people know.

Ruth Stenton still has the memory of how she felt when she got the second registered letter containing seventeen thousand dollars. You start to forget. You start to realize that hard as it may be, some little girl do ask for it.

Grace McDonald still has the memory of what it felt like when she got to work early on the morning after the one a.m. phone call.

You pick up the phone to call the police, then you put it down because the police might be in on it too. You remember a song that you have no reason to remember because you too old for loud American music despite all those years at Georgetown, but it said, just because you're paranoid don't mean they're not after you. You close the door to your office and pull a chair behind your door and a credenza behind the chair and you wait. You try to think but all you can do is wait. You touch your shoulder and wince because the pain is still raw. You try to think, to remember if you saw this Land Rover before Marescaux Road. No, not when you left your home on Lady Musgrave Road. Not when you turned left on Old Hope Road, then right, heading south to downtown. Not when you turned right again on Marescaux Road to bypass Crossroads congestion. The white Land Rover seemed to come out of a childhood fear of blackheart man, it just appeared, fully formed and ready. It rammed into the back of your car first and you cussed, slowed down for a stop to get out and swap insurance docs or something. You stopped but the Land Rover did not. It kept coming and when it rammed into you the second time your head clobbered the steering wheel. It pulled back and you stomped the gas pedal and drove off, but it followed, came up to the side, you saw schoolgirls crossing further down the road and hoped they run fast, but they're not running, they're not running, move! Two dove to the side of the road. The Land Rover swung into yours, shoving you into the sidewalk. It came again and you swerved out of the way, almost hitting a stop sign. The vehicle dogged you all the way around National Heroes Circle and swerved into you again on the driver's side and you screamed. Then, as you drove out of Heroes Circle to head south, to the police station near South Parade, the Land Rover turned and headed north.

You parked you car in two spots at the Kingston Public Hospital and ran five flights up the stairs to your office. You locked the door and you waited. The phone rang. You waited. It rang seven times and stopped. You turned away but it rang again. It sounded insistent. It would not be denied, bitch.

—Hello.

—You want to know a joke about dogs?

—Who is this?

—You want to know a joke about dogs?

—Who is this?

—Did I utter, mutter, or stutter? I said if you want to know one bomboclaat joke bout dog.

—No.

—Most times they have more empathy than humans. The son of a bitch was actually trying to help her. Can you imagine that? Only one person in the room behaving like a decent human being and it was the bomboclaat dog.

—Why you telling me this?

—You seem like you were looking for an answer so I thought I should just save you the trouble and give it to you. Baby—

—Not your fucking baby.

—Rass, baby have one serious potty mouth, though. You mother didn't wash it out with soap? Should I send somebody over to her house to ask her? You want to know, don't it?

—I want to know what, son of a bitch.

—You want to know if I send in Caesar pre or post mortem?

—You think you're scaring me?

—Not at all. If I wanted to scare you I would tell you bout the part of Jamaica that is always night, that you don't know fuck about. I would have pulled that *Sandals Negril* T-shirt you were wearing to bed last night over your head and make you choose which one of your nipples I bite off. If I wanted to scare you I'd say look out your window right now, north a few parking spots then center. I'd say wait until you see me wave back at you. If I wanted to scare you I would tell you how many times I have to change the lining of that car trunk. You know how hard it is to find parts for a Saab 900 Ruby? Only 600 made, 599 of them in the UK. If I wanted to scare you I would remind you that is not even me that come after you just awhile ago. Couldn't, too busy waiting on you right here. And is not me that would come after you again. You know, we used to just set up in the next room when him or me dealing with a bitch. I mean, how else the little boy going to learn? But man, since hidden camera, I can be anywhere and still see everything. You know the other thing about video? You can see what you do wrong and correct it. Now every man in uptown can do the work and is all cause of me. Pity things get out of hand. So you going to thank me?

—Thank you for what, you son of a bitch.

—I don't know. For starters, that I'm not coming after you.

—What you want?

—I already get it, baby.

—Fuck you.

—In good time, maybe?

You hung up. You wished a phone slam had an echo.

This is what Alicia Mowatt wore to Jacqueline Stenton's funeral: her school uniform. White blouse, white skirt below the knee, and a royal-blue tie.

The Sisters insisted that Immaculate girls represent the school at so somber an occasion. Jacqueline was buried at Dovecot Cemetery, an expensive burial grounds usually reserved for the rich and their chidren.

The prime minister had business, but the ministers of education and national security were there.

Rain threatened to but did not fall. The cemetery was packed with people who never knew Jacqueline, most in black, gray, and white, including seven old women from miles away who bawled throughout the whole service despite asking for the poor girl's name twice.

Alicia didn't notice any of this, her eyes were so fixed on one thing, refusing to blink until they burned. Far off, maybe two hundred feet, the red Saab pulled up and paused. She wondered if she was the only one who saw. Nobody else seem to be looking west, only south to the hole in the ground and Jacqueline's pink box sinking. The red Saab did not stay.

Melissa Leo smoothed out her white skirt and straightened her tie when she got out.

ROLL IT

BY LEONE ROSS

Mona

T he woman has fifteen minutes before she dies on the
catwalk.

She stands behind the cheap black curtain that separates backstage from runway, peeping out at the audience as
they clap and su-su behind their hands.

It's so dark, she thinks.

The open-air runway loops through the botanical garden
and the murmuring spectators. No one in Jamaica has seen a
fashion show like this before. Strobe lights and naked torches
blend, mottling the faces of the barefooted models as they ne-
gotiate hundreds of golden candles scattered across the stage.

They are all dressed as monsters.

A hot gust of wind bursts through the palms and banana
trees, pushing against the curtain where the woman is waiting to die. She watches as one of the models onstage stumbles,
steps on a candle, and stretches her long neck up to the sky: a
wordless screaming, like eating the air. The audience laugh and
gasp and admire the vivid blue dress clinging to her body and the
thick blood on her arms and clumped in her long, processed hair.
She is dressed as a vampire, what country people call Old Higue.

—*Gimme more blood, nuh.* That was what Parker said at re-
hearsal last week and he was surprised when the stage manager
explained it was vegetable dye. —*So where is the artistic integrity?*
Parker: her husband. Not handsome. His father broke his nose

before he was fourteen and it always seemed on the brink of splintering again. At school they'd called him battyman and so his eyes are watchful.

He'd walked over to her and bent down so close his eyelashes touched her cheek, not caring about the jealous glances around them.

—*You all right, baby? When we go home, I rub your . . . feet.*

The other models watched, and thought of his voice, poured over their wrists; of adjusted hems and skillfully placed pins and the hold-breath moment when his quick fingers brushed their bare skin.

The woman moaned quietly against his shoulder and he'd laughed, whirling to face the rest of them, fierce and happy.

—*You are all my beautiful ghosts.*

Fourteen minutes: the woman sweats. Behind her and the black curtain, a white passage looms, ending in a makeshift tent, where the models go to change. Girls run to and fro, on and off stage, or stand and wait in the passage, like her. She can hear the clapping each time the curtain opens, like the ticking of a clock. It is midsummer and Kingston seems hotter than ever, despite the whirring, upright fans around her, that only stir the heavy air. Sweat trickles down her neck-back and between her thighs. Moisture beads on her top lip. She's used to being the hottest person in the room. She hopes her makeup won't run. At home she cranks the air-conditioning high until Parker arrives and always slips a hand-fan in her purse for the walk between the car park and the supermarket.

The waiting girls sigh and murmur, strung along the passage, cutting shadowed eyes at her. She's used to the way their dangling thighs and backbones remind her of an abattoir. She's seen many of them come and go through the years, so beautiful, but never friendly. Chandelier silver earrings tangle in shop-bought hair; golden creole earrings pull at piercings, fall and are scooped up again, teeth sucked in irritation; bells and beads tinkle and clack; they pull at hems and wrists and feathered details; crochet and hand embroidery.

"Anybody have a nail clipper?" The girl asking looks anxious. Parker doesn't allow long fingernails. The woman looks at the ground, littered with tiny white nail crescents. No one else sees these things.

She watches as the girls climb the six steps up to the stage; disappear through the curtain slit and return minutes later, triumphant. Some pant and pump the air with their fists, others are silent and professional; they dash back up the passage and into the tent for the next costume.

She will only walk one dress tonight.

Thirteen minutes. Maybe twelve, now.

Two girls slink past.

"She get the best dress again?"

"Weh yuh expec?"

Years of people saying things faraway that she shouldn't be able to hear, but does. The sweat prickles. She pulls the soft fabric away from her chest, blows down her cleavage gently, rocking.

Another girl comes back through the curtain: her transparent black lace dress exposes flat, dark breasts and a g-string that is scarlet and wet, like wearing a wound. Red contact lenses, flaming red hair. In the countryside, the old men who work as ghost hunters give girls red underwear to fend off the succubus at night.

The woman shudders.

"Move, nuh," says the red girl, and runs up the passage.

The hot woman watches her go, then turns back to the curtain.

Parker gave all the models ghost stories to read, even before he began to sketch and cut and sew.

—*This is not just duppy story. I want you to* embody *them.*

One girl looked confused. Later, the woman took her aside to explain what *embody* meant.

Twelve, oh twelve minutes. She could sing eleven. The air stinks of the blood Parker mixed in with the vegetable dye and body paint. Each time a girl slithers through the curtain the woman thinks of a goat giving birth, legs first, a glut of liquid.

Slip in, slip out.

The albino girl up next is new. She wears a cream wedding dress the exact color of her skin and a tattered veil over the yellow dreadlocks weaved into her yellow hair. Hundreds of cream silk roses fall from the bodice, pour down the back of her, and weep into the ground.

Parker heard about her: a tall dundus girl, living near Matilda's Corner who wanted to be a model. He paraded her through their living room, with her hair the color of straw and her golden eyes.

—*Now that is my white witch of Rose Hall.* Later he told the woman how angry he was about the way the dundus was treated. —*Ignorant rassclaat dem. You can call a girl like that ugly?*

The woman watches the dundus and her wide, nervous eyes and thinks of the legend of the white witch: a young English bride, brought over to the Rose Hall slave plantation to live like the Queen. She had children whipped in the front yard of her great house and disemboweled one of her maids just after breakfast. And when the slaves rose to kill her, her ghost returned to slaughter them in their dreams.

What could have made her cruel, so?

The dundus hoists herself up the steps: two-three, another girl lifting the bans o' roses train so she doesn't trip.

* * *

Parker was happy when things went to plan. And sometimes, when he was happy and sleeping, she slipped out and walked the cooling Kingston roads, too late even for gunman. Found her way in pitch blackness: she'd never needed lamp or torch. People driving home late caught her in the headlights: whizzed past her, open-mouthed.

When she was tired, she clanked home.

—*Aaaah*, say the fashionista crowd, out under the stars and in the green expanse of Hope Gardens.

She came here for the first time as a girl: on a school trip to the funfair, where there were American things like bumper cars and whirl-a-gigs and a train and the older girls laughed at her barely hidden delight. They would rather be in the plaza, eating banana chips, and what you wearing to the party up Norbrook tonight, who driving? But she remembered the whoosh and creak of the rides and the pink bouffant candyfloss. It all seemed magical, this fairground in the middle of a place called Hope.

Nine minutes: who can she say these things to?

Parker found her sitting under a bougainvillea tree, far away from the funfair, when the teasing from the girls got bad. Fifteen years old, long bare legs, and trying to do her homework. She was already a year behind, 'sake of stupid, her mother said, and how she couldn't bother beat her anymore because if you beat even a mule too much, it back bow and the only chance she had for a life was her looks. Even though men said she was too maaga and tall, and what a way she *black*, they took great pleasure in her oval face and the way she moved down the street.

The woman didn't care what she looked like because what she really wanted, more than anything else, was to get three A's and go to the law school at UWI. She'd been up there to watch the student mock trials and the black robes. But what happened to her every day was that she picked up the history book and the letters jittered like kumina dancers and slid away—now why did that *B* have to move its way back behind the *H*? It was the misbehaving letters standing between she and UWI and her mother's belt and a chance to come and sit here in Hope Gardens and read law books; her mother said she was lazy but it wasn't true, and eventually she'd put on a black robe and say, I'm a lawyer, Mama, and what you think about that?

One day, her mother would burn.

Parker saved her.

She must walk well in eight minutes. She still walks from her hips; all Jamaican models do. It is something they hear when they go abroad. You have to walk runway with your legs and shoulders; only Naomi Campbell can get away with a hip-sway, and everyone knows she's old school anyway.

Once in New York, the stage manager screamed at her: —*I told you not to walk like a whore, bitch. How many times?*

She thinks that Parker is a visionary. That is what they call him in the newspapers. But so many people here misunderstand him. They say he's weird and wacky and that the heavy jewelry he wears would look better on a woman.

People are stupid.

She must remember her walk, yes, when she gets on the stage to die.

—*I going make you famous, sweet gyal*, Parker said, under the bougainvillea tree. And he did. At her first runway show he dressed them all in exquisitely tailored black dresses and masks like fly eyes and gave them small, sharp machetes to carry. He said they were mosquitos, the kind that gave you dengue fever.

She understood him immediately.

—*Walk like your back is broken*, he said. —*You know how mosquitos crouch on your arm before they bite you?* He made a claw with his hand to demonstrate.

She wasn't thinking much when she corrected him: —*Mosquitos don't bite, they push in a tube thing*, and she was struggling to remember the word *proboscis*, one of those words that danced across the page and slipped off into the grass, when his backhand pitched her over a table and she landed before she had a chance to think about falling and lay bent in three different shapes, too incredulous to be frightened, and here was a *P* by her throbbing head and was there a golden *R* by her broken fingernail—*I never tell you, cut your nails?*—and she thought: You lie; no, is not so it go. He never just. He never.

And the jealous eyes.

—*Him beat her because him love her.*

Was that true? He'd picked her, sweating in Hope Gardens like a red hibiscus.

Seconds are precious, long, bare things. She experiences them as if she were walking through a rainforest, thin green branches sticking into her flesh. She shifts her bare feet, catches the eye of another girl waiting to go onstage. The girl smiles and sharp molars poke over her lips. She is a river mumma, her dress made of silver-green fish scales, but she is also like fruit, a nobbled soursop.

The woman recalls her mother telling duppy stories at night, she facedown in her bed, the wheals on her back and shoulders too fresh to lie any other way: stories about the man who picked up a stranger in his car, and the stranger had long, jagged teeth, and the driver jumped out of his car and ran and ran and ran;

gasping, sweating, begged shelter from a woman fishing by the riverbank.

—*Sistren, I just pick up a duppy wid long teeth*, and the river mumma turned around and smiled.

—*Teeth like these?*

—*Smile, let them see your teeth*, Parker instructed. —*And when you reach the front, cry. A river mumma is a wet thing.*

Even now, she can't read like everybody else. Even the most ignorant people can read the ingredients on a juice box and the words on a billboard, and she likes the matinees on Sunday television because she doesn't have to read, although Parker's mother likes foreign movies with subtitles and when they visit she's glad she's picked up a little *parley vous français* and can say something when Parker's mother asks her what she thinks.

The dundus girl is back through the curtain in her wedding dress, happy face like a peeled egg: she can rest now, there's no other work for her tonight, and the woman wonders, now that she's been his white witch will there be work ever again?

She watches the yellow girl walk away, sees her reach down and pluck one of the cream raw-silk roses from the train and slip it in her mouth. They are so succulent; no wonder she's moved to stealing.

The woman has stood in her own front door, dressed in Parker's beautiful clothing, which is always so light and expensive, so kind to a woman's body. Has felt the maid passing, sweeping, looking.

—*You going out, miss . . . ?*

—*No.*

Nobody remembers her name: has no one at the *Gleaner* or the *Observer* or on JMTV ever noticed that?

Parker James's favorite model . . .
Parker James's model wife considers retirement at thirty . . .

The woman leans toward the river mumma model, who leans back toward her as the seconds thunder past. The chains around the woman's bare feet crackle. Parker says the chains have to be heavy.

More than anything else, she knows he will never change. "What is my name?" she asks.

River mumma frowns. "How you mean?"

She slips past her and away.

She remembers Parker sitting beside her, under the bougainvillea tree, picking up her history book, and she could hardly breathe, his voice was so pretty. He had the right kind of voice for reading bedtime stories. He read the first page and the second and the third, and she found herself melting against the tree trunk. He still reads to her at night, fifteen years later, everything she's ever loved: Shakespeare and Jean "Binta" Breeze and Naipaul and Dickens. She can lean back and lose herself in a sea of words and different worlds, his voice deep and sure, his hands on her waist afterward, so gentle and hissing into her neck.

—You hot inside, sweet gyal.

She used to hope that someone else would come along one day and read her stories. But she knew it wouldn't happen. No one would sound like him and she didn't have to fill in her name on the forms at the UWI hospital because everyone there knew who she was.

She brushes her hand up and down her body; up and down and the chains jingle and she tells herself it is just like jewelry. Parker usually hides the damage in her scalp, in the cleft of her buttocks and between her thighs. This week, he has been glee-ful and unrestrained. The bruises are purple and yellow and black; fist-sized lumps across her shoulders. There is a bruise on the sole of her left foot. All for his artistic integrity.

Four minutes; river mumma is finishing her circuit—the woman knows by the rising claps—has she cried enough to please Parker? He is waiting in the front row, at the foot of the stage. The woman always walks ramp as his last model, the best in show. He will mount the stage to hold her hand and take the final bow.

—*Perfect*, Parker said, when the makeup artist brought the chains to loop around her feet and throat. His fingers trembled as he clothed her in chain, and turned her, so she could see her-self in the full-length mirror. His eyes were wet. —*Did I make you beautiful?*

Scrabbling fingers on her concave belly.

—*Oh, yes.*

She can't leave this love. And Parker will be what he is, forever.

The woman remembers her mother's stories.

—*You can hear it?*

She reaches up, mimics her mother, cupping her ear.

—*Listen good: rolling calf a-walk.*

She has always shivered at the strength and power of the rolling calf story. There are so few details, as if people have been struck dumb with the terror. They say that your head swells and lifts before the rolling calf comes; that you can feel your feet ris-ing from the floor. Clanking chain and hoarse panting. Is that a roar outside? Hooves clitter-clatter, clunk. Hiss of fire, smell of smoke. Never, ever-ever look into its burning orange eyes, and if you hear it coming, curse bad words! Curse as loud and long as you can and pray the rolling calf go on past. It can bruise you with its flailing chain, even with its back turned.

Flame eyes, dragging broken chain, ripped free . . . from what?

Hell, hell. She knows.

She climbs the steps and parts the curtains: —*Aaaaaah*, say the audience.

Flame creeps up the cheap black fabric where her fingers cling. The orange dress he made especially for her crackles on her skin; her nostrils flare at the smell of ash. The chains are hot and violent snakes, undulating down her thighs.

Her belly is suffused in golden fire. She laughs at the candles. Thrusts her hand into a naked torch, up to the armpit; there is no pain anymore.

People scream and clutch their heads; scatter and pray. A few curse: rich and juicy epithets through the dark night air. Others float, inches from the steaming grass. She can hear Parker screaming at the end of the catwalk.

"No, no, no!"

Whoomph! Her hair burns. Her bruises peel away under the heat, like black paper.

Walk and roll, she thinks.

Her eyes burn last.

ONE-GIRL HALF WAY TREE CONCERT

BY MARCIA DOUGLAS

Half Way Tree

Kingston full of them. But this one take the cake. Short shorts and a silver kitchen knife to rhaatid. People call her mad but before that them used to call her dance-hall queen and before that she was Mrs. Anderson daughter and before that somebody did leave her in the trash up Premier Plaza.

Is Patsy she name. One week now she standing here, with a knife in her hand, right across from the clock tower in the middle of the four-directions square.

Traffic back up and people full up the street, but she don't look neither left nor right. She just watch the door at the foot of the clock. And she don't talk neither, except middle day. Every twelve o'clock—to no one in particular.

Yesterday, hear her: *Watch me and them. My feet will never have enough.* And she laugh one long forever laugh and fling back her head then get all quiet and gone back deep-deep in herself. Whole time she just rubbing her finger along the edge of the blade. Today now, is like she pick up her thought from the day before—hear her: *Trust me. There's more to me than this badass weave.* After that, she tug up the zip on her boots and watch back the clock. The door lock with a padlock and mark with four letters: N-O-I-Z. The sky over Half Way Tree vex with electric wire. Hungry birds all over.

* * *

We are the children of Jah-Jah/Don't let Babylon catch-ya—is a one-foot dread outside the electronics shop on the other side of the street. Him sell cell phone cover and brassiere and panty—pink nylon that smell like ganja.

People say Patsy waiting for a DJ to step out the clock. A man with a razor-sweet mouth who will kiss her up and make her put down the knife all slow. That's what she waiting for, they say. Some of them say she waiting for Governor General to step out. She did have a baby for him, them say. People say plenty things. Let them talk—they don't know nothing. Maybe is all Jesus Christ she waiting for. Her weave long and black like john crow tail-feather. Maybe is duppy she waiting for too. Let them talk.

We are kings and queens here/The dawtas need my brassiere—the dread tapping his one-foot.

Tuesday, twelve o'clock, hear her: *Run the tune.* Nobody don't hardly notice. She say it small like she talking to the door. She look bad now—her weave don't comb and her centipede eye-lashes soon fall off. *Run the tune,* she say again. This time louder. One centipede fall and she don't even blink; she just watching the door. *Run the tune!* Her voice fill with barbwire and coral weed. Play her the dancehall, people say. No, is roots cure she need, some say. Everybody think them know what Patsy need. Maybe is all hey-diddle-diddle she want, or #386 in the Sankey Hymnal. Is so Half Way Tree tune clash.

Long time before the clock build there was a cotton tree on the same-same spot—a big slave-time tree—right where the clock tower standing. That tree knew every historyness. An English soldier kill a boy under it one time. The boy spit on the ground and the spit catch the soldier's boots and that's

how the fight start. And years later, an ole woman dead under it. She dead with a farthing in one shoe and a free paper in the other. She walk from Trelawny to St. Andrew and was so tired; she just lay down and dead. For there is a tiredness so deep it can kill you; a tiredness that trace straight back through your blood to a far-off shore.

Nighttime, Patsy sleep not far from the clock, in Mandela Park. Rats in the park big as puss. She curl up on the concrete with two crocus bag. She is not a fool. If any man bother her she say, *I am HIV positive. I am HIV positive. I am HIV positive,* over and over. As soon as day light, she gone back to watch the clock. Mrs. Anderson live in Canada and have relatives in Buff Bay, but them don't want anything to do with Patsy. They write letter to Mrs. Anderson that her save-from-trash daughter standing up in front the clock at HWT. Last July Patsy come home late one night from party with wildness in her eye. My *feet,* is all she say; and from that she not herself. But Mrs. Anderson can't do anything. She have Parkinson's and live in government housing with her niece.

I&I am a witness/This one for the empress—Dread business going good today—*Hotness is a gift!*

Only one person bother with Patsy—a high school girl that cross the street sometime and leave a patty or box drinks. Patsy don't even look on it, but when night come she take it. The girl leave a shoulder bag with a box of Tampax in it and every day now Patsy sport the bag on her shoulder; a nice bag too—shine-black with a silver buckle. The girl just leave the things, quick, and walk off; don't even look behind. A bow-leg girl—Merle Grove High—with her backpack and cornrow hair. Wednesday, twelve o'clock, hear Patsy: *I dance for them on the ship; 1792.*

She don't say it to nobody special, but she still watching the door.

They say the ancestor tree was silk cotton—one massive trunk, so big you could keep session in it. Still, the only thing cottonwood use for is canoe and cricket bat. And coffin. But the roots-them travel far-far underground, down and across. People don't know it, but is only the grace of God and the leftover roots holding up Half Way Tree; after all this time, those roots still span under the earth clear to York Pharmacy and the Tastee's patty shop; they even travel below Hope Road, deep under the bus stop and the schoolchildren feet. Those roots suck plenty spill blood and cares-of-life tears. Watch yourself, people. One day sorrow ground will cry out.

Thursday, hear Patsy: *They made me do it.* Rain falling in Half Way Tree and she don't have no umbrella. The rain coming down, coming down. She hold the bag closed, but water fill up her boots.

Rain a fall/breeze a blow/Jah-Jah call us way down low—the dread laugh and open his mouth to let the rain fall inside, every drop of Jah-Jah water numbered. The bra and panties cover with plastic.

Friday, sun-hot; hear her: *I wheel and dance for I think they would free me.* The street busy with buses and cars and police. Public Works employees on strike. A roadblock on Hagley Park Road. An evangelist preaching dutty hell. None of that bother Patsy— her eyes on the door like is Zion gate.

Saturday, hear her: *The white man pull an ostrich feather out his hat and put in my hair. That's when I know I can't fly home.* People say Patsy waiting for Bob Marley to come out the clock.

When Prophet Bob come she will take it as a sign to cut off the weave and turn rasta. Bob will hold up Manley arm on one side and Seaga arm on the other, just like the old days. Manley will be on the downtown side of the clock and Seaga will be on the uptown side. People say a lot of things.

Sunday, rain again. The sky gray like dutty dishwater. Funeral up at Holy Cross Church. The procession pass and three crows circle behind. Patsy look hungry. No high school girl today. This time Patsy have a broken umbrella though. Blue with *Fi Wi Versal Studio, Ltd.* mark all around; and one spoke that stick out. Twelve o'clock, hear her: *Fly away home to Zion/ Fly away home.* The birds gone and the patty shop closed. Her shorts not so tight anymore.

One time they hang a girl from the silk cotton tree. Is the kind of historyness that get tear out the book, but bad-mind can't stop story from coming out. The girl said a brazen thing and for that they hang her. Just a young girl—with a fever baby left in the crib. They hang her from a high-high branch and when they pull the rope she hear a strange music that come from afar—from way out in the future, two hundred years. She never hear a music like that before, all roots and bassfull and one-drop beat; and her two feet dance a dance right over the spot where you see Patsy looking. And she let out a sound, jah, and give up the ghost.

Monday, again, and early. The high school girl leave a plantain tart and a bottle soda. She leave quick and catch her bus. Nice girl. Jamaica need more like that. People say if Bob Marley come out the clock, he will come holding one arm of Selassie and one arm of his father—the white man, Norval, who run leave him. Three short little man stand up together. Some of them say no, he will come with Queen Nanny, the maroon warrior sistah, and her adversary, Cuffee. For don't historyness can keel over and change that way? Patsy watching close now, like her eyes picking the lock. The wheels in them turning. A man take a photo but she don't even see the flash.

Calling children of the Most High/We don't want no sufferation—

Hear Patsy: *I dance so hard, my feet couldn't stop.* People say Patsy boots fill with American dollars. She standing on money, they say. People like to guess how much money in her shoes. One thousand dollar in each boot, a schoolboy say. How you mean? say the other one. Five thousand. No, a million. She sell her soul to DJ; is must at least one million she have. People say her poom-poom fill with evidence. She have a flash drive in there that could bring down the whole Jamaica government. Somebody give her the cash in exchange for shutting her mouth, they say. People like to talk. They madder than Patsy. Let them run their mouth.

Tuesday early-early; tropical storm warning and where Patsy going to go? Rain falling; shop soon lock up and everyone gone home. Only two dog under the piazza across the street. Hear her: *Who can't fly, run. Who can't run, dance.* And her two knees touch and part touch and part; then stop. Rain fall and make a pool, up to her ankles. Her made-in-China hair blow across her face. Rain beat the door, but not a soul come out.

When they cut her from the tree, the girl's two eyes was still open, for she dead watching the future—schoolchildren running toward her; and music-music; a woman with a knife; rain falling against a gray door. To this day, you can still smell her soul-rebel piss on the ground—all nanny goat and guinea weed strong. Go Half Way Tree, sun-hot, and check for yourself if is not true. No water wash away that smell.

* * *

Three days and three nights rain fall, then Friday morning rain clear up and the smell right there again: womanish and fortify. Patsy hair dry now, but water dripping from the handbag.

Dread in the oven baking/Baking—I-rical dread top ranking today; he even rhyme in his dreams now. *See mi little sistah, call her/call her*—

That slave girl did not know her place, they say. She was too force ripe. The day they hang her, people come to Half Way Tree all the way from St. Catherine. When they see the way her feet dance, everybody captive. One man take a piece of the rope for souvenir; another a bit of the branch. Cotton tree draw spirit tings, that's what they never know.

Patsy, twelve o'clock: *Them can't take away my dancing feet; them can't take away my dancing feet.* The sky over Kingston all dutty-gal bathwater. After school, and a boy bet another one he can make Patsy move. He throw a stone and hit her on her shoulder. Patsy don't move not even a finger. Then he throw another one. Then the other boy throw a piece of bottle glass. Patsy eyelid flinch, but still she don't move. Soon more stones coming; one hit the door on the clock tower. Her neck-back bleeding. She grip the knife tight, but she don't turn or shift her eyes, not one rass.

After that, market people sell under the tree—navel orange and fall-down mango; naseberry and custard apple in season; sweet sop and sour tamarind. Sometimes evening when they clear up, they feel a shift in the air; hear the young girl skirt shuffle; fruit flies over the spot where her feet did dance; her breath smell like spirit weed. For not

even fire or frankincense and myrrh can stop a duppy like that.

Bloodfiah! The dread leave his ganja nylon and run grab the boys by their two shirt collar. They tear from his hands and take off down the street. Patsy still stand up same place, her head cock to the side like she listening something—a sound past the cars and shot-dead news on the radio, past screeching birds, cuss-cuss, and baby cry. Is a tune she hear, people say. No, is murder duppy she hear, a man say. And for once someone is right. Hear her: *jah.*

A woman took the girl's lace-up shoes as a souvenir. She put them in her garden in Liguanea and planted flowers in them. Purple and white periwinkle. *You should have seen her feet dance,* she said to lady guests on the terrace. The shoes had been a gift from mistress before the girl turn ripe and talk-back. The girl sprinkle arrow root in one sole and put leaf-of-life in the other. Is powerful herb and balmnation that. There was Spanish needle in her pockets and ram-goat-dash-along in her hair—

And look, two tears fall down Patsy face—is the first people see her cry. They roll like slow-motion movie. When they get to her cheekbone, they pause, then start again. Her head tilt to the side; her eyes fix on the padlock, the spot where the shoes did dance.

Early-early Sunday morning the door wide open and Patsy stand up in the clock with her knife raise in the air like statue of conspiracy. How she pick the lock, only God know. Is her eyes she use to open it, people say. Three police car with bluelights-bluelights. Murder in the clock, the people say. Patsy come with a knife to cut her rope; to stop the past and change the future—

* * *

To run, run, run with leaf-of-life and Spanish needle to save the baby with colic and too-hot fever; to dance him in her arms with balm and deliverance; before him dead and take away forever. Brazen girl, she said she would not work with baby sick in crib. Said she heard the baby cry out for her from afar-afar on the other side. *Let me dance with him,* she said. And when they tried to stop her, she took off through the field, then turned, picked up a stone, and threw it right in overseer's eye. *Is you the father!* she shout. And she take up her foot and run toward the crying in her heart—

But Babylon handcuff her already. They taking her straight to Bellevue. Hear her in the police car: *I dance at my graveside, the year with no number. Nobody see me, but I dance there.* Sunday organ obituaries playing on the radio, but tomorrow is reggae and dancehall again. *Judgment!* the dread call. Half Way Tree back to business as usual. A strong woman-piss smell, and fruit flies.

LEIGHTON   LEIGH ANNE
NORBROOK

BY Thomas Glave

Norbrook

But now the secret, *that* secret—his, and the nasty-dutty (but rass *gorgeous*) black bwoy's—is at rest in the corpse. The corpse that cannot be hers, he thinks. Insists. But it is. The corpse that fits so snugly—so snug it is obscene, death being the final and most repugnant obscenity, an *absolute execration,* to use the phrasing of a friend from some years ago, a friend he now remembers he had secretly loathed. No. That cannot be her corpse. Not in this casket bedecked (no, *festooned,* he thinks, curling a lip although he is hardly aware of it) with these most outrageous flowers . . . with these impossibly mawkish arrangements. Not here in this Anglican church of his childhood, with the late morning's invincible sunlight slanting down through the church's stained-glass windows, through those not particularly interesting windows his grown-up architect's eye had learned to disdain . . . a church and all of its outfittings should be lean and clean, he thinks . . . at least a church that serves the sort of people this one serves: their sort of people. Those who know where particular forks on the table belong and how crystal ought to be arranged for christenings. Leanness and cleanness, to facilitate entry of . . . what? The spirit? The Lord? But whatever, he thinks, just not dark like this one. Not flanked by too-tall, dark mango trees on one side, like this one. Not, like this one, obscenely, unforgivably containing her body. The body of his sister. The only one he had ever known. Lying on her back with those *flowers*—

She, a well-brought-up Norbrook girl and a child, like himself, not only of the Shepherds, but of *those* Shepherds, their parents: *those* Shepherds of the best part of Norbrook not yet invaded by swaggering drug-trade butus in Benzes and gold chain–wearing never-see-come-sees who had finally managed, after years of clawing, to crawl so far above the Half Way Tree clock. Those Shepherds, known well enough by residents of the older, unostentatiously stately homes along upper Norbrook Road and even in certain apartments in Grosvenor Terrace and Manor Park, who, if more good sense and less lacerating grief had attended them, surely would have despised those flowers; surely under different circumstances would have regarded them, as she would have, with a special and unmistakable brand of scorn. For indeed, in regard to the bouquets and displays, what in God's name had his parents been thinking? Thinking, to have placed upon the coffin and at its right side such violently red roses that, virtually shouting their presence from the front of the church and the casket, suggested something quite beyond the quotidian normalities of the heart—something tawdry, even, well beyond the dignified and restrained realm of the eminently respectable church in which he, his parents, and that vast blur of close friends, more distant friends, and other family members whose names he could, on this sultry and impossible morning, barely remember, now stood? The church in which he could not possibly, he had told himself as the service began, be standing now beside his parents, the both of them completely silent but, he had noticed, uncharacteristically stooped; his grandmother, off there to the side just past his father and three uncles, barely able to stand (her aged face wet, her face so very very wet, the faces of two of his three uncles so unbearably and impossibly wet—but still they, those tall, straight-backed men,

like his father, and his mother, remained standing, actually able
to stand). What had any of them been thinking?

But then, of course, none of them—no, not one, not even
one of his deeply pragmatic aunts who had returned to Jamaica
from Fort Lauderdale for the service as soon as she had heard
the news of Leigh Anne's death—or, rather (but *say* it, he
thinks, damnit, the fucking word, the word that none of them
had been able to utter) *murder*—none of them had been thinking clearly over the past eight days. Not thinking clearly ever
since the police—ever since—

Four shots to the chest and one to the neck, one of the policemen had said, *severing* or *rupturing the* (the medical someone or
other had said that, dear God)—

But then *say* it, you—what was the word he had heard one
of those men in London, when he had traveled there with two
cousins last summer, call another man? *Cunt.* In Sloane Square,
of all places, to which he had dragged his cousins one unexpectedly warm, in fact sunny, afternoon in search of a pair of
Victorian buildings he had wanted to photograph for one of his
bosses who had always nurtured a passion for the more fanciful
aspects of Victorian design—"an architect's delight," the boss,
an Appleton-loving man named David, had said more than
once—when they all had witnessed that man (a white man, yet,
though obviously grubby, pasty, and clearly not from that part of
London) shouting in the street to another man (also a grubby,
pasty type—the sort who looked as if, with his gray crew cut
and incipient beer belly that matched his comrade's, he would
without question have to get rowdy and belch volcanically between brews at football matches)—shouting something like,
Well go on, then, and take it all the way if you like, and see if I care,
you stupid cunt.

Sounds like a pussy with teeth, one of his cousins had snorted,
laughing at the vulgarity of that type of Englishman. *Not top-*

drawer, his deceased grandfather would have said. *Not quite out of the top drawer*, his Uncle Wilson, longtime admirer of Her Majesty, would have sniffed.

And so then say it, you cunt, he thinks. *Tell the fucking truth, for once in your life. (But do not think of the nasty-dutty black bwoy. Do not think—no, don't dare—about how Leigh Anne, upon learning about that, had looked at him. Had not looked at him.) Say that she is dead. Leigh Anne Faith Shepherd, your only sister and only sibling, is dead.*

She, he does not want to think, *the only one who had ever known. Known about that.* She who, after knowing, for years, had looked at him. Had not looked at him. She who had been murdered.

That's the word, you stupid cunt. *Murder.*

But then there had been no time, really, since the news, this news, for any of them to think. No time for them to reflect on the utterly incomprehensible news that some gunmen—possibly two or three, although an elderly neighbor who had heard the shots from her front veranda swore that she had in fact seen four men (although in truth the darkness had obscured their precise number)—had "surprised" her.

Surprised her, the police had said. This deduced from their initial investigations. Surprised at the gate of her driveway the lovely twenty-six-year-old Miss Shepherd, lately of Cherry Gardens, where she and her fiancé Peter, to whom she would have been married at the end of next month, had moved only six weeks ago.

"Surprised" her, yes—something deeply hideous about the word, as if the event had been somehow akin to a birthday party—and had shot her to death in a "fusillade" of bullets—that was the phrase, wasn't it, that you often saw these days in the media accounts of such events in Jamaica? Surprised her early that evening, eight or so evenings ago, as she had pulled into the driveway of the new house that she and Peter had been fixing up slowly, lovingly. Meticulously. She had pulled in at just a little past seven while perhaps listening on the Land Rover's radio to Irie-FM, which she had always loved; thinking perhaps that she and Peter might that evening make an early night of it, since he was due to depart for a six-day work trip to Cayman the following morning. Pulled in, lovely girl, sweet adorable younger sister, younger by two years, thinking nothing of her imminent death in a "fusillade of bullets." Surprised and—

Red? Would there have been a great deal of red across her form suddenly slumped behind the Land Rover's wheel, and on its front seats? But the flowers, he thinks. Yes, much too red. Not at all our way of doing things, he thinks. We were not thinking. Nobody was thinking.

But then, how can he possibly be thinking now, right now, his sobbing parents beside him, of what the nasty-dutty black bwoy thought of all this? Of the flowers? How can he possibly be thinking of him now as he stands here among his family? Standing here feeling what cannot be possible, and must not be now nor ever again: that *obscene* stirring in his—oh, but yes, exactly. There. The place where that kind of movement begins, down there, where the drowsing curled animal stirs until, awakened by the slightest secret start or shudder, it presses itself outward, *out*, in search of the warmth and the grip that is the outer flesh's resistance and welcome. Feeling all that and then the drowsing animal's stretching to attention as, that suddenly, all at once, he smells once again the flesh and stink of the nasty-dutty black bwoy, it is simply not possible for him to be standing as tall as he now stands, next to his bending parents . . . standing and trying to be . . . trying to be himself, Leighton, whoever "Leighton" is and has always been to them, to all those aunts and uncles and the grandparents . . . and to his parents, by God. *And how can I be here?* he thinks. *I don't know. No, I really don't. I'm standing*

here thinking of him and feeling him on me again because . . . because she was there. Because on that particular night she saw, and
remembered—or at least never forgot.

Saw, yes. She saw, having walked in on them. Four years ago.
Him and the nasty-dutty black bwoy, in their parents' house on that
lovely and still, so still, Norbrook night. Still but for the peepers. Still
for once, miraculously, with no noise of traffic at that hour from
Norbrook Road; no dogs in neighbors' gardens barking in argument
with dogs barking in rage; and a moon, a moon as generous as gold,
that had gleamed its determined but gentle white through so many
Upper St. Andrew streetlights. That night, in the blood, in the flesh:
remember it. Remember, as you knew then, that there are times when
people, people like your beloved younger sister, should have stayed
as late at the party to which she had gone with those several friends
as she had said with such certainty only a few hours before she had
planned to do—because if she had done that, if she had kept to her
word, you would then finally, finally have been able to do all the
things that you had so longed to do and had never done, never dared
to do, even if, especially if, they were things to do with and to a big-
hooded nasty-dutty black bwoy who labored, sweaty and dirty as
those people always were, with his sweaty-dirty, but not young and
gorgeous and big-hooded, uncle in your parents' garden. Then, in
those most secret times, you can at last be free, you can soar, you
can even be dangerous and disgusting and take some of the nasty-
dutty black bwoy all the way down your throat (Jesus Christ, the
hood), and taste him in the very back-back of your throat, Massa
God, before he pulls it out and whips you with it in the face because
no one will know, no one who knows you will ever know. There are
times when you know, as you knew that night, that your parents
were indeed in Fort Lauderdale for the weekend (they had called
back to the house only a few hours before that evening, and Yes,
dear, your mother had said—her voice as always so warm but cool,
her voice as always so assured provided that your father was not

anywhere nearby—we arrived safely, though Daddy is a bit cross because, well, you know, he's tired, eh? But everything is fine so far . . . Yes, my dear, and Aunt Hyacinth says hello again). In Florida for the weekend and not due to return until the following Tuesday . . . you and Leigh Anne by that time of course old enough to stay at the house on your own, the two of you well into your twenties; knowing that they were away visiting the aunt who lived there and several other relatives, and shopping up there as people like themselves so loved to do when provided the slightest opportunity; knowing that your sister was going to her blasted party over in Russell Heights shortly, so that you had been able to tell the helper, Yeah man, go home at five thirty, Leigh Anne and I can take care of everything from here, no problem—you so confidently told the helper, although you did not, in that moment, actually anticipate that anything would really be possible with the nasty-dutty black bwoy who still, that late afternoon, sauntered about the grounds with his machete looped on the side of his pants: the gardener's nephew who came often to assist his uncle, and whom you had imagined on first glancing at him to be named Ransford or Davion or one of those typical ghetto names that black ghetto dwellers love to give their children.

But the bwoy's name had in fact been Michael: a slender black Michael with beautiful teeth and lips—beautiful everything, as it turned out—who, like his uncle, your parents' elderly gardener, had always smelled of the garden and of the sun, sun and earth and sweat: a younger, always bare-chested man with those nipples, that stomach, those narrow hips, that backside, and with who knew, until that night, what size and shape of hood: that nasty-dutty black bwoy who, like his uncle the gardener, walked always with a machete slung in such a manly way on his waist and had learned from an early age, like his uncle, to call you "sah"; that bwoy who had actually looked at you and looked at you so many times over the years—he, the gardener's nephew, daring to look at you, the Shepherds' son—as you, sometimes just as daring if not more, had looked back at him, at

that blackness that had never been yours: those Shepherds were not
black, they were most certainly not black. You looked, though care-
fully, quietly, with lowered glance; sometimes even daring, gazing out
from your grilled bedroom window, to watch him water the hanging
baskets or bend over to chop away weeds from the ornamentals . . .
he being nearly the same age as you, perhaps a year or so older? Yes,
he had actually told you his age when, at last, impossibly, your hand,
that night, had found its place on his hood, as he had gripped you at
the neck and forced your face into his chest—

(But Leigh Anne is—is—is dead, he thinks. The one person who knew, the only person aside from the gardener's nephew
and himself who *knew*.)

It was not supposed to be. Never supposed to be. But yes, you'll be
back late, nuh? he had asked his sister. Yeah man, she had replied—
murmured, actually, momentarily distracted with pulling some loose
thread out of her skirt—and had mentioned something about maybe
staying late at her friend Jessica's, in Allerdyce. She and Peter had
known each other even then, and Peter, soon to be her fiancé, had ar-
rived not long after that to drive her over to their friends', though she
had always preferred to do her own driving whenever possible . . . that
was Leigh Anne, that was her very independent streak. And she had,
not long after that, departed . . . leaving him alone on the grounds
with the nasty-dutty black bwoy walking around, swinging his hips
and machete—for by that time the gardener-uncle also had gone,
had in fact taken off early that afternoon and left his nephew behind
to do the rest of the cutting and chopping and cleaning up. Cutting
and chopping . . . and thinking about those words, and seeing the
machete gleaming on the black bwoy's hip had given him some pause
. . . for hadn't there been so many stories in recent years about men
being "chopped up" by gardeners? Something gone wrong one day? A
bit of temper in one, a slip of cruelty in the other? A demeaning word
tossed just once too often from brown to black? The final comprehen-
sion, by the black, that the brown's lowered gaze barely concealed an

abiding contempt? The black perhaps finally understanding, perhaps after fifteen or twenty years of service chopping back their damned trees and cutting back their blasted bougainvilleas, that the words "dutty" and "nasty," if never uttered directly to him, were most certainly thought by several (if not all) members of the household about him? Yes, maybe a definite Yes to all, and the possible Yes had, for at least a few moments, given him considerable pause . . . yet that evening, at last, impossibly, they had met. Brown, black. After dark, well after twilight. Met in the washing room with its washing machine, heavy sink, and constant smell of chlorine, amidst which the helper—Carlene, a young black woman from Trelawny whose only enemies on earth were dirt and Satan—in daylight hours scrubbed and wrung stains from clothing, curtains, bed linens soiled by brown people's sweat.

Just a glance and a very slight smile that could not truly be a smile but was—that was all it took, it seemed, as he found himself there, in the washing room where he never went, when the gardener's nephew was at last there, with grave concentration washing his hands and forearms before leaving for the evening. Yes sah, de bus mi a tek a T'ree Mile, the bwoy had said (beautiful teeth, he had noticed again; black skin, gorgeous teeth): full patois, not one English sentence in there. Bus a T'ree Mile, den mi haffi walk. Although he did not think of it at the time, he would remember later that the bwoy had not mentioned that, upon leaving the house, he was also required to walk all the way down the long stretch of Norbrook Road to Olivier Road, then past the golf course to Constant Spring Road, then take the Constant Spring bus to Half Way Tree where he would change for a bus that would take him closer to Three Mile. For some reason the bwoy—machete still shining on his hip—had not mentioned any of that.

But really, there had not been much else. They had not had to make uneasy talk about football, or the weather; they had not had to talk about how wonderful Henry, the bwoy's uncle, had been all those years, working such long hours and so reliably for the family; they had not had to say anything about the amount of traffic on Norbrook Road these days, nor about the number of doctor birds that had dived into the garden one afternoon, spun in ever-widening circles, and then departed almost as suddenly as they had appeared, never reappearing in the family garden in that number. It had seemed as if all at once, their faces had come together. Hands. Arms. Crotches, and hands in crotches. Without the saddling or comfort of language, except for a few very soft words the bwoy had whispered in his ear— "You can suck m'hood?" and "Gwan, hold it tight fi mek i' 'tand up"—words like that, which he was sure he had returned with similar requests—little had been said. Suddenly he was smelling, tasting that black bwoy in him, within him, on him, and, impossibly, himself on the black bwoy, the bwoy who did not speak or chose not to speak English, and that fast, yes, that fast, he remembers, everything was black: night, skin, and the space in the throat that aims to grip the tightest. Although it was not possible, the black bwoy's tongue was in his mouth, his in the black bwoy's, and—

(Smells. Sweat. Armpit stink, mansmell, crotch. Sweat, crotch, hoodsmell. Lift up the hood and sniff the tip. Sniff it before you suck it. Before you put your mouth on it, smell it. Breathe it. Taste. Unwashed hood after a full day, rass, and rank crotch. He was smelling it. I am smelling it, he had thought. Smelling you. I am smelling your fleshsmell ranksweatfleshsmell and

Yes. Yes. Tasting it. Tasting you. Michael. Nasty-dutty black bwoy. Sucking me sucking you. Here.)

"Michael," the bwoy had said while somehow managing to keep his tongue pressing against the other's—lowering a hand to his machete for only a moment, to in fact release it as he released the button that clipped his trousers closed—saying the name again, "Michael": his name, simply his name.

There are times, even if you are standing in shock at your sister's funeral, gripping the pew railing in front of you as the organ, in all

*its sorrow and wail, begins to call your name, when you can hate
her with every inch of your blood and bone, and wish her dead yet
again for having done certain things: for having once called you that
name, "Chunkybatty," when you were all children and you'd had,
in truth, a chunky batty, though you gradually outgrew it in adoles-
cence, in fact grew by all accounts into a slender young man: but
that name and its humiliation, Chunkybatty, remained and scalded
the scorn of childhood awkwardness and shame that three of your
favorite cousins never forgot, and laughed over every chance they
got—laughed over for years as you, small boy at the time, had stood
there, Chunkybatty, stood there and looked at them. Or you could
hate her, deadsister, for telling your parents, although you had sworn
her to confidence, that one of your teachers had severely scolded you
for looking "unkempt" in your uniform in an afternoon class; or hate
her for snapping at you, "No, stupid," when you as her older caring
brother had merely asked a question about one of her friends who
had been ill, and had later, most unexpectedly, at a tender age, died;
or hate her and very much wish her dead, again and again, for returning home early from a party when she had told you several times
only hours before, No, she would definitely be home late, of course,
with Peter, with Andrea, maybe with Karen too: with all of them, she
would be home late. But no, not late that evening, because she and
Peter had had a rare disagreement early on that had escalated into
a bitter fight, and "Home," she had angrily said, "Enough already,
man. I'm leaving. Home," she had said—and home she had come,
in someone else's car—in Andrea's car, or Deirdre's; in the car of
one of those friends who were now somewhere behind you in the
organ-wailing church. There are times when you should know that
these things might happen. But when you cannot take your tongue
out of a nasty-dutty black bwoy's mouth and cannot stop inhaling
the smell of his sweat and tasting it too, the sweat and smell and
kisses and cock pressing against you, inside you, and then deeper
inside still, of a black bwoy gardener who is in fact not at all either*

nasty or dutty; when you cannot, will not, give up the feeling of his warm warm strong black, so black, arms about you holding, holding, like that, and the feeling of his mouth upon your neck, warm, soft, moist, whispering into your most receptive ear his name, his most holy beautiful two-syllabled name; when you have sucked and kissed and even, oh my God, swallowed his rank hood and everything that makes his flesh, that flesh, possible, and he has kissed your belly and then so easily, so calmly and gently, eased his thick black hood into your backside hole, your battyhole, and fucked you, fucked you standing up with his gleaming machete on the concrete floor of your parents' washing room, his trousers on the floor tangled up in yours and his hood pushing, pushing inside you as you gasp and shudder and reach behind you for his neck, his arms, for something to grab onto because the pain and pleasure and sheer raw burn of his flesh are too much, beyond all things, beyond imagining, beyond even "Michael!" *you had actually called out, calling his name in spite of yourself,* "Michael—"

There are times like these when you simply cannot be as aware of things, of sounds and vibrations and suddenly approaching lights, as you ought to be, as you must be. As you must be, by God, especially inna Jamaica, bomborassclaat. Receiving him, receiving his warm rush inside yourself with no thought in those moments of danger or disease or even his black skin so far up inside you, against you, on you, you cannot completely be in your "right mind": *you are in fact deluded, diverted, disoriented unto joy, freedom, release: release from the black bwoy, the brown boy, the black bwoy and the brown boy kissing and sucking, and if only, oh my God, you thought, if only we could—*

But then. Then. Then she was there. Standing there, the person who drove her home mercifully having left her by the front veranda because she had wanted to be "alone," *as she had said as the car pulled up the driveway.* "Just leave me at the house, I'll be fine. Anyway, Leighton is home."

"*But are you sure?*" *the other person had asked as she had pre-pared to get out of the car—the driver had in fact been Andrea, dear Andrea Harvey now sobbing quietly in the third row on the right, clasping her hands beneath her chin and rocking back and forth as her parents, beside her, hold her, or at least her father does.* "*Are you sure? You seemed really upset when Peter said—*"

But she had almost snapped at Andrea as she occasionally snapped at him: "*I'll call you tomorrow, man. Thanks for the ride, Andrea, but really, man, I'll be fine. Good night.*" *And had walked away from the departing car and—perhaps more rapidly because she had indeed been on the verge of tears, or, in fact, had actually been crying, thinking of some of the things that Peter had, so unexpectedly, said during their foolish argument—she had walked faster, faster, and that quickly, without of course at all expecting to, had come upon—*

Them.

Them, there and—there.

Black, brown. No, not a woman and a man, but—the gar-dener's—the gardener's nephew? And her (but No. No. No no no)—her brother?

There. In the concrete washroom smelling as always of chlorine and—and what else? Flesh? Sweat? And something else, the smell of—

Oh yes. My God. The smell of—

Unmistakable. That smell, and men. Two men. Flesh. Sweat.

In the concrete washroom, the first and only time she had seen her brother's . . . her brother's . . . yes, bending; yes, engorged; yes, and the black bwoy, the gardener's nephew, holding it in his hand, in his hand, as he had moved and rocked and pushed behind, behind, behind her brother. Behind Leighton Andrew Shepherd. Her brother.

She had looked at him. She had not looked at him.

He had looked at her. He had—

(But then she had been so upset upon leaving the party that she

had not even thought to call, and would he have heard his phone ringing anyway if she had called? Would he have heeded the ringing? Would he have stopped? Where was his phone anyway, just then? And would he have cared?)

And Michael—

Not again. No. After that evening, none of them had ever seen him again. Never seen again the nasty-dutty black bwoy who somehow in one of those smell-and-suck moments, one of those oh-my-God-he-is-inside-me moments, had become to him, finally, "Michael." Not the nasty-dutty black bwoy, but . . . "Michael," he had thought and thinks now in the church, his parents bent beside him. Yes.

She had looked at him that way every day she had seen him for the couple of years she'd had left to live. She had looked and not looked at him that way especially in his dreams: dreams of broken twisting stairs, dreams of drowning . . . dreams of reaching hands cut off at the wrists. Dreams of black bwoy kisses, thrusts, embraces. Dreams of that one. Michael. And dreams of faces. Hers. His.

There are times when you know that you should not be standing—somehow managing to stand—during your sister's funeral, feeling glad, as you do now, and happy—oh, rass, tell the truth, *relieved*—as you feel now, that she is dead. Though you are sad, devastated (well, no, actually, much much more than devastated), that she died as she did and that, oh God, you never had a chance to say goodbye or I love you, or a chance to tell her how much how much how *much* . . . and only you can know what the rest of that sentence would say—you know that you should not feel this most secret feeling of deliverance, yes God, and safety, God, that she who knew about *that* and *him* and all of *it*, though it was only one evening and little more in fact than an hour, if that, is now dead. Though you may hate the roses that surround her corpse and wonder why the bomborassclaat your parents chose all these outdated Anglican songs for the organist to play as the minister proceeds onward and onward still, you know that, though this secret mixture of hatred and relief just may kill you one day, if you are fortunate, it will not. It may not kill you, this enormous hatred and relief, if you . . . if you *what*? Yes, what? But you do not know the answer to that question right now. Do not know it, and will not, until—yes, you think, closing your eyes briefly, exactly: until. Until that day, whichever day that will be. And then, dear Lord. Oh, *then*, Jesus. Fury. Fury like fucking. Glory.

But for now, perhaps, for him—for all of them—what follows will be enough: the moment when the organ begins once again to wail and soar as the minister's voice carries over all of their heads its long and incantatory litany of woe; the ancient keening of *On this day, dearly beloved*, and *We ask this of our Lord, Heavenly Father,* toward climax unto crescendo unto the deeper breath that is no breath at all—that is in truth scarcely a sigh, the gasp and gape of loss: the loss that unleashes all manner of good sense from the hands, that undoes the reliably quiet dignity of the wrists, and rips open the chest for the returning raven's descending glide *in* and *in*.

His mother has begun to shudder and give way even more beside him, he feels it; his father has at last slackened and surrendered his shoulders to the raven's claws and the dip of its narrow beak over the exposed neck so pathetic and vulnerable before the soundless glide: this he knows also. Knows it as he feels the hand that cannot possibly be his hand, but is, rise not to his face (to his shock now wet, then wetter, then warmer still), but to his mother's shaking arm; his hand that speaks to her the words that his mouth, so dry, unlike his face, cannot.

She would not have wanted those roses.

And what would . . . what would the nasty-dutty . . . what would *Michael* have thought of—what would Michael have felt about the—

It is only then that he notices that Michael's uncle is not anywhere in the church.

But now—is it in fact now that he becomes aware of that great dark bird—the raven, perhaps, or some other creature—descending over his head, as if to enclose his wet, warm face between its wings? *And then what will happen next?* he thinks. But never mind: for, as he already knows, there are times when, even though you are secretly glad someone is dead, and even though the brief grip of a beautiful nasty-dutty black bwoy *Michael*'s arms about your straining body reached deeper into your *cunt*, yes, *say it!*—deeper into your brown male cunt than you could possibly have imagined, to the point even of bringing you dreams of hood smell and the incipient taste of piss as you bend once again to suck and kiss it, you know that somehow, even with the great dark bird descending over you and your mother and father giving way next to you, you will somehow continue standing. And, at the dreadful service's end, you will walk with everyone else out of the church, away from the awful flowers. Away from that thing dressed up to be her—the thing that is *not* her, no, and that will never speak. At least, so he hopes. He hopes it will never speak. Let him believe so, at any rate: believe in the possibilities of the spreading day outside and all the silences and accompanying noise, as the dark bird's wings now almost completely cover his face and its beak poises as if to take aim where his skull is thinnest, as it now wraps itself entirely, ever so gently, in the way of a shroud, about his head.

PART III

Pressure Drop

PART III

"54-46 (THAT'S MY NUMBER)"

BY CHRISTOPHER JOHN FARLEY

Trench Town

There have been so many lies told about my late brother in the Jamaican press that I feel compelled to send this e-mail to the *Gleaner*, especially since many of the falsehoods originated with me.

I don't expect you to publish all of this, or even most of it, but rest assured that I will post the entirety of it on my new website: TheRealProofWatson.com. Unfortunately, ProofWatson. com had already been taken and is selling unauthorized paraphernalia—hash pipes, roach clips, rolling paper, etc.—bearing my brother's image. My lawyers are looking into it.

In the wake of my recent early retirement—something that the *Gleaner* issued not a tweet about—I have finally been able to speak freely about some of the cases that I worked on with the assistance of my brother Proof. I had always wanted to be a writer of some sort—buy me a few Red Stripes and I'll recite most of the Claude McKay canon—but I was derailed from that track by a family tragedy early in my life, and any poems I might have had in my heart I covered with my badge. Surprisingly, in the wake of the media frenzy brought about when tales of some of his exploits surfaced, many of my colleagues on the Jamaican Constabulary Force, some of whom I served with for a decade, were stunned to hear that Proof and I were related. I would have thought our shared surname would have been a clue, but following up on evidence was never a strong suit of members of the department. Which is precisely why my brother's mysterious gifts were so extraordinarily useful during our collaborations . . .

On my first morning as assistant commissioner, I decided to enter the Kingston Central Police Station through the back door. The rainy season had begun, and it seemed the showers would never stop, and the wet had soaked my uniform to my skin in just the brief time it took me to dash from the front door of my apartment building to the front seat of my secondhand Fiat 500. I was particularly perturbed by the drenching because I had gone to great difficulty to iron my clothes the night before, hoping, almost certainly in vain, that creased pants and a pressed collar would boost my standing with veterans of the force who had been dismayed about having a thirty-year-old as the second-in-command, and someone largely raised in America, besides.

So I went round to the back alley, intending to dry off in one of the rear rooms before making a grand, sartorially correct entrance. But before going into the stocky brick-walled headquarters, I spied in a back alley strewn with garbage a rastaman with Rapunzel-length dreads taking the kind of hits that would make a cricket ball wince. Two men held the rasta's arms as a third delivered head and body shots; a fourth man watched, every so often punching numbers into an incongruously pink cell phone. To my shock and disgust, the assailants were cops. The sun was just rising, and the rain was still falling, and so it was hard to see exactly who was doing what to whom. But as I sprinted through the mud to offer assistance, the identities of all the figures in this drama soon became clear. I recognized the one delivering the blows as a man everyone called Officer Coconut, a sour brute with a roundish skull and wispy hair like his namesake; the man on the pink phone was my superior, Commissioner Manatt.

"Wa a gwaan?" I asked. (When I'm excited, my patois tends to come out.)

The commissioner put away his phone. The officers let the rasta drop and, limp as a banana peel, he tumbled into the commissioner, who pushed him roughly, face first, into the muddy ground.

"'Im two ears hard," the commissioner growled, giving a dismissive wave to the beaten man.

With that, he lit a cigarette, looked at me, and laughed; his officers joined in. The commissioner had an acne-scarred face and a nicotine-stained voice and his laugh was anything but mirthful. I always did dislike him—never trust a man who enjoys wearing epaulets.

"A good mek 'im tengle up," the commissioner continued. "Dat deh a fi uno!"

He thrust a soggy manila folder into my arms, flicked away his cigarette, and went into the station and out of the rain. His men followed him, with Officer Coconut shooting me a last smirk before closing the double doors behind him.

I bent over the rasta, rolling him faceup. He was shoeless, as usual, and his black shirt and jeans were caked in mud. And of course, though it had been a number of years, I instantly recognized his thick-featured face: the full lips, the flat pharaonic nose, the heavy serious brow. In fact, his looks very closely resembled my own. I knew him all too well, even better than the others.

"Do you have a spliff?" my brother Proof asked.

The commissioner had given me a case to solve on this, my first day in my exalted office. This was preemptive punishment, of course, an attempt to taint the golden bwoy before he became the heir apparent. Personally investigating a crime was substantially below my new rank, but after what I had witnessed in the alley, I quickly decided I couldn't trust whatever was going on to anyone else. Officers all around stared as I led Proof through the station, and the buzz continued, like the sound of angry bees, as I ushered the mud-dripping dreadlock into my office. I had been set up in a glass cubicle that was less private than I desired, and smaller than I deserved given my new station. My office was full of light, but it might as well have been a dank dungeon with bars; I felt like I was both incarcerated and on display, like Rilke's panther. I had moved in days ago, but I had yet to unpack my boxes, and I had put but a single picture on my desk. As Proof dried off and cleaned up, I pulled down the blinds in my fishbowl workspace, and then flipped through the manila folder to familiarize myself with the case.

The folder contained a small sheath of damp papers. On top was a Post-it from the commissioner's secretary that the prime minister's office had called—this case was high priority. Beneath that was a news clipping from the front page of the Sunday *Observer* featuring a woman, maybe twenty years old, with cocoa-colored skin and sea-green eyes with a slight Asian tilt. She had a long, lithe body and was looking back at the camera over her shoulder with a Mona Lisa smile. She was wearing red running shorts, track cleats, and a midriff-bearing, crimson jersey with the number 45. She had the sort of face that launched ships, the kind of behind that inspired dancehall hits, and a pair of legs that looked as sweet as stalks of sugarcane.

"Soledad Chin, the sprinter?" I murmured to myself. "She's the vic?"

Proof was now doing some odd stretching moves that were something like yoga crossed with mixed martial arts. For a man who had just gotten the Rodney King kicked out of him, he seemed no worse for wear. "I kept my ears open the whole time the cops were doing their thing," Proof grunted, as he arched his back. "Soledad left her room at the Marriott last night and never returned. Could be a kidnapping, could be something else."

"I didn't even know she was on the island. Every time I see her in the sports pages she's at an American track meet in her Harvard uniform."

"She left Kingston when her aunt died a few years back. She returned with a group of students as part of a cultural program—the International Returning Immigrants Exchange."

"IRIE?"

"The PM invited her to be part of it. Jamaican-American makes good and all of that. A murder won't be good for tourism."

"I assume the commissioner brought me in because of my Cambridge connections. How did you get mixed up in this?"

"Chin isn't just a world-class sprinter. She's a math major. The cops thought there was some link. But I didn't tell them anything. Which is why we had our little disagreement outside."

It was too much of a coincidence that my long-lost brother turned up on my first day in my new position. Word of my promotion had no doubt hit the street; perhaps Proof wanted to check up on me and got caught when he got too near the station. In any case, I needed to find out what he knew. "So what can you tell me?"

Proof smiled. "Cockroach nuh business inna fowl fight."

"Cho! You and I both know what you really are."

"What's that, braa?"

"You solved math problems as a teen that professors had been working on for decades. If you're a rasta, I'm Peter Tosh."

"And wa mek you so speaky spokey, Hahvard boy? You're a poet, not a cop!"

He still knew how to press my buttons, and he was getting them all, like a child punching every floor on an elevator. My parents had given us both the choice to go to high school in America, but only I had taken them up on it. I remained stateside for college, completing my undergraduate degree in English literature at Harvard—but after my parents' passing, I changed course and pursued a masters in criminology at Northeastern. Career sacrifice was the least I could do after what my family had suffered. "You didn't have to stay here," I admonished Proof. "And at least I came back."

"You have this fancy office and you haven't even unpacked. You know you don't belong here."

"And where do you belong? Do you even have an address in Trench Town?"

Proof spat at my feet.

Blood rushed to my head. "A fuckery dat," I choked.

"Yu waan tess mi?" Proof replied.

And just like that we were teenaged boys again. I balled my fists and stepped toward him; he struck a pose I swear I saw in *Crouching Tiger, Hidden Dragon*. In my rage I knocked down the one photo I had on my desk. It fell faceup, and the glass protecting it shattered. We both looked at it, and a certain calm came over the room. I unclenched my fists, and Proof bent to pick up the photo. It was a portrait of my parents shortly before the attack.

"We're coming up on seven years," I murmured.

"Six years, ten months, three days, nine hours, and twenty-seven minutes," Proof responded.

There was silence between us, and after a moment, I broke it. "What was that Xbox *Mortal Kombat* shit you pulled just now? You know karate?"

"I don't know . . . karate," Proof smiled.

There was a knock outside my office and through the shades, I could see somebody that had to be Officer Coconut—even his shadow had muscles. I turned toward the door to see what he wanted, but Proof grabbed my arm. Then he pulled out a cell phone and placed it on the desk—it was the same pink phone the commissioner had had before. Officer Coconut knocked on the door again, a little louder this time.

I looked hard at Proof. "Wha! This has to be put into evidence. There are forms that need to be—"

"Cho! Don't go all poet on me, Miss Lou. Are you running this case or are you running this case? We have about a minute to figure out what's on this before they come through that door."

I picked up the phone. "It's locked!"

"The commissioner was trying a code to unlock it. I heard the tones that he was punching and figured out the numbers: 1092."

"The files say she was born in October 1992 . . ."

"That was the commissioner's mistake. Soledad was a math major. She's too smart to pick a static number. If she wanted a code that she could change every few weeks, what number would be most meaningful to her?"

"Her 100-meter time?"

Proof nodded.

I tried variations on the number, each one a tenth of a second lower.

"Try higher. The files also say she's been fighting the flu, throwing up a lot."

The phone unlocked with 10.94.

Officer Coconut was trying the door handle again. "I can hear you in there! You have something that belongs to the commissioner!" he bellowed, rattling the glass windows.

Proof closed his eyes. "We have about thirty seconds. Do you have a spliff?"

"What? No. What are you doing?" I asked.

"Focusing. This would be easier with a spliff. Look at her text messages."

"There are a couple from the commissioner. Looks like she didn't answer any of them."

"Sexting must be as far as fat boy got. What else?"

"Texts from Smith, Jean, Patton, Marple, Wolitzer, Bour-baki—"

"Bourbaki? What does that one say?"

"It's blank. But she responded with a number: 423."

"That's likely a hotel room. A meeting place. Spike the message."

The door burst open. Officer Coconut had kicked it and broken the lock. Quick as a spider, Proof grabbed Officer Coconut's arm and used his momentum to throw him to the floor. Proof bent over the man; he was out cold.

"You just assaulted a police officer," I said to Proof.

Proof stood up. "You can file your report later. We'd better get to where we're going before the commissioner figures out we actually have some evidence."

We took my car and drove through the rain. Soledad had been staying at the Marriott, but room 423 had been empty for a week; the closest hotel where that particular room was booked was the Pegasus, which is where we were headed. The rain was coming down even harder now and my Fiat's wipers, even at the fastest setting, couldn't sweep the windshield clear fast enough. All around us, the city of Kingston was a submarine blur of greens and browns and yellows.

I dived in: "You want to tell me where you've been for seven years?"

Proof ignored my question entirely, stole a glance in the rearview mirror as if he was looking for someone, and then lit up a spliff.

"What the hell are you doing?" I asked.

"Ease up. Everything cook and curry."

"I can't have that in my car, mon. Did you tief that from Officer Coconut?"

Proof exhaled smoke.

"I get it. This is all Babylon and I'm a baldhead. So why are you on this case?"

"It's hard for a mathematician to resist a puzzle. There's something fascinating going on here."

"Does this have to do with the name on the cell phone? Bourbaki? You know him?"

"I know his work. But him nah real."

I looked at him blankly.

Proof took a long toke. "In the 1930s, French mathematicians collectively agreed to publish math papers under that pseudonym."

"To avoid the Nazis?"

"Something like dat."

"What's going on here? Is this just about a missing girl?"

"One-one coco full basket," Proof said.

Like many readers of the *Gleaner*, I'm sure, I did my time in the tourist trade. The Pegasus is where I worked, along with Proof, over a long slow summer in our youth when our more professional internships fell through. As we pulled up to the monolithic hotel now, memories flooded back into my mind of a juvenile bet we'd made over who could romance the most women during our summer break. When, early in June, Proof fell for Beatrice, an American tourist who checkmated Proof at chess (the only time I'd seen him lose) and then mated him without the check in the hotel sauna, I thought for sure that I would post the higher number, as he was entrapped by the bane of all playas: love. Proof always had a sentimental streak—he once nursed a baby hummingbird back to health. So I thought I had this numbers game won. But like most things arithmetic, when it comes to my brother, I lost anyway, one to zed.

As we entered the lobby, which was crowded with collegiate tourists with mango-orange tans, the ivory-uniformed doorman moved to stop Proof, who was barefoot with mud in his dreads, from going too far in. I flashed my badge, but the doorman refused to let my brother pass.

"I'm the assistant police commissioner!" I protested. It was the first time I'd said it out loud and, although I must admit it felt good, it would have felt even better had it prompted the desired response of shock, awe, and obsequious compliance.

"I'll have to get the manager," the doorman responded.

Proof just smiled, seemingly used to this kind of rasta harassment.

The manager, a red-haired black man with freckles, came striding over. It was Foster Forest, who had worked alongside Proof and me that same summer but had remained to rise up the ranks. He was an exuberant man whose every feeling could be read on his face as easily as an emoticon.

:-D

"Zed!" he called out, grinning and clasping my hand. (Unfortunately, word of my bet with my brother, along with the unfortunate results, had leaked out that season, resulting in an even more unfortunate nickname among people that knew me back then.)

"I'm the assistant police commissioner now," I repeated. "My brother and I have business in the hotel."

Foster turned to Proof, recognizing him for the first time.

:-o

"Wah! Proof Watson—a yu!" Foster blurted out. "Sorry bout the holdup!"

"Nuh nuttin," Proof shrugged.

"Yuh changed, mon! I remember—sixteen years old, you rewrote the accounting program, boosted hotel revenue 20 percent! The Jamrock Genius! I always thought you'd win a Nobel Prize!"

"Actually, they don't give Nobels for math," Proof replied.

"I heard you got into Harvard, Stanford, MIT. You teaching now?"

"Not exactly. I have to learn about myself first, mon."

"So you're at UWI?"

"I'm in Trench Town. I smoke ganja, meditate, and play chess against tourists for money."

:-/

Foster clearly didn't know how to process that information and neither did I. But he seemed to be finished catching up with Proof, and turned to me. "Well, sorry for the caution before. It's just that a few minutes ago we had an incident . . ."

"What kind?"

"A man with a face tattoo—like teeth or something—tried to use the elevator. When we started asking him questions, him leave. We called it in to the station."

I took down his statement in a little more detail, but this was not good news. The whole thing sounded like the work of Lil Croc—one of the most feared posse leaders in the city. All of his men, as part of an initiation rite, were given face tattoos in the shape of crocodile teeth—one tooth for every year they were in the gang. Some of the veteran members of the group were so tatted up it looked like they were being swallowed whole.

I shook hands with Forest and then Proof and I headed to the elevators.

"The Island Einstein—back in action," Forest called out after us. "Walk good, mon!"

Proof and I entered the elevator and let the doors shut.

"I wish I had a spliff," muttered Proof.

"Cho! Never mind that. Lil Croc's men are poking around. We need to figure out his game."

"You're the cop. You tell me."

"I know he wants to be an outlaw hero to the masses—like the Godfather, Rhygin, or Jimmy Cliff in *The Harder They Come*. He's even sponsoring a track team."

"There's your answer. Getting Soledad to join would be a coup. The man keeps a dozen crocodiles in his yard—he'll make her an offer she cyann refuse."

The doors to the elevator opened on the fourth floor, and we walked briskly down the hall to room 423. I turned to Proof. "Let me do the talking. We have to follow procedure."

Proof pulled an imaginary zipper across his mouth, but what reassurance I got from that gesture was swiftly undone when he performed a similar zipping pantomime over his eyes, ears, crotch, and buttocks.

I knocked twice on the door, but before I rapped a third time it swung open.

A short young man in heavy black glasses stood in the entryway. He was missing much of his left arm, which ended in a reddish stump just below his elbow.

"Bourbaki?" I asked.

"Excuse me?" the young man answered.

He looked Middle Eastern, and was wearing a long flowy shirt. "Who are you?" I asked.

"Albert Aziz." He had a Middle Eastern accent too.

"What are you doing here?" I asked him.

"This is my room."

"No—what are you doing in Jamaica?"

"I'm a senior at Harvard. I'm with IRIE—the student exchange. Who are you?"

I brushed by him, with Proof following. Room service trays were scattered about the place.

"Have you seen Soledad Chin?" I inquired.

"Yeah, yesterday afternoon," Aziz answered. "What's this about? Who are you again?"

Aziz was twitchy and thin and looked ready to bolt at any second, like a lizard on a wall. "We're with the police," I told him.

Aziz pointed at my brother, who was poking around the textbooks scattered around the room, which mostly seemed to be historical in nature. "This guy is with the cops?"

"He's with me," I said. "He's just observing, not commenting in any way."

"I'm a mathematician," Proof smiled.

"A rasta mathematician?"

"Six and Seven Books of Moses. *Two Sevens Clash*. Dreads the biggest numerologists around."

"Numerology isn't mathematics."

"So you say. So you're from Afghanistan, correct?"

"Why do you say that?"

"You're reading Abu Rayhan Biruni, one of the great Persian mathematicians and philosophers."

Proof displayed a copy of the book he had picked up. I snatched it from him.

"We're of course not interfering with anything that could be used as evidence," I said, handing the book back to Aziz.

Aziz fumbled it in his one good hand.

"Where's your prosthetic today?" my brother asked.

Aziz turned away from Proof, who clearly unnerved him. "I'd really like it if you left now—and took him with you," he said to me.

"Not just yet," I said. "You didn't get worried when Soledad didn't come back last night?"

"She's from Kingston—she knows her way around. Is she okay?"

He didn't seem at all concerned—or surprised. "We have some evidence indicating she was in this room."

"We're study partners."

"Nothing more?"

"She's got a million jocks after her. Like I said, we're just study partners. Not that it's any of your business. I really don't want to answer any more questions until—"

"Last time you saw her—where was she headed?" Proof asked.

"She always gets a million invites to parties. People kept slipping them under her door at the Marriott. She came over here to get away. What happened to her?"

"Did you see these invitations?"

"Sure. She even left a bunch."

Aziz opened a desk drawer stuffed with papers and he pulled out some fliers of various colors—red, blue, green, white. They were all invitations of one kind or another to clubs, dances, and various functions. Proof slipped one out of the pile. It was a handwritten note with an equation written on it.

$$\frac{dx}{dt} = x(\alpha - \beta y)$$
$$\frac{dy}{dt} = -y(\gamma - \delta x)$$

I looked at Aziz.

"Beats me," he shrugged. "I'm a history major."

Proof peered at the invite. "Those are the Lotka-Volterra equations."

That meant nothing to me and he knew it by the look on my face.

"A.k.a. the predator-prey formulae," Proof continued. "They describe the interaction of two species where y is a predator, x is the prey. Lions eat sheep, lions increase, sheep decrease. Lions die off, sheep increase, lions eat more sheep, increase again. Circle of life, expressed in math."

I escorted Proof by the arm out of earshot of Aziz. I wrote the Lotka-Volterra equations on my left palm.

"You used to do that when we were kids," Proof grinned.

"Yeah, well, you got the math gene," I shot back. "I had to do something to help me keep up. Back to the equations: just who is the lion and which is the sheep?"

"There's more to it than that," Proof replied. He held the invite closer to a floor lamp.

Below the Lotka-Volterra equations was the faint impression of something that had been scrawled in haste on whatever paper had once been on top of this one. I could only just barely make it out. The impression read: *dutty tower*.

"What does that mean?" I asked.

"It means we're going to Trench Town."

Afternoon had arrived but the rain remained. As we drove into Trench Town the showers continued. The rain beat on the roof of the car like nyahbingi drums. Through the curtains of rain, at the intersections, I could see men under tin-roofed stands cooking things on sticks over trash cans lit on fire.

"So what do you think Mama and Dada would have thought, you living here?" I wondered aloud, hoping to draw my brother into conversation. I had so many questions. I knew he was living in Trench Town, but where? Was he still doing any math? Did he have a woman?

Proof said nothing, but he stole another glance in the rearview mirror.

"What are you looking for?"

Proof didn't answer and lit up a spliff.

"You can't smoke that in here," I complained.

"Nuh ramp wid mi! I need a smoke."

"You think you're the only one who could use one? That you're the only one hurting?"

Proof kept smoking.

"Nobody blames you," I began. "ATM robberies happen every day—truss mi. I get that it's hard to deal with. But we're from Cherry Garden, mon. What you doing in Trench Town?"

Proof exhaled so much ganja smoke I had to open a window. Rain poured through the crack as Trench Town passed.

"This was all low-income housing in the 1920s," Proof said at last. "There used to be an actual trench that ran right through town. Like the canals in Venice, only filled with piss and shit."

"You're schooling me in stuff I know. I thought we were talking about you. And how you're wasting your brain."

"There's history here that you can't see. I'm learning things that can't be taught."

"Like how to fight like you're in a video game?"

"It's called Bangaran. It's older than Capoeira."

"Never heard of it. I think you made that up."

"Truth. The Maroon warriors developed it in the seventeenth century. How do you think they managed to fight off the British for two hundred years?"

"So why do you need to know it?" I asked. "What war are you fighting?"

Proof smiled and kept blowing smoke.

* * *

I parked the car on a backstreet in Trench Town. It was early evening and we were in front of a seven-story apartment building that had been hit by Hurricane Ivan back in 2004 and now tilted at a twenty-degree angle like a hooker leaning against a lamppost. The Dutty Tower, people called the place. The building had been home to some minor stars on the Studio One record label and had been declared a national landmark years ago, and so developers, even ones who regularly paid off local public officials, couldn't get the place torn down, even though it was perpetually on the verge of collapse. Squatters had colonized every floor and the general consensus was that it was a matter of time before one of them burned the building down.

We got out of the car. The rain hit us hard and sudden like a hotel shower with controls you can't figure out. We ran up to the Dutty Tower and opened the front door.

Inside the building was a disaster. The air smelled like curry and ganja and Noah's ark. The hallways were parallelograms clogged with junk—palm tree trunks, old motorcycle engines, tables, coils of wire. Goats wandered around, munching on whatever they could find. Homeless people—dreadlocked men and women, small children—milled around the passageways, or sat boiling pots and cooking meals. Some of them turned to me, looking at my uniform before turning back to their cooking pots, rolling papers, or tattered Bibles. To look a little less like a cop, I quickly stripped to the waist, leaving only my undershirt and soggy once-pressed pants.

"It's going to take days to search inside this place," I moaned to Proof. "Any ideas?"

"Do you have another spliff?"

"Can't you get inspired without violating the drug laws of the island?"

Proof headed back out into the rain.

"Where are you going?" I shouted.

"I need to overstand."

"A wha u a say?"

Proof headed through the open door of the Dutty Tower and I chased after him. Night had come and it was dark outside. The rain, if it was possible, was coming down even harder now.

"When I used to do math, it helped to look at a problem from a fresh angle," Proof explained. "Do you have a torch?"

I got a flashlight from the car. Proof shined the light up at the leaning apartment building, illuminating one window at a time. The outside of the building was just as chaotic as the inside. The squatters had hung all sorts of things out of the windows—soaking wet laundry that someone had forgotten to bring out of the rain, clanging wind chimes, empty bird cages. Some windows were shuttered, others were cracked, some were lit, others were darkened, some had been painted green or yellow or black or bricked over. Proof let the light linger on one apartment on the seventh floor. The window had something odd painted on the outside:

$$Z$$

"What's the Z stand for?" I asked.

"That Z is not a Z. Look closely."

"Is this some sort of math thing?"

"Actually, yes. But we'd better go up to the seventh floor—fast."

The Z that was not a Z still looked like a Z to me. I copied the symbol onto my left palm as carefully as I could and followed him.

We tried to quickly make our way through the tangle inside of the Dutty Tower. The antiquated elevator wasn't working—naturally—so we took the stairs, which were unlit. Proof led the way with his flashlight, every so often bumping into a child, a goat, or a dread heading in the opposite direction. Even though I was carrying my uniform folded up in my hand, people still eyed me with suspicion—I guess I still walked, talked, and smelled like a police officer. As for Proof, he got friendly nods and the occasional "Walk good, mon."

"What are we looking for?" I asked as we passed the fifth floor. "What did that symbol mean?"

"The Bourbaki came up with it. 'The dangerous bend.' They used it whenever they wrote about an idea that could get people into trouble."

We had reached the seventh floor. This portion of the Dutty Tower seemed mostly uninhabited. The hallway was dim, and the floor was clear, but when Proof pointed the flashlight at the ceiling, the air came to life. A dozen whatsits and whosits buzzed by my head in a stream of green and black and red.

One of the UFOs hovered before my eyes. With its long curling tail feathers, it was unmistakably a doctor bird. I'd just never seen them nest inside a building before. The bird buzzed away. Proof pushed on.

"Hold up!" I told him.

"What?"

"We don't know what's in that room. We have no backup, and you're not a cop. If we're gonna do this, we have to do it my way. Now get behind me." I pulled out my gun.

Proof looked at me and my Glock 22. He reached in his pocket and pulled out a pen. He clicked it and moved beside me down the passageway.

We were in front of the room with the marked window. I tried the door handle—it wasn't locked. Proof pushed it open, slowly.

The room was completely empty. It was a studio apartment

with two large picture windows, one marked with the Bourbaki symbol that looked out over Trench Town. The room's fixtures had been stripped—the electrical outlets had been pulled out, and there were holes where the faucets and toilets perhaps once were. But the most striking thing was painted on the wall opposite the window: a huge golden triangle, six feet tall, bordered in red flames. Beneath the image was a series of Roman numerals painted in black:

$$0\ I\ I\ II\ III\ V\ VIII\ XXI$$

"Fascinating," Proof breathed.

"You know what this means?"

"The flaming triangle is the symbol for the Black Star Brotherhood."

"I know all the posses. I've never heard of that one."

"That's because it's not exactly a posse. Have you ever fallen into a Wiki wormhole?"

"What?"

"A Wiki wormhole. You start looking into something on Wikipedia, and in that entry something else catches your eye, and then you read that entry and click on something else, and pretty soon you're reading about latrines in seventeenth-century Holland and it's four a.m. Well, at the bottom of the deepest, darkest Wiki wormhole you ever fell into is a thing called the Black Star Brotherhood."

"Are they Garveyites?"

"Not exactly. Rastafari isn't the only religion with roots in Jamaica. I heard some of this when I was doing my dissertation, but more from the Trench Town rastas. The Black Star Brotherhood is kind of a numerology cult that traces its history to Ancient Egypt. Basically, the members believe that math was started by Africans in Africa and we have to protect it from infidels. Legend has it that as the ancient library of Alexandria was burning down in 48 B.C., members of the brotherhood saved the scrolls and protect them to this day. You might want to write this down."

Proof handed me his pen and I drew the triangle symbol with the flames on the palm of my right hand, and the Roman numeral sequence beneath that. "Let me get this straight. You think that the Black Star Brotherhood—"

The window to the apartment shattered. Proof hit the ground and I went down too.

Crawling on my elbows, I moved over to the window. I saw two men on the street in front of the Dutty Tower. I pulled a spyglass from my belt.

Peering through the small telescope, I could see the distinctive face tattoos. These were Croc Posse veterans. Lil Croc was known to be a superstitious man, fascinated by stories about obeah, duppies, and strange symbols. Perhaps that Z that was not a Z had attracted his men. He probably saw in a dream that Soledad was his destiny.

"Fuckery!" I cursed. "If we don't find Soledad soon . . ."

When I turned around from the window, Proof was standing up, heedless of bullets and posse members, staring intently at the sequence of Roman numerals on the wall.

"Everything cook and curry," Proof declared. "I know where Soledad is!"

I had to call for backup. The police arrived quickly, a surprise for Trench Town. The commissioner was among the first to show up, with a typically sour expression on his pitted face. He was accompanied by the hulking Officer Coconut who had a broken nose and a bruised ego, but had likely not said anything to anyone about the assault thanks to what Proof had picked from his pockets.

"Wa'ppun?" the commissioner growled, as we met him out-side the Dutty Tower. "Where's the girl?"

"Have you ever heard of Fibonacci?" Proof asked.

"Is that the perp?"

"Not exactly. Fibonacci numbers were named after the Ital-ian merchant Leonardo Fibonacci of Pisa—"

"A wad di rassclaat yuh a chat bout?" the commissioner in-terrupted. "I read your file, mon!"

Proof just looked at him.

Right there, in the rain, the commissioner let my brother have it. As I listened, I grew enraged, and two of his men had to hold me back. The commissioner had grown suspicious of how well Proof and I had worked together, and had quickly speed-read everything the department had on him. He knew now that we were brothers. He also knew about the robbery that took our parents' lives. I had removed mention of it from my records, and I never talked about it at work. I didn't want armchair psy-chologists to try to use it to figure me out—though, if I'm being honest, maybe it explains a lot about my life. It had been rain-ing that night too. Proof had just been accepted to Harvard, and we were headed to a restaurant on Braemar Avenue to celebrate. We needed a little cash, but none of us took note of the man who slipped into the ATM with us. I don't even recall his face—I only remember the gun. Proof had been standing at the machine. The man ordered him twice to clear his account. After the third time, the man fired two shots.

The commissioner laughed. "Island Einstein, dem call you. Genius of Jamrock. But when tief kill your parents, you couldn't remember your own ATM code! Now stop pretending you're better than us and tell me: where is the girl?"

Proof smiled placidly, betraying none of the emotions he may have buried in his heart.

"The Fibonacci sequence begins with 0 and I, and each

subsequent number is the sum of the previous two," Proof continued, as if he'd never been interrupted. "My brother's investigation led us to a room. On the wall was written a Fibonacci sequence in Roman numerals. One entry was missing: 13. I believe Soledad is at a Trench Town address that begins with that number."

"That could be dozens of addresses!" the commissioner blustered. "Naa mek mi vex, mon! Is this some sort of joke?"

Proof smiled again. "Mi naa jesta."

An army of policemen descended on Trench Town. I had thought the best way to proceed was to keep things quiet, but I was overruled by the commissioner, who wanted to move ahead with all deliberate speed. He also relieved me of my duties on the investigation; I could see by the glint in his eyes that he hoped to gain favor with the PM when the girl was found, the case was solved, and tourists everywhere on the island could continue tanning themselves in blissful ignorance.

I offered to give Proof a ride home to wherever it was in Trench Town that he lived, but he didn't answer me or even meet my gaze. He was somewhere deep within himself, his eyes staring at a ghost ship far out to sea.

"Let's not lose touch again, okay?" I pleaded. "Can you give me an address, an e-mail, something?"

Proof was surrounded by Beethoven's silence, deaf to the world, hearing only his own music. He wandered off, barefoot, down the street, away from the lights and the sirens. "Mi dun d'weet!"

So that was it. After years apart, and my younger brother, having solved the case, was strolling back out of Babylon and exiting my life.

But why had he helped the police—why had he helped me—in the first place?

I got out of my Fiat and followed Proof on foot.

If some sort of back-to-Africa math cult had kidnapped Soledad, possibly even murdered her, why were they using Roman numerals, Fibonacci numbers, and Lotka-Volterra equations? Why were they using pseudonyms and symbols from a French math group?

Still the rain kept falling.

Proof's first stop was a curious one. He visited a jewelry store on the fringes of Trench Town. The place was a modest affair, more of a storefront than a full store, more of a pawnshop than a real shop. Through the window I could see my brother asking the man behind the counter some questions. The man disappeared into a back room for a second, and when he returned he was holding something—what appeared to be a prosthetic limb.

Proof exited the shop soon afterward. Setting off at a fast pace—I had to jog to keep up—he headed deep into Trench Town.

The rain would not let up. Darkness had enveloped Trench Town, and the only light spilled over from the illuminated windows of the houses. I watched as Proof strode down one dead-end street and paused in front of a cottage at the end of it. The place was small—maybe a single room—and looked fairly abandoned. But I could see, inside, the faint glow of flashlights. Proof leaped over the waist-high white gate and walked up to the front door. He knocked, and it opened a crack. He seemed to be holding a brief conversation with whomever was on the other side. I don't know what he said but it worked. The door opened wider, Proof stepped in, and it shut behind him.

I went down the street at a run. Who was inside the house? What web was Proof spinning?

I came to the front door. 45 Star-Apple Lane. I kicked open the door, took one step inside, and found myself knocked back into a wall by a blast of gunfire.

* * *

When I came to my senses, I didn't know how much time had passed. The room was dark and a single window looked out on a full moon mostly hidden behind a cloud. The only sounds were the bark of a dog outside in the street, the intermittent rain on the roof, and my own labored breathing. I hadn't gotten a clear look at whoever shot me, or the gun, or even the rest of the room.

Against the wall I could see a woman, dressed in black jeans and a dark T-shirt, sobbing and shivering and holding a shotgun in her hands.

Soledad Chin.

Then the moon disappeared and the room was black again.

"What's going on?" I asked into the darkness.

Proof shushed me, and tugged at a makeshift bandage he had wrapped around my torso. "You've lost a lot of blood. Try not to move around."

My side was throbbing with pain.

"I didn't mean to shoot you," Soledad cried.

"That's comforting," I groaned.

"She thought you were one of Lil Croc's men," Proof explained.

"I don't understand any of this," I said. "Why are you here?"

Proof offered a grim smile. "I knew from the start the math cult was a ruse. But I had to wait until I could sidetrack the police. I knew that if Soledad and Aziz were on the run, they certainly didn't want the law catching up to them. We have worries worse than the police now."

Soledad began to sob loudly, but then pulled herself together. "Lil Croc is coming."

"How does he know where we are?" I asked.

Soledad wiped her face with her T-shirt. "I left Kingston because Lil Croc's men killed my aunt, threatened my family—he wanted me to join his crazy track team. I told Albert everything one night." As she spoke, she unconsciously rubbed her belly.

"You're pregnant?" I asked.

She nodded. "Albert told me we were going to be together. He had a plan."

I turned to Proof: "How did you know where to find them?"

"His left stump was rubbed raw—clearly he had recently worn a prosthetic device," Proof answered. "There was only one pawn shop in the area that had recently purchased a limb. I found out from the owner that Aziz had left an address, because he wanted to be given a chance to buy it back in case a buyer put in an offer. It's hard to part with an arm—even a fake one."

"We wanted to disappear for a year," Soledad said. "I was getting pressure from everywhere—the cops, the gangs, my sponsors. Albert said I should fake my death. He came up with a crazy math conspiracy to occupy everyone until we got away. He patched it all together."

"I thought he was a history major," I interjected.

"History of mathematics," Proof broke in. "Judging by his textbooks."

Soledad continued: "The arm gave us the money we needed to lay low. Albert figured staying at my aunt's house would be the last place anyone would look. He went back to the Pegasus so nobody would connect us, and so he could help throw the cops off track."

I was about to ask where the hell Aziz was now, when the moon peeked out and answered the question for me.

I could now see that I was lying next to a body—it was Albert Aziz. His flowing Afghan shirt was dark with blood. I jerked back with surprise. Soledad began to cry once more; Proof put an arm around her.

"Lil Croc had men watching the Pegasus," Proof said to me.

"One of them followed Albert here and shot him as he entered. He'll no doubt be back with reinforcements."

"Then what are we doing here?" I struggled to get to my feet but my side was in too much pain. I slid back to the ground.

"We're not going anywhere," Proof said. "You're in no condition to travel."

"Can't we call for help?" I said.

"Soledad ditched her cell so she couldn't be tracked. Your cell was destroyed when she shot you. And I haven't carried a phone since I started living in Trench Town. But we have other options."

Soledad peered out the window. "They're coming."

The moon disappeared again and the room was in shadow.

"We've only got a few seconds of complete darkness," Proof told Soledad. "We're going to stay here and distract them."

Soledad looked at him for an explanation.

"You have to make a break for it," Proof said. "Even if they take us out, at least you'll be safe. That's the most important thing. I want you to keep on running until you see a cop or a police station. Then you ask for the commissioner, you understand me? He'll be so embarrassed that his search failed, he'll send the whole department to save us."

Soledad wiped the tears off her cheeks and nodded. "I'm out of bullets," she said.

I handed her my Glock; she smiled at me and rested her empty shotgun against the wall.

"I want to see gold medal speed, you hear?" I said. "Silver will get us killed. Run quick noh!"

Gun in hand, Soledad dashed out of the door and into the shadows.

After a few moments, the moon lit up the neighborhood again. Every shingled roof, every wattle wall, every picket fence was cast in cold white illumination.

I crawled into a corner that was furthest from the window.

Three shadows peeked in—they'd be breaking into the shack soon.

"Now I wish I had that gun," I moaned.

"I wish I had a spliff," Proof replied.

The busted door flew open. Two of Lil Croc's tattooed men stood in the doorway, guns in one hand, flashlights in the other.

Proof moved as quickly as a spider. He disarmed the first two intruders with a Bangaran kick and a flip, but three posse members rushed into the room and pinned him down.

Then, through the doorway, stepped Lil Croc.

Lil Croc was a fireplug of a man—steely and short. He was bare-chested and massively muscled, with a huge tattoo of a crocodile winding around his torso, up his neck, and covering his face, merging his head with that of the reptile.

Lil Croc stomped one foot.

Two of his men raised their guns, one aimed at Proof, the other at me. Moonlight glinted off the metal of their weapons.

Acting on reflex, I extended my hands, palms out, waiting for the shot.

Lil Croc stopped. He stared, wide-eyed, at one of my hands.

As speedily as he had entered, Lil Croc turned and ran out of the cottage, his posse close behind him. Soon all the shadows were flying down the street, through the rain, and melting back into the urban darkness.

"Wha-what just happened?" I asked.

Proof grabbed my left hand, tracing with his finger the pyramid fringed by flame I had sketched in the center of my palm. The rain had blurred—but thankfully not erased—the symbol. "Apparently, there's at least one person on this island who still believes in the Black Star Brotherhood," Proof laughed. "Who born fi heng cyaan drown!"

I started to laugh too, but my ribs hurt too much. I had lost a lot of blood. The room was spinning—I didn't have as long as

I'd thought I did. The last thing I remember thinking that night is this: I hope Soledad is as fast as everyone says she is.

So, as you can see, readers of the *Gleaner* deserve to know the truth. The Soledad Chin case was extensively covered in the paper and hardly a word of it was true—especially the stories that detailed how the commissioner cracked the case. Much of the misunderstanding, of course, was my fault. The report I filed for the department left out several key elements of the narrative: Proof's role in solving the crime, the identity of the suspect who shot me, and the fact that Soledad was still alive. After she made an anonymous call to the station house, and a patrol car took me to the hospital, Proof helped her disappear. Then he vanished as well and a *Gleaner* reporter went so far as to tweet that he was dead.

I had slipped my brother my e-mail address and he had promised to stay in touch—but, naturally, he did no such thing. Weeks went by and then months, holidays, birthdays, anniversaries, with nary a word. I looked for him in Trench Town, but heard nothing; stories came back to me about sightings, but nothing definite. He was a duppy.

A year later, long after I had unpacked the boxes in my fishbowl office (but wasn't feeling any more at home), I received a tip from an informant that my brother had been spotted in a store buying sacks of sugar, red ribbons, and several small plastic cups. But nobody knew where he had gone after making the odd purchase.

None of it made sense to me either, until, driving home one night, I heard "Three Little Birds" on the radio of my Fiat. I continued driving straight over to Trench Town.

When I got to the seventh floor, a dozen hummingbirds buzzed around my head. Their numbers had increased—this had to be the place. I knocked on every entryway on the leaning hallway until finally, at room 721B, Proof came to the door. He was holding a narrow plastic cup with a red ribbon tied around it. Three doctor birds, attracted by the color, zipped around his hand, sipping at the sugar water in his cup.

"You don't call, you don't write . . ." I joked.

Proof didn't seem surprised that I had found him. He yawned, put down the cup, and lit a spliff.

"Lil Croc is still out there. A lot of his business is running numbers. With your particular skill set, you could help bring him down. Will you help?"

Proof, sucking on his spliff, said nothing.

"I don't understand you," I complained. "You hate cops. You cut me off. So why did you help with the case? There must be some reason you got involved."

Proof was as silent as a calculator.

I continued: "Here's my theory—I think, because of what happened to our parents, you want to give back. You want to use your math skills to fight crime. Tell me I'm wrong. Tell me I haven't cracked your formula."

From inside the apartment I heard the cry of a baby.

"Honey, are you coming back to bed?" a woman's voice called out.

That sounded like Soledad.

I looked at Proof.

He smiled, exhaled a cloud of smoke, and slowly shut the door.

SUNRISE

BY CHRIS ABANI

Greenwich Town

The rising sun picked out the points of the old tin roofs. Soon it would fill the narrow, potholed street with flame. Petunia wore a brown dress and white sneakers as she sat on the small veranda of her two-room, wood and concrete house, erect in her wicker chair, slurping her coffee, looking down the littered street from this small elevation over the hibiscus hedge to that house, that house, that damn house eight gates down, where that sports car was parked, that house with the coconut tree in the front yard and that bright red door.

This is fuckeries . . . you are fuckeries, she muttered. She put the tin mug down on the table next to her and reached for her phone.

Hunts Bay? Beg you send a squad car now. A girl and her baby dead in Greenwich Town . . . please, sir, as there is a God I not going answer any questions. What more you want but that a girl and a baby dead in Greenwich Town? I done give you the address already, sir. Don't worry yourself with who me is. Just come. Just come. Just come.

When she got off the phone she thought of what she'd say when she was asked in person. Who she was?

If she'd been asked before two a.m. this morning, she would have mentioned four things: the daughter of a fisherman from Treasure Beach; a dropout from a nursing school in Mandeville; a woman who'd lived her forty-three years in the light of the gospel; and a former sinner who did not do what an older married man had commanded—which was to abort her child.

Her scalp itched under her store-bought hair as her mind took her back to that time.

When her mother had found out she was fooling with Mr. Gladstone, she'd beaten her with a mop stick and called her Jezebel and said if she ever took no more man again she was going to tie her up. And she'd been so afraid—not so much of getting hit again, but of being restrained—that she ran away to her father's fishing shack one night when he was gone to sea. When he returned, she told him that her mother now had a new boyfriend and she, Petunia, didn't like the man, and so she got put out.

She was seventeen then, but so small that folks who didn't know her used to think she was twelve. Her father didn't question her. He simply took her in.

She began to wish now in this moment of waiting that her father was alive. He would have taken care of Linton, that nasty, stinking dog. She wouldn't have had to try.

In her mind she saw the shack where she used to walk down from their little house to meet her father just before sunrise, making sure to get there in time to hear the slither of wood on wet sand as he dragged his canoe ashore on Frenchman's Cove beach. She saw in her mind the bright blue of the boat, and the way it glistened in the soft light of predawn, saw also the other men all along the beach, pulling their canoes ashore until the beach looked like it was littered with toy dolphins.

Her father's face always broke into a smile when he saw her.

After a few weeks with him, when she was sure her belly would begin to show, she stopped going to school. Her father was not the kind of man who paid attention to this sort of thing. Though she knew now that she'd have been better off in life if he had. But he was a good man, and they grew closer as she lingered with him in the mornings when the boats came in. With school off her agenda, she had time to just sit with him on the prow of his blue boat named for her and give him his breakfast and ginger coffee—which she, Petunia, was drinking now on her veranda as she waited for the sirens to come.

Looking back now, with the eye of an adult, she understood a look that used to confuse her then, the look of a parent marveling at the miracle of his child while feeling the weight of sorrow. In her recollection, it was a look that never lasted. Like lightning, it would come in a flash, then her father would begin to laugh again, and rub his hands in her hair, and she would giggle and tell him not to wipe the saltfish oil 'pon her head.

On some mornings, though, there was not much laughter. At these times, he'd ask her when she planned to go back to her mother. As she complained, he'd say her mother was good, that he'd shamed her, that's all.

She is from a good family, he would say. A better class than mine. I couldn't married her—and they wouldn'ta let me marry her—so is like the shame is mine too. I feel that's why bad luck take me and I mash up like this, just drinking rum and can't even take proper care of me daughter. One day, though, one day, God might take a chance on me and give me a little grace.

The next thing Petunia saw, as she sat on her veranda, was her seventeen-year-old self waddling barefoot on the hot gray sand, her shame six months prominent, living off the fish and kindness of her father's friends, and hearing someone calling her from behind. It was a young white man from Ohio who had come down from the Seventh Day Adventist church up in Mandeville to take her to the new home for unwed mothers.

We are a place of acceptance, he'd told her, where we believe you can be reborn.

And who wouldn't want that? she thought, as some schoolchildren walked by her house in their uniforms, and radios and TVs sounded in the houses on her street. Who wouldn't want that? So she went with him the next morning to Mandeville. And that is where her pickney Grace was born, and where she'd entered the college run by the Adventist church. But the same man who had saved her wanted her body in return so she left, ran away again.

She found a job at Kingston Public Hospital as a ward assistant, and settled in Greenwich Town. Rough place, everybody used to tell her. Out there is West Kingston. But at least, she told herself, it's down by the waterfront, and her happiest times ever had been with her father, who had since died, down by the sea. And she needed to save money for Grace's future. And in this neighborhood the rent was cheap.

Oh Grace, oh Grace, oh Grace—she glanced down the road at the red front door—why you cause this kind of crosses on me? But is not like nobody never tell you, said a chorus of voices in her head.

The girl grew pretty. On top of that she had tall hair and light skin. People used to say she look half Chiney. Went to good school too, Ardenne Prep. The kinda school that made her, Petunia, have to work two shifts three times a week and take the long bus ride up to Mona Heights on weekends to clean and cook, and wash married women's skimpy underwear and exercise clothes.

But she didn't used to mind the ride up there, in truth, because that is where she had found what she came to know as her rightful church.

One Sunday afternoon, her bus broke down near the US embassy on Old Hope Road, near Lane Plaza, and as she waited for another one to come she heard a glorious singing, and the spirit of the Lord led her to follow it, and she ended up going into the heart of a ghetto hidden away in the middle of that uptown splendor in a place called Stand Pipe; there she met the sisters of the Church of the Pentecostal Fire, Clarisse and Millicent and Hildred. And soon after she met them, they began to warn her that she had to think about where she was living, because a girl like Grace would not survive slum life.

That one did hurt her for true. *Slum life.* Like where they lived was any better, just because it wasn't in West Kingston or felt like it was in the country, as people still fished out there by the waterside.

But who could have seen it coming?

Grace was a good girl, churchgoing and choir-singing all along. Then she turned thirteen and began to notice boys, and boys began to notice her, and what should have been an inno-cent time of bad perfume, and fumbled school fetes, and gossip, and giggles, and bad makeup, and the uncertain swaying of hips noticed mostly by boys her age, whom God in His mercy made inept and shy to protect the world from unfolding too soon, became something else.

Here in this place where the Lord had let the devil have free reign, thirteen-year-old boys weren't the only ones to watch young girls. And Grace came to the attention of him, the one who drove that sports car parked before that house with that damn red door—and where is the damn police?—and nothing she could say seemed to deter her child from sneaking out.

She began to think now of the story she'd tried to use to scare her.

One night when I used to live with my father, the story had begun, I heard a commotion as I was walking past a bar, and when I went in there I see a man grabbing him up. My father was drunk already even though it was just past lunchtime, and the man was three times bigger than him, and the man had him down, you know, had bend him over and my father was down on one knee struggling, and then him see me, and when him see me him just twist the man and flip him over, and as the man was flipping over, my father just come up with him fishing knife and slit the man crossway from him right shoulder down to him left side, but not too deep. No guts did spill. And after that him just come to me and gave me some pocket money and order another Red Stripe. And I want you to know something, Grace: I might be a woman of God, but I know I have the devil inside. And sometimes when I see you with that damn Linton, or hear that you driving up and down beside him in him car in your school uniform, and going over there and passing through that red door, I get the look on my face that my father had when he saw me watching him fight that man that time. And let me tell you this, and I am only going to tell you one time: if you look under my bed, you will see my father's knife.

And is not like I tried only one way, thought Petunia. She'd even tried to work with the other side.

One night she'd come home from her second shift and Grace wasn't there, and she just knew she was over there behind that damn red door, and she'd marched over with a New Testament clutched to her bosom, and when the hooligans who worked for the dog saw the shape of her coming through the night, they met her halfway, stopped her in the public street, and roughed her up, and during the roughing up, Linton himself came out. He was dressed in just his underpants and a baseball cap, which did not prevent him from sauntering up the street.

I promise you, he'd said, that if you ever come over here and disrespect me like that, you going find Grace—and I don't even know where the little stink-pussy red gal bloodclaat is— you going find her in a bag out at sea. And trust me, I was going leave her alone, but because of this now, I just going keep fucking her. And if she listen to you and bring some argument to me I going take it one step further and fuck her up. So if is that you want as her mother, then come over here and fuck with me again. Me no frighten for nobody. Is me run this place, and trust me, Mother, me can fuck any gal, anywhere, anyhow, anytime.

As she'd walked back to her house while those hooligans laughed, Petunia thought of all she'd seen those years at KPH, all those dark inventive ways in which men hurt women and young girls.

She'd waited on this same damn veranda the next morning, had watched her daughter leave that godforsaken house at sunrise and take that shameful walk while other girls were going to school. And she had tried to talk to her—nobody can say she didn't try—but the gal wanted to walk inside the house without answering her mother, and when she grabbed her and slapped her, the bitch hacked and spat in her eye.

That night she did not work her second shift as scheduled, she went up to Stand Pipe to church, and there over a votive lit in the corner of the tabernacle she made her pledge.

Almighty Lord, the one true God who smote the enemies of David and Solomon, she invoked. The prayer was elaborate, the calling down of the ghost to witness, the calling down of fire, but the pact was straight. If you don't protect my child, Lord, she said, I will have to bring the fire down on the enemy myself, like Elijah did to Baal on that holy mountain. So help me Lord to stay true and straight.

And even when Grace got pregnant by Linton, said Petunia to herself as she heard the sirens in the distance, she was patient with God. Had Job himself not endured more than that and without even the blessings that she had?

One night, when Grace was just two months pregnant and was still spending nights with that nasty thirty-odd-year-old Linton boy, and she, Petunia, confessed that she was losing faith, sisters Clarisse, Millicent, and Hildred reassured her.

Put it to God again in prayer, child. Put it strong-strong this time. We have a mighty friend.

And she smiled up at the big picture of Jesus over the altar, and in her heart she felt as if she and that man had an understanding, and as the sisters lay hands on her she bowed her head and smiled.

She said, Don't pray for me or with me no more, my sisters. I have heard directly from the Lord.

What did the Lord tell her? Take the pickney out of school before she start to show. Lock her up in her room. Look for a new place. And move. When you go to work, tie her to her bed. Use tape and seal her. Put up black curtains. Lock every door.

As the daughter of a fisherman, she knew all about knots, and there was no slipping out of the ones she made.

It was risky to keep a pregnant girl tied up and immobilized, she knew, but she'd worked at KPH for a very long time, so she kept Grace hydrated with saline drips. Hand-fed her fish soup and chicken with dumplings at night.

The girl began to behave herself under this regimen. Full compliance came in only four weeks time. After this, she merely had to threaten and the girl would get in line.

What had she been thinking? Jesus Christ.

One thing ended up leading to another. She, a God-fearing woman, began to weave a net of lies—like, Grace gone America to live with her father, or, She going to finish high school over there; I want her to go medical school for she is a girl that want to reach very high.

When the girl became very quiet, she wasn't sure if she was just depressed like most women are when they are pregnant. But it was clear that she'd lost all of her vitality and had begun to drift around the little house.

What had she planned to say when the baby was born? She'd never gotten that far in her thoughts. And she began to wonder now, as the heat rose up with the full morning, if she'd simply been testing God, or if it had been a matter of crossing that bridge when she got there, or if she'd been teetering on the edge of madness. It was possible. For wasn't it madness that made mortals challenge the Almighty?

What struck her now as she drained what was left of the cold coffee in the mug was that Linton had never once asked her about Grace, never cared to find out where she had gone during the time when she'd disappeared, and she'd passed his house and he'd driven by her in his sports car many times.

One time as she passed him hanging out outside his house, she cut her eyes and railed in tongues. He said: Witchy Poo, you think throw-word can frighten badman? Hey, you know why I don't bloodclaat shoot you? Is through I love your daughter. Don't worry, when she legal I going give you a money for her and put on a ring. I going make sure you don't change bed pan and wash sore foot forever. So don't gimme bad eye too tough.

She spoke more tongues and shook out her skirt and went home to her daughter, whom she'd been caring for with saline drips and fish soup and chicken with dumplings for six whole months, and God saw that it was good.

Petunia stood up. There were sirens coming fast from up the block. She threw the mug away into the garden and wept for what she'd seen and done just hours before.

When she'd come home from her night shift, Grace was splayed out on her bedroom floor, legs so wide they looked unhinged. And blood. Lord have mercy! Blood everywhere. The sheets. The floor. The walls. It was like an evil spirit had been called from hell to rip her child apart, to tear the baby from her womb.

The baby, such as it was, was in its own splatter on the floor near Grace's feet. Someone would have come if she'd been screaming. This Petunia knew. But she, her mother, had done her job too well, had broken her daughter's will so badly that the girl had been alive but not living, walking but dead.

The cry that came from Petunia was so old, so primal, and

yet so soft, a whisper swaddled in a rasp, a sound one hears from feral cats. As she cried this soft cry, there was a flutter, a movement so subtle it could have been imagined, could have been a trick. And she paused and stared, and noticed it again, a slight tremor of breathing at her daughter's neck.

What must a mother do for the suffering child? What must a mother do if she wants to keep her pledge to God?

Petunia went into her room, kneeled beside her bed, and reached below it for her father's knife. With her hand over her daughter's eyes, she put the edge against her throat and flinched, repeating to herself that she was saving her from suffering, that this was a mercy like Abraham had offered to Isaac before the Lord had stayed his hand, and that even though God had neglected her, she would be strong. Like Cain, she would have to make her own way.

But then she peeled her hand from Grace's face and saw the dead-fish eyes, and relented. Tried to wake her. Call her back.

She knew from all those moments down at KPH that when the breath was gone it's too late, but she tried anyway, because there is no training or experience for death happening to your own daughter, especially at your own hands.

Nothing to do but sit in all that blood and cry until there is nothing but air, a choking that in its own way brings comfort. Then you shower. Then you change.

You make your coffee. You go on your veranda. You make the call.

You wait.

MONKEY MAN

BY COLIN CHANNER

Hughenden

Would someone adjust this mike just a *little* for me, please? That's good. How do I sound?

So, in 1975—what's that? About thirty-five years ago?—I got myself into a really bad situation in Jamaica. Needless to say, it was a very different time from now. For one, there was still something called a left in this country. There was also something called a right, a recognizably rational position like the one held by my old friend—and I use this term despite the many times we disagreed—Bill Buckley.

As you may know, it was hard for me to get work in this country for years and years after the Davis case, so I went into exile in France.

I had never been good with money, and almost all I'd earned was gone. So I didn't think twice about saying yes to the BBC when they asked me to travel to Kingston to do voice-overs and interviews for a two-part series on dub.

For those of you who don't know what dub is—well, lemme see if I can explain. It's a kind of reggae. And we all know what that is. But imagine a kind of spacey, warpy, instrumental reggae with snatches of sound—voices, clock chimes, bird calls—pretty much anything an engineer could imagine while smoking pot (which could be anything, couldn't it?), drifting out and in.

I was one of a crew of six. In addition to me there was a producer, two camera operators, a lighting tech, and a sound engineer. At forty-five, I was the oldest, and the only girl.

Anyway, within an hour or so of settling down at the Sheraton, just as I had lit my second spliff, Nigel, the producer, phoned to say our driver had relayed instructions that we shouldn't order dinner because he'd be coming back to take us out.

Well, I became quite grumbly—believe it or not, I can be a bitch—but Nigel convinced me I should go, that it made sense to play nice, especially since he had the sense that the invitation had come from high up. And we needed protection. Most of the recording studios in Kingston were in or near the slums.

So we piled into a cream and white VW camper and off we went. We were staying in New Kingston, a rather optimistic grid of new streets with few buildings, but as far as streets go, well laid out.

From there we drove in light traffic through neighborhoods with large colonial homes and old trees. I remember one of these districts being referred to by the driver as Trafalgar Park.

The driver. Ahhhh. The driver. I'd paid no attention to him at the airport. His name was Wayne Haddad, and he was about twenty-one. From the conversation he was having with the lighting tech, I gathered he was in his last year at the university, in his parlance, reading history with econ.

He was short and slim with an afro that was turning into something else. I remember thinking as we drove that if he turned up in Brazil or Venezuela he would easily blend in.

After a twenty-minute drive, which took us up along a well-populated ridge, we arrived at what we learned was his parents' house. Like its far-flung neighbors it looked like something from the hills of LA. Lots of cut stone and plate glass. And a huge veranda reaching way over a cliff.

We dined with Wayne's parents—Maylynn and Clive—at a long white table set beneath some sort of fruit tree strung with lights. The broad city lay below us like a beaded cloth.

Maylynn looked and sounded slightly Irish. Clive was black,

light brown, but called himself Lebanese. We had duck, I re-member. And fish. There might have also been roast beef. But I'll never forget the turtle soup, which I'd only had before in New Orleans. And booby eggs. Small brown speckled things. They were poached.

Anyway, Wayne drifted away from the table midcourse and didn't return. He paused for a moment between his mother and me, leaned on the backs of our chairs and kissed her neck, then reached through the spindles and tugged my dress.

By this time, small conversation groups had sprung up. I asked Maylynn about her son. He was nearly fluent in French, she said. But before more came out a sonic fog began to creep across the lawn. As the bass increased in volume, the forks and china shook.

Clive shouted, "Turn off that damn Bob Marley! Don't you see we have guests from abroad?" He began to stand, but May-lynn fanned him down.

I asked about Wayne again. His mother put her hand on mine and leaned in close. He'd only been allowed to work in the family business earlier that year. He was a bright boy, but unappreciated by his father, which sometimes made him—she gestured with her hand—erratic. She and Clive owned a few gift shops, including the one at our hotel. They also owned a pharmacy, a hardware store, two supermarkets, a fleet of rental cars, and the camper, which she called a tour bus.

Wayne, I found out, wasn't actually a driver. He'd somehow found out there was a French speaker in our group, at which point he'd told her that he wasn't going to simply organize our transportation, he'd do the job himself.

Clive began to fan his nose. The music was bringing with it a certain herbal scent.

After being in Kingston for about ten days, most of them on

the hot plains interviewing men with nicknames like Niney and Leggo and Yabby You, we were invited up to Maylynn and Clive's again.

This time when Wayne reached between the spindles I waited till the music started, asked for directions to the bathroom, and met him in his flat, a wooden cottage set way off from his parents' modern, concrete house.

I was so self-conscious, getting into bed with him. Since that first time he'd touched me, all our screwing had been done in the parking lot of the Sheraton against the Camper, standing up.

"We should have a proper date one day," I said as I walked out.

The music was so loud I didn't think he'd even hear. I'd been in movies since I was fourteen. To me, lights, cameras, and travel had always meant sex.

I didn't need Wayne to show me any kind of serious intent. I was twice his age to begin with. And he wasn't really my type. I liked men with presence. But he was convenient. And good looking. And most importantly, his parents owned a pharmacy, and for the last week or so he'd been getting me my stuff.

The gardener drove us back to the hotel that night. I waited up. Wayne didn't call. I took a Valium with my rum.

The next day I took amphetamines to keep me up. Wayne seemed quite distant. Even cross. Barely spoke to anyone.

It was about nine or so when we arrived at the hotel. We'd spent all morning with Augustus Pablo at a sophisticated-looking studio near a skating rink.

The phone rang at close to midnight. It was Wayne. I had just finished up a phone call with a casting agent. Another job had fallen through. Before I went downstairs I took a few Pertranquils then drew a line of coke to balance out.

Wayne was leaning on a blue Citroën 2CV. This was his car. He kissed me for the first time ever. Opened my door. I was wearing bell-bottom jeans and a pink tube top. He was wearing a black leather jacket despite the heat.

When I got inside the car it seemed that Wayne was unsure what to do. We drove for about fifteen minutes with the radio off before we even spoke.

"So what do you have in mind?" I asked.

"Kingston is not like Montego Bay," he mumbled. "We close down kinda early. We don't have a lot of tourists here. But don't worry. I know where the action is."

We kept driving, mostly in silence. The bug-eyed car nosed like a rodent through the empty streets. Shopping centers with *For Rent* signs drifted by. At traffic lights we'd sometimes see half-naked men just lying on the sidewalk or walking in circles talking to themselves. A few clicks down from a late-night burger place we saw a car pull over and a male arm holding out a lunch box and gesturing come-ons to children who were looking through a garbage bin.

Each time I saw something like this I'd stare at Wayne. This world outside his window meant nothing. He just kept driving toward the distant sparkling hills.

We eventually came upon a stretch of road completely given over to bars and clubs, simple buildings in bright colors with hand lettering and makeshift designs. Cars were parked two wheels up on the curb. Rough men in knit caps and newsboys milled about. The music was constant but not loud.

Wayne led me upstairs to a spot called the Stable. It was a go-go joint—something anyone could tell from its name.

In some kind of weird pretense of actually dating, he sat beside me with his hand on my leg, but we didn't really speak. His perspiration made the odor of his jacket rise up.

Anyway, we stayed there for hours, shoulders touching in the dim blue light, watching black girls in white boots shake it. The speakers in the ceiling made the disco rain down. He drank beer. I drank rum. We shared a pack of Rothmans.

"Mind if I smoke a spliff?" I asked.

"One whiff of weed," he told me, "and they'd throw us out."

"So, blow," I joked, "would get us banned for life."

"No," he said. "They wouldn't even know what it was."

Bingo!

I reached for the foil in my purse. He raked his fingers through his hair, and reached inside his jacket for some aviator shades. It felt thrilling to sit there in front of everyone doing lines, almost as thrilling as the times we'd screwed unnoticed in the parking lot of the Sheraton while cars passed by.

He leaned into me. My lips fell apart. But he didn't kiss me. He put his mouth against my ear and said, "Let's speak in fucking French."

Now, I had been with weird men before. But aren't men in general a little weird? And as far as weirdness goes, it wasn't such a strange request. The way I read it, he wanted to show me he was hip.

So while the guys at the rusting iron tables all around us chewed ice cubes and drank Guinness and talked about which of the naked girls they'd done or would like to do, Wayne spoke to me in French.

With rough pronunciation but very good vocab, he told me that he'd learned to parlez-vous in high school and that he'd chosen Spanish at first but had dropped it because the French class had more girls and that he'd taken weekend classes at Alliance and that's why his accent was so good and why French films were his favorite because at Alliance that's all they showed there and did I know why he liked French films so much and NO the answer was not because they were French and YES you could say that he loved all French things but the *real* reason he loved French films so much was that they taught him a lot about those damn French girls and did I know what that was so lemme tell you then French girls were easy and what about American girls well what do you mean what about American girls what have I learned about American girls from movies well from movies I learned that American girls scream for every fucking thing especially when they are in the shower or think red Indians are around—

In retrospect I should have known he was a little off. What can I say? I was a little off myself. I threw my head back and laughed. Laid out another line.

Then he asked me about me . . .

I steered the subject back to film. To my mild surprise, he became quite sober, introspective, charming. Even showed a little wit. He knew a lot about Cassavetes, Peckinpah, and Varda. And a little bit about me. He used a film I'd done many years before with Agnès to shift the conversation back to me. He seemed to have a list of things he wanted cleared up, like why I took the name Arielle Béchard when I'd been born Georgette Michel. And is it true that I'd come to America as a baby after being born in Quebec?

I was getting around to answering some of these questions when he said in English: "You're cool."

I said, "Oh yeah?"

He squeezed my thigh. "You know why I brought you here?" he asked. "To freak you out. Yeah man. I wanted to bring you to a way-out place. I wanted you to just lose your head. But you're cool. You're just so cool. I like girls that are cool. A lot of girls my age aren't cool, you know. A lot of people period aren't cool. But you're cool. You like my jacket? I wore it for you because it's cool."

I told him in French that I wasn't really cool, that I only seemed cool because he was so easy to be with. To myself I said, I've been to this joint many times. I know its sound. I know its mood. Its smell. I've been here in Rio. Watts. Kinshasa. France, in the banlieues. In Chicago, on the South Side. Always the rare white woman. Always with colored men.

This discussion with myself made me a little ashamed and self-conscious. I wanted to get away. With each passing second I felt older, whiter. More intoxicated. More broke. The room felt too hot and dark.

I said to him, "Allons-y."

It was about one in the morning when we left. I figured we were going to his bungalow or my hotel. Most of the other bars and clubs were closed. There were a few men milling about. Standing still with little motorbikes between their legs.

Before Wayne put the car in gear I asked him to roll me a spliff. He asked for the foil. My mouth felt dry and my joints tightened as I watched.

My hair was long in those days, and dark, and as we zoomed along in the 2CV the wind came through the window and splashed it on my face.

So there we were, moving easy down this dark road, lit hills behind us. Every now and then a car came around a corner, stunning our gaping pupils with its high beams, and Wayne would brake or swerve. The little shops and houses were all shut.

After we'd driven a mile or so I saw a billboard with a photo of the island's leader shaking hands with Fidel. I asked where we were.

Wayne said, "Red Hills Road." He tossed his head to indicate the hills behind us. "Go past the Stable and down and round you'll eventually get up there."

As we passed the billboard I began to think of how the CIA was working hard to sink this island, just like they'd worked to sink me. Sure—some bad choices had been made. Sure—this pressure had been in some ways brought on.

Look, I'm no political theorist. I dropped out of Bard in

my junior year. But I know a thing or two. The Jamaican government had made it illegal for women to be paid less than men; had made university free for all; had offered free lunch to kids in elementary school. In other words, they'd been messing around with the fundamental laws of social equilibrium in this hemisphere, so damn them. Damn them the way you damn an actress who harbors the falsely accused, or calls out Israel on Palestine, or publishes op-eds in the *Washington Post* about America's hypocrisy on apartheid. Damn you. Damn you. Damn you.

But anyway, there we were, moving along this Red Hills Road, heading either to Wayne's bed or mine, when out of his mouth comes a question. Whose dubs did I like the most?

This isn't how he said it, but it's what he wanted to know. I paused before I answered. The truth is that I couldn't tell the sounds apart. As I thought of what to say he asked: "Aren't you curious why we turned off Red Hills Road?"

"I didn't notice."

He slapped the dashboard and whispered, "I'm going to take you to meet the greatest producer this country has ever known."

"Where?" I asked.

"At her home."

"Which is where?"

"In this housing scheme called Hughenden. A decent place. Nurses. Teachers. And civil servants. Nothing to worry about. Folks like that."

We drove on for a few minutes, slower now, on very small streets, and made a few more turns. I closed my eyes. We were still moving when I opened them. The houses were close. The yards were small. The rooflines were flat. Most porch lights were on.

I leaned my head outside the window. I'd begun to feel really, really scared. And tired, but not sleepy. And sick.

We stopped. Wayne tapped my shoulder then stepped out of the car. I held the seat cushion with both hands and tried to bring my heart rate down. He knocked on a burglar bar. I drew on the spliff.

A curving quarter-mile of fences stretched before me. From my perspective they'd began to warp and shake. A door clunked open. My name called out.

I didn't move or answer. Wayne approached the gate, stood there sweating in his leather jacket, waiting for me.

I said, "This is just not how these things are done, babe. We've got a schedule, you know. But I don't have to tell you. You know. And . . . and the poor guy . . . what's his name. He wouldn't like to be ambushed in the night by a journalist or whatever it is I'm supposed to be. Let's go home, babe. I'm getting kinda sick. You gonna take me home?"

"It's not a he," he said. "It's a she."

At this point I took mild interest. All the people on our list of subjects were men.

"But she probably isn't even up," I said. "Let's just go home. Tomorrow, I'll run it by Nigel. The producer decides this kind of thing."

"But she's about to let us in," he said. "Come on, Georgette."

"What do I even call her?"

I missed what he said.

The small, dark house smelled of ripe bananas and curry. The louvers were all shut. My toes were sweaty on the cool floor tiles. I tracked Wayne by the odor of his jacket and the padding of his boots, then I found myself waking up. It took a few seconds to realize this. Sometimes awareness is slow to seep in.

I opened my eyes. It was still dark. But dark in a peculiar way. And although I was tired, I couldn't figure out why it was so hard to move. And there was a woman there. I sensed this. She was naked, I felt. Spread-eagled. Tied up.

She was me.

I tried to free myself. I shook my head. The bag was fairly loose around my neck, so maybe I could thrash it off. My legs were pulled so far apart my groin began to hurt. Fuck, I wasn't wearing any clothes.

I screamed. I tried at least. My lips were taped down.

For the next hour or so I wrenched and pulled. What was outside the darkness? Was there someone standing silently a foot away? Was I even in the house I'd entered with Wayne? And where the hell was Wayne? Was he hurt? Had someone killed him?

When this kind of thing happens, you don't think about your loved ones. You don't think about God. You think of being tortured with simple things. A cheese grater on your nipple. A citrus spoon in your eye. An iron pressing your vagina shut.

That's what happened to me. I kept picturing awful things, and the more I thought about them the more I *knew* they would occur.

I began to breathe so hard and sweat so much that the bag started clinging to my nose. I began to lurch and wrench. Which made things worse. But I couldn't stop myself. But I *had* to stop myself. And somehow I did.

I can't say it was anything more than will that made me slow my breathing down. Long in, long out. Long in, long out. No holding. Keep going. This wasn't yoga class.

With my breathing fairly settled, I was able to concentrate enough to plan. Where was I?

I heard light traffic moving back and forth in the distance. Every now and then, a van or motorbike would pass along the nearby streets. There were daytime voices spilling from a house to the left of me. It was hard for me to follow the conversations. Their accents were rough. But I could pick out words like *starch* and *sheets*. In the background I could hear a radio. Right above me, the branches of a tree scraped the roof. A small fruit fell.

As I struggled to hear all these sounds in isolation I detected another, fainter noise beneath them. At first I couldn't tell what it was or where it was coming from. A kind of shushing. At one point I thought it was a broom. I slowly realized I was hearing human voices . . . coming from . . . no . . . not the house next door, but from somewhere behind me. Same house. Other room.

A serious whispered conversation was going on. One voice belonged to Wayne. It was snappy. Angry. The other voice was deep. It would go silent for long stretches, then continue in reasoned tones.

A door opened. The voices and footfalls grew louder. Came close. I played dead.

Two pairs of feet entered the room. A hot body sat beside me on the bed, inches from my hip. From the smell of the jacket, I could tell it was Wayne.

"Arielle," he said, nervously. "Arielle."

He shook me. I willed my body not to move. At the foot of the bed, a calloused hand began to softly pinch and stroke my toes.

"Go home," said the other voice, which belonged to the person who had touched my feet. "We not doing this thing. She is all right. But not so well though. Look how her foot is cold."

The bed lurched and creaked as Wayne jumped up. From the direction of my feet I heard a jangle then a swoosh. A belt had come off.

A scuffle began. Small things fell over. Bottles broke. Wayne and the other person were breathing hard. One of them banged into something big and wooden. Clothes were ripped. Then all of a sudden a great tumbling rushed toward me. I had no time to brace. The air was blown out of my lungs.

Wayne was on top of me. His wet mouth and hot breath

were on my face and neck. The other person jumped on top of him. I began to suffocate under the weight of both of them. The mattress fell. The mattress slid and twisted. A fist caught my ribs.

I could tell that Wayne was throwing lots of elbows by the way his weight was being thrashed around. But he couldn't get away. He was pinned, it seemed. I don't know what he did, but suddenly space opened up between us and I caught a breath before his chest came down. Then all I heard was *whack, whack, whack-whack-whack-whack-whack.* Just hard and fast and rough like that. And he began to grab onto me like I could give him shelter. And squirm on me like my body had a door that he could open and lock behind him after running in.

I was so focused on Wayne that I didn't realize the other body had gotten off him, and the weight on me was not as bad as it had been, but it was still awful, so awful, so awful to be tied up and then grabbed onto, especially by someone being flogged. And I kept moaning for him to get off me, and for one of them to untie me, and for both of them to leave the goddamn room, but no one heard me, no one cared. So there I was, still beneath this jerking body, forced to take its spreading weight.

The beating finally slowed then stopped.

"Get the fuck out of here," said the deep voice. "Fuck around, I'll beat your ass again."

Wayne stood up. I could hear him to my right in what I imagined as a corner, sniffling.

The person with the deep voice sat on the bed at my left shoulder. I lay still and kept my eyes closed when the bag was eased off. The tape on my lips was inched off. No skin was lost. The fingers that unbound my wrists and ankles were thin but rough.

"Put on your clothes, miss," said the deep voice. "We're leaving."

I listened to them tramping out. A door opened. More outside noises drifted in. The door was closed again. The Citroën started up and drove away.

I lay there for another five minutes without opening my eyes. The smell of ripe bananas and curry sauntered in. I knew now I was in the house I'd entered the night before.

I looked.

It was a small room of which I had no memory. It had gray walls and white and yellow checkered tiles. There was little furniture—an armoire and a postered bed. The stuff on the dresser was scattered—figurines mostly and papers. This is what I recall.

I became concerned, as I put on my clothes, that there might be other people in the house, so I was careful. Tried to make no sound. I pulled away the gauzy curtains and cranked the louvers open and peaked out.

The day was beautiful. Red crotons marked the boundary of the yard next door. An orange kite was pinned like a brooch to the sky. A bird was roosting in the almond tree. I wanted it to sing.

Anyway, after I finished going through my oh-God-I'm-so-glad-to-be-alive-the-birds-are-chirping moment, common sense returned. "You need to get the hell out of here," I said to myself. No, I didn't think this. I said it aloud, softly.

I grabbed my purse and put on my shoes and ran to the door, opened it, and paused. Standing by the gate, inside the driveway, back turned to me, was a slim figure in a Panama hat and a baggy suit.

"So you're awake," the deep voice said. "I was worried. That boy Wayne is something else. You're lucky I came home."

I had nowhere to go. I couldn't go back inside the house. I mean I could, but why do that? My eyes flitted round for ways to escape. The prickly hedges were head height on either side. The front fence would catch me at my chest. The top of it was lined with broken glass. If I had to, I could take it—maybe—with a running start.

"Is this your house?" I asked.

"Is this my house? What kind of question is that? Of course."

I put a foot outside on the sunbaked slab that was the porch.

"So where's Wayne?"

"I don't give a fuck, miss. Excuse my French. You're not the first person he did that way. Damn boy sick." He opened one half of the gate without looking back at me, then added, "Pass and go your way. You have money? I can give you some to take a bus. I can't manage the taxi fare though."

It was less than ten paces to the gate. I edged along the driveway, my elbows brushing on the prickly hedge. I closed my eyes when I reached the gate. If anything bad was going to happen I didn't want to see.

It was easy enough to get back to the Sheraton. I hailed a passing cab. It was around four in the afternoon when I got there. I felt as if the receptionists and bellboys knew something from the way they said hello and looked at me. In my room I found my drawers open. All my drugs were gone.

I called Nigel. As soon as I began to speak he said, "Darling, we've been worried sick. Take some time. Put yourself together and come have a chat by the pool."

I went to meet him in a long white dress. I wore a wide hat and butterfly shades to hide my face. He was already sitting at a poolside table. A large umbrella gave him shade.

When the waiter came to take our order, Nigel asked for Pepsis. He leaned back in his polo shirt, crossed his legs, and looked toward the diving board, fingering his smooth blond beard.

By this time I'd learned that everyone had been in a panic. The police had gone to search my room. They'd found what they'd found, which was bad, very bad; but the good news was that the BBC had worked it out for me to leave the following day without getting locked up. For use and distribution.

"Distribution?"

"Oh Arielle, shut up. And another thing"—he looked at me directly for the first time—"we'll have to sacrifice somebody's head."

"So, you're asking me to come up with a list?"

"Oh Arielle, go fuck yourself."

I am the first to say that what I did after this defies all logic. But the truth is that I felt a deep urge to return to that house to find out what had occurred. I also felt I needed to thank the brute who'd come to my assistance. And determined to discover the details of the whispered conversation I'd overheard.

Wayne? He could not be trusted. This was certain. But the person with the deep voice? I wasn't sure.

I returned to the neighborhood at about five thirty. I was too unsettled to go to the house directly and I didn't remember exactly where it was, so I asked the cabby to just drive me around.

All the houses had been built alike, I saw; but many of them had front rooms and enclosed verandas added on. There were lots of trees here, and kids. On every other block I saw boys playing soccer in the road. It was close to dinnertime. The smell of beef and chicken leaped over the hibiscus hedge of almost every fence.

It was about six or so when we found the place. The sky was turning orange. The sun was edging down. I asked the driver to wait as I got out. I used a stone to rap on the red mailbox, and the front door swung out.

No one could be seen.

"Oh, it's you, miss. You're back again. Please come."

"Can you come out here, please?"

"You have nothing to fear, m'love. I am relaxing. If you want to come, you can come."

I opened the gate and went in slowly in the long white dress in which I'd lost my job. The louvers were all shut. A dog began to bark next door. An okra tree in the front yard was in lavender bloom. A few houses down, a boy was on his flat roof launching a kite. I stood on the uncovered patio three or so feet from the redwood door.

"So can you tell me what happened?"

"What you want to know?"

I'd have to step inside to see for sure where the voice was coming from, but it was clear that the speaker was seated near a corner to my right.

"Well, I came home this morning at around eleven o'clock, and saw Wayne like he was in panic, and I asked him what happened, and he told me that he came here with a woman last night, that woman being you of course, and further, that while he was making love to her she get paranoid and start to talk all kinds of things about the CIA and how they mash up her life, and as he was trying to calm her down she start to fight him. Every time he try and calm her down she would settle for a while, then get enrage again. So I asked him where the woman was and he took me into the room and I saw you sleeping and then I got a little panic because all the time I been thinking it was a local girl. For if you fuck with a tourist in this country you will hang. At least that is how I see it. So I say to him, maybe you should take her back to her place, but then he started to say that he couldn't do that. And he wasn't giving me any sensible reason. But I know is a fellow like the drugs, so I ask him if you was that type too and he said yes and that he was afraid that you might dead on him and that he might get the blame, so maybe we should just kill you and dump your body. And I said, well, that might not be the best thing, that maybe what we should do is just tie you down to the bed so that whatever was in your system could wear off."

"So I was just acting crazy?"

"That is what he said to me. I never see it myself."

"But you believed him?"

"I saw how you scratch him up, miss. His face was scratch up bad-bad. Look under your fingernails. If you don't bathe yet you might still see some skin."

I looked; the evidence was there. The cab driver called out to me, and I told him things were okay.

"So if you weren't here last night then how did Wayne get in?"

"He has a key. I let him use the place sometimes, if you know what I mean."

"So are you related to the woman who lives here then?"

"That is a long story, m'love."

"What do you mean?"

"I am the only one who lives here. Wayne is my nephew. His father Clive is my half-brother. I am half-sister to him."

I thought I'd misheard because of the accent.

"Who's your sister?" I asked.

"I don't have any sister, m'love."

"So who is the record producer? Does a record producer even live here? Wayne said that."

"That is me, m'love."

"And what is your name then?"

"They call me Monkey Man."

"So who's the—"

I heard a body shifting in a chair. A skid. A squeak. I removed my shades.

"Wayne told me you were someone of substance"—long pause—"and that I should let you interview me." Another long pause. "You don't sound like you have much sense."

It began to occur to me that the woman Wayne had spoken of and the man who had rescued me might be one and the same.

I went to the gate and cupped my mouth and spoke to the cabbie at a low volume: "Pay attention. I am going to go in."

I stopped at the doorway though. Afraid. It took some time for my vision to adjust to the low gray light. There was a figure with a rowdy head of white hair sitting on a small blue couch. In front of it there was a low table. At one short end of the table was a Danish chair with wooden arms. Off to the side against a wall there was some sort of credenza. Figurines and a creeping plant in a shallow bowl stood on top of it. A turntable as well.

There were pictures of Jesus, Martin Luther King Jr., Fidel Castro, and the prime minister on the walls.

"Come. Sit."

"Is it okay if I stand?"

"Suit yourself."

"So what happened between you and Wayne?"

"Nothing happened between me and Wayne."

"You beat him. Quite badly."

"Well, Wayne is a child to me."

"But you can't just beat people like that."

"So I shoulda just let him kill you and dump you."

"Was he really going to do that? I mean—really?"

"He was going to do something worse."

"What could be worse than that?"

"How old are you?"

"Doesn't matter. What's the point?"

"The point is that I saved you from something really bad and something in your heart made you come back. You know within yourself that you owe me something. How we going to work this out?"

A bad feeling came over me. I had gone too far. "I have to go," I said.

"So go on. Nobody not stopping you."

"But can I ask you something?"

"This is a free country, m'dear."

"What were you and Wayne talking about before you came into the room? I wasn't sleeping. I was only pretending. I heard you. But not really. What was going on?"

"How you going to pay me back for saving your life?"

"I dunno. I mean . . . what?"

"You tell me."

"Tell you what?"

"That is my point exactly. You tell me what. You tell me how you going pay me back."

"I can't. Honestly, I'm broke."

"I don't need money, m'love. I need time."

"What were you and Wayne fucking talking about before you came into the room? Please tell me. I have to go."

"I don't take bad words from women, sweetheart."

"I'm sorry."

"As they say, teeth and tongue will meet. But okay, let me tell you something. Wayne was planning to rape you, miss. He was going to rape you, then kill you, then dump you. This is what he said to me. I said to him that no raping not going to go on in my house. We can kill you, yes, but we not raping you. No raping not going on in here. And he said okay. So when we came in to seriously see if we should kill you now, I saw the look in his face. But I couldn't believe it, because we had talked about it already say that no raping was going to go on. But then him sit down on the bed and reach out and I saw the intention and I remember what they do to me and I just . . . well, I just . . . is like I just lose my mind. My nephew. My own nephew. His father and me is blood. Is not like he didn't know what they do to me. Cause one day I told him. And for him to come now and want to do that in front my face, well, that was a disrespect, and certain kind of disrespect can't stand."

My arms began to shake. Although it was hot in there I

began to feel cold. The smell of curry mixed with bananas made me want to throw up.

"I have to go," I said. "Really. I must."

"Not before you pay your dues."

Then I saw the gun.

I got instructions. I obeyed. I shouted to the cabbie that I'd need another twenty minutes. I stepped inside and locked the door.

My purse fell from my grasp. I closed my eyes and braced for the fury of the shot. I heard movement. Shuffling. Cloth on cloth. Cloth on floor. Piling. *Flop. Flop.*

When I opened my eyes I saw a woman reborn. All her hairs were gray. Her chin was strong but her eyebrows arched like they'd been plucked. You could see that she and Clive were relatives but she was lighter in color than him.

"Don't shoot me, please," I said. "I'm a good person in my heart."

She used one hand to cover her almost nonexistent breasts. Her skin was slack on her bones.

"So why you didn't come and talk to me?"

"What do you mean?"

"Everybody come and talk to everybody all the time, but nobody ever come and talk to me. Is like they forget about me."

"Please," I said. "I'll do anything you ask. Don't shoot, please. Don't shoot. I have had a very, very, very, very bad last few days."

"You're a journalist, right?"

"Yes."

"Come sit next to me." She kept her free hand to her chest and gestured with the gun. "I not going hurt you. Don't make this thing here throw you off." There was a tin of butter cookies on the table. She used her chin to point to it. "Make yourself at home, m'love. Eat one. Them nice."

She picked through the pile of clothes on the floor and put

on some boxers and a tank top. She seemed comfy, as if this was the way she dressed around the house.

"What do you want from me?" I asked.

"I just want you to pay your dues like how I paid my dues," she said, her voice breaking up into a rougher kind of patois now. "I paid my dues for this music, but nobody remembers me. Nobody talks to me. Is like I don't exist. And Wayne told me around a month ago that some people were coming down here to do a reggae flim and that he was going to make sure they talk to me. And every day I check him is pure tomorrow business, and more tomorrow business, and sometimes—I don't know if you know, but is a fellow that like to put on airs and get french fried so sometimes you not getting tomorrow-tomorrow. Instead you getting dummay-dummay. You know how many times I put on a suit and sit down here waiting for you? You think I like wear suit? So honestly, I did really give up on the thing. When I talk to my friend them like Keith Hudson and Errol T and people like that and they tell me how you interview them and how you nice and all that, I just feel like say my time will never come."

"But what do you want from me?" I asked.

"I want you to interview me."

"But I am not here with the cameramen . . ."

"Well, a man can't get everything every time. You can come tomorrow?"

"I'm leaving."

"How you mean?"

"They fired me today. It's a long story. While I was gone they searched my room and found things that shouldn't be there in the eyes of the police."

"Taste the cookie. Don't just play with it. It nice."

"It's okay."

"Pass one for me."

We fell into silence.

"So why do they call you Monkey Man?" I asked

"That is what I wanted to tell you on the camera, miss. You see, I might look healthy. But doctor told me that I sick. Said I can die any time."

She reached under the table for a photo album, opened it, flipped through some pages, and gave it to me.

"Look at me," she said. "Look at me now how I meager, and look at me just three years ago how I used to stout. They said it reach the liver. Can be any time now."

I began to sniffle as I looked at the photos. She'd lost nearly fifty pounds. As a man she'd been compact. Strong in the arms. In some images her hair was slicked and parted like a movie gangster. In a few she wore a penciled-in mustache. There she was in London with Jimmy Cliff. At a bar looking chummy with Johnny Cash. Always styled in well-made suits. Yeah, she used to be someone.

"Can I have one of these?" I asked.

"You'd really want one?"

"Yes."

"For what?"

"Just to keep. I like to keep beautiful things."

Her cheeks tightened. But her lips said, softly, "The taxi man waiting. Go on."

At this point, I needed no convincing that I owed her. Even though she'd been fully prepared to kill me earlier that morning, she had also, in one day, twice spared my life. But I was in danger. She was holding a gun. I stood up. I looked around the room. Lots was going through my mind. Just a mess of things. How many people knew her secret? Who would remember her as *her* at the end of her life? And I found myself reflecting on why I had become an actor—to preserve for all eternity the essences of evanescent lives.

My hands reached out and I held her face. She held my

arms. We stood. She inched around the table and we drew each other close. And with all the deep affection that rose up in my heart, I said, "Tell me your story, in your voice, sweet love. I promise you I'll tell it one day for all the world to hear. Tell me your story, sweet love."

After a short pause, she began: "From I was little I knew I was a boy. I wasn't born here, y'know. I was born in Costa Rica, a place name Port Limón, a place by the seaside with lots of houses on stilts. People there speak English and are more like West Indians than say Spanish.

"I came here to Jamaica in 1957. But I had run away from my mother long before that because she used to beat me to wear girl clothes. So I run away from her when I was around twelve and just moving round and moving round ended up in Colón in Panama, just hustling and doing odd jobs, but mostly street fighting, and from there I came to Jamaica to work.

"By that time I had found out that Abe Haddad was my father, and he had a big electronics store downtown on King Street. Same kinda setup like he used to have in Limón. So I turned up there one day and lay in wait for him and when he got inside his fishtail Chevrolet I got in there with him and acted like I had a gun and told him to turn down a lane and I showed him a picture of me and my mother and my brother and pointed at my brother and said to Mr. Abe that I was his son. I could tell he didn't really remember us so well, so I bluff him, and he took my word. So that's why I get away with saying my name was Joe. So he asked what I wanted him to do for me and I said nothing more really than a job. And in his own way Mr. Abe was responsible, so he forgive me for the gun thing and blood thicker than water and all that, so that is how I got my start.

"So yes, that is how I establish myself in this country as a man. I never had any hard time catching on because how we used to talk in Limón and how they were talking here was the same thing. Call it like a Canadian going to America then. You just fit in.

"So I am a man who can learn anything. My head is good. When I started working at Mr. Abe's store now I learned how to fix all electrical and electronic things. And gradually I start to experiment with building PA systems and amplifiers and all those things with tubes, the good old vacuum tubes.

"When this whole music business started later in the '60s now, most producers used to buy their amps from me. Go to anybody who know the business and they will tell you that I was the one who establish how this music sound. I was the one who go to Mr. Abe and say he should go into this music thing. I was the one who built everything in that studio at 4 Chancery Lane, right round the corner from the Ward Theater. Mr. Abe might have owned it, but I was the one who used to run everything, even the board. In fact, I build that four-track board. I never had any music training but I had the ears. I knew a hit song. You know how much hits I make for Prince Buster? Derrick Morgan? Bob Marley? Jimmy Cliff?

"Suffice it to say, there was a lot of jealousy, and one day I came to the studio and everything was destroyed. Two whole shelves of equipment gone. What was left was mashed up. Just mashed up. My Ampex. My Scully. Three Shure microphone. Like somebody beat them with an iron pipe. I knew who it was. I won't call no name.

"Look, by that time I had killed about three people. People used to hire me to collect money for them and all that, because I was rough. So I knew it wasn't a coward who did it. There was only one other producer who was bad enough to try and do such a thing, and the only reason he was so bad was because he a former light-heavyweight boxer, and on top of that, an ex-police.

"So one night I waylaid him when he was going home. His

business was over on Darling Street near Coronation Market and the railway. Rain was falling. Downtown lock up. Not even ghost outside. What they call a dark and stormy night. I had a gun in my waist. A little pistol named Ernie. I trail him, watching him move under the shop piazzas with him hat and umbrella. I was wearing black from head to toe, moving mystically right against the curb, but in the street. Then, just as I was about to grab him, I slide in some gutter water and fall down and he turn around and jump on me. The gun flew outta my hand and he drew his own. And what I could do but put up my hands and beg for me life?

"By the way, thanks for rubbing my neck, miss. Thank you. Some of this is hard.

"So anyway, he put the gun in my back and march me over to his studio and open the door and push me inside. There was a back room where he used to keep old equipment and he took me in there and put one piece of beating on me. If you notice, in the front I wear false teeth.

"After he beat me up now, he made me crawl out the back door on my knees like a dog. When I got outside he admitted that he was the one who'd mashed up my studio and he took off his belt and ordered me to take off my clothes, said he was going to beat me like a little boy. Well, of course I wouldn't do that, because he'd know. So I dare him to shoot me. I said, *Shoot me if you bad*. And he was bad. The bullet grazed my temple. I don't know what kinda police he could have been to graze a man point blank. But what happen really is that I fell and hit my head and while I was stunned and couldn't help myself he took off my clothes to beat me and disgrace me, and well . . . you know what he saw . . .

"To even talk about it now just take me right back there. Truly, this is not what I really wanted to talk to you about. I wanted to talk to you about my music. I wanted to talk to you about that, but look now, look now. All these things is coming on. Maybe I'm talking too much . . . Is okay?

"Well, the fucker took a picture of me out there like that. I don't know where he got the camera from. But I remember how my eyes hurt from the flash.

"One day later on now, I was working at Mr. Abe store, which is what I had to go back to again, and a man came in and drop off an envelop with the picture. Shortly after, the store phone ring and they call me and a voice say, *As long as you stay out of the music business your secret well safe with me.*

"The next few months was really hard. I just feel like everybody could look at me and know. A lot of women used to like me, and I used to fool around with a few of them, but I used to mostly just keep to myself. And I started to drink hard, and fight.

"The position that I was in force me to do something I have regretted to this day, even though it end up changing the world. When you know what it is to be your own man, it is hard to go back and be just ordinary. You understand? Is like if emancipation come and then the boss come a year later and say, well, they check the date and, well, right now it look like you get let go too early so you have to come outta your hammock or whatever and go back and cut cane.

"Miss, you know what I end up having to do? Work in secret for other producers. When they do the recording they would call me in to the mix and the mastering. You see this dub thing, I was the one who invented it in 1965. People think it came later. But sometimes when I got a song to mix I used to just rub out the lyrics and remake it, and add in all kind of echoes and reverb and all that. Cause to tell you the truth, that is how I was seeing myself—like somebody whose voice got rubbed out. The echoes and all that now, that was the way my heart was trembling inside. I make that music, that dub music for myself, as a way for me to express my way of feeling, and later on they pirate me and don't give me credit. But one day, my life took a turn.

"It was the thirteenth of May. I will never forget. I was at Randy's mixing the whole day and a musician came in and asked if I heard what happen and I said no. Well, suffice it to say, it was all over the radio that the car lick down the same producer who did mash up my life and he was in the hospital with a broke foot—man in there can hardly walk. And I say, *Yeah?*

"By the way, my back hurting me. I need to sit. You want a cookie? Them nice, man. Eat one.

"So, remember I told you I used to collect money? Well, when you have that kind of background you know all kinds of folks. So here is what I did. I organized some men who had just come out of prison and was looking for something to do, to go to the hospital dressed in khaki shirt and pants like porters and kidnap that fucker for me.

"No joke, no lie. They followed my instructions. Waited for him to go to the bathroom on the crutches. One went in there with the chloroform to knock him out and two roll in with a laundry trolley and cover him up and bring him out and put him in the back of a Transit van and bring him to me.

"You know where I asked them to bring him? The same studio him mash up. When the chloroform wore off the fucker was so frightened. At first he didn't know where he was. He was just lying there on the floor in his pajamas with the heavy cast.

"Don't ask if I didn't beat him. Don't ask if I never kicked him. But that is not all I did. I did worse. If he was going to hold a secret over me, the only way for me to win was to have a bigger secret over him. There was a reason why I got men from prison as compañeros. They good at that thing called rape. Five of them. Two turns each. No grease. The last thing I said to him was, *You think is you alone have camera?* Snap. Snap. Snap.

"For four years that fucker stayed out of my life. I rebuilt my studio and I was riding high again. I even got married. Met a little Christian girl from the country and took her for a wife. She was so simple. I used to tell her that if I use my thing on her she would cry. But it looked like she met a man who was giving her something extra, so after a while she told me that the devil come and take her and that although she wasn't right to be involved in adultery she just couldn't stand the constant mouthing off for the rest of her life.

"Suffice it to say, everybody wanted to work with me. And I worked with everyone. Johnny Nash came and worked with me. Bob Andy worked with me. Everybody who wanted a hit song came to work with me. And the musicians used to love to work with me, because I used to have the best equipment. If they wanted something custom I used to sometimes even build it for them.

"But when my wife left me I felt bad in truth. Is not an easy thing to live a secret life. I used to hear people say all kinds of things about people like me. I myself see people laugh at them. Sometimes I myself used to hate them because it was like they just brought so much unnecessary attention to themselves. Especially the men.

"It was around this time—1969—the same year I bought this house, that I myself started to go to church, to St. Mary's down the road. And for the first time in my life I started to dream about myself as a child and see myself as a girl again, in frocks. Sometimes I used to wake up frightened. I really didn't know what this mean. Because it wasn't like I wanted to wear woman clothes in real life. But it was a thing that just began to come up over and over again in my dreams. Most of the times, though, I used to just wake up and kiss me teeth and just go on with my life. But truly, really and truly, some of the times I used to just wake up and bawl and ask God why. And I am not sure if

I even wanted to get an answer, because honestly, I didn't know what I was asking, like why what?

"I didn't want to be a woman. I wasn't asking for that. I didn't want to be something I was not.

"Oh, what did I want to be? I never really think of it that way. Well, as you put it to me that way . . . well . . . just me.

"But you cutting my story and you say you have to go. Well, one Friday morning after having one of those dreams I was telling you about, I decided to go to a different church. On top of that I decide to go as a different person. As a person in woman's clothes.

"Luckily, I am not a tall person, so it wasn't too hard for me to get things in my size. Saturday now, I went to look. I didn't go downtown, though, where people knew me. I went uptown to Half Way Tree and got a purse and stockings and a hat, and a frock and everything, and I packed them up in my Zephyr Zodiac and drove from there quite all the way down to Westmoreland. It took me about six hours going over all them hills, and I found a little guest house in Negril, right up on the cliffs, looking out over onto the sea. And it was only hippies down there those days. And those kind of people I figured didn't really care. Some of them was just walking round naked. I saw two women ones that looked like they were friends, but I couldn't stand to look at them.

"What I didn't know was that I was being followed, that all this time that fucker had been plotting his revenge. When I got back to the guest house to change and come back to Kingston, is three gunmen I meet up in my room. I heard one say, *Gunbutt him*. Then everything went white.

"When I woke up I was in some kind of storeroom somewhere. My clothes were gone. There was a line of breezeblocks toward the ceiling so a little bit of air and light could come in. It had no color. Just the raw concrete. Like how it is in jail.

"I had a sense like I was in the country somewhere, because

the only sounds I heard for two days was wind. No cars. No children. The whole time I think I heard one animal—a goat. And as much as I bawl out, nobody didn't hear me and come.

"After three days or so passed now, one evening as the sun was going down I heard a car. I got nervous because I had gotten accustomed to being by myself and I never know who it was. But I was hungry and thirsty. Is not easy to go so long without water and food.

"As I listened, I heard doors opening and closing and footsteps coming toward me down a passageway. Before they got to me they stopped and entered an adjoining room. I heard them leave, drive away, but something had been left in there. For the next two days and nights I heard this thing moving around in there. Something of a good size. Breathing. Scratching itself. Sometimes in the night I would hear this *Uuh-uuh* sound, and I kept thinking to myself, *Jesus, what is that?*

"Well, I eventually found out. Two evenings later the car returned again. The footsteps—sounded like the same ones— came down the passageway again. By this time I am hungry and weak. The door opened slightly. I could see into the passage a little bit. What light existed was coming from another room somewhere, so all I could see was shadows, but everything was really dark. I smelled food and saw someone bend down and slide a plate across the concrete floor. Then someone put what I found out was a bucket of water and a cup and a towel and a rag. I asked the man who he was and where he was but he didn't answer me.

"It wasn't much. Just some fish and bread. I was so thirsty I nearly drink the bucket of water, but I was thinking that maybe they give me the towel and all that so I could get cleaned up before they let me out. Like maybe someone had paid ransom or whatever for me.

"I took my time to wash myself. It was like I didn't know if

I was going backward or forward in time. What I mean is that I didn't want the life I had for the last few days but I didn't know exactly what was going to happen ahead. I mean, why all of a sudden they were being nice to me? Feed me, and all that? Allow me to bathe?

"But it felt good to clean all the muck off me. For my skin to not feel sticky. To lose that sour smell. To smell good.

"Now, while I was eating, the room next door had been quiet for some time, but then some movement again. My skin right away just fill with cold bumps. I put my ears to the wall to listen. Through my other ear I heard footsteps coming. They stopped next door.

"I heard one man say, *Watch it, it will bite*. Another one say, *What a damn thing big*. Then a third one say, *So what they plan to do with this 'rangutang though, eeh?* Now, I knew what a 'rangutang was. It was a like a cousin to gorilla. The two of them is ape.

"I started to get a little nervous because I started to imagine this thing getting away. But then I heard a fourth voice, and this one sounded like it had some knowledge, so although I was tense, I kind of start calm down. This voice say, *Look, all you louts need to do is move the damn thing to the other room. This thing has been brought into the country illegally and if anything happens to it at all, it is going to be hell to pay*. And when he said that I heard a big commotion and a *Uuh uuh uuh uuh*.

"Then I heard them open the door over there and like a chain dragging, and like fighting and flailing and *uuh uuh uuh uuh* and like something big and heavy and thick bouncing off the walls and people running away and falling down, and I began to imagine them leading this thing outside, but I began to get really frightened when instead of going back the way they came, they move toward my door.

"Miss, when my door open and I saw the shadow of this big everlasting hairy thing, I ran to the back of the room and bawl out, *Lord God, Jesus Christ, deliver me from evil*, and they slam the door and is pure darkness again. And I could hear heavy, dragging footsteps inside, just feet away from me.

"I said to myself that if I just keep quiet it maybe wouldn't bother me. I heard like sniffing. And scratching. Then nothing at all. My heart was beating hard. Then it began to beat harder when I hear one of the man them say, *So this 'rangutang thing will really sex a human being for true?* and another one say, *I hear them have nature for woman just like man.* Then the first one say, *No, me can't believe that,* and the other one say, *So what the bloodclaat you think we leggo him inside there for?*

"Then all of a sudden I heard one loud noise and something charging toward me. And I start to kick and punch before I felt the grab.

"The two of us now start to tussle on the floor. I hadn't really eaten for a while, as I said, and it was bigger than me and stronger than me too, and as I was fighting with it I feel like it was trying to get me on my back and between my legs. And lemme tell the truth. Before that I was thinking it just wanted to eat me or kill me. I wasn't no kind of animal expert or whatever. It was just survival I was dealing with. But when this thing had me on my back in the corner and I realize what was going to happen, I really start to fight now. Cause I heard when the man say this thing will fuck a human being and the other one say it have nature, and I put the two of them together and say that, well, they say monkey is second to man and that this monkey now, maybe his nature tell him to take me as a wife, and you know what? Nobody was going to help me.

"And I knew this but I was still shouting out. And I'm getting shaken. And I'm getting hit. My head lick against the wall a dozen times. And you know what? After a while I just give myself over to what's going to happen. I just accept that this is what was going to happen to me. And I felt something inside me in that place for the first and only time. It was painful. It was strange. And I tighten up to lock it out. But there was so much force. So much pressure.

"And you know what I did? I just put my mind to it. Thinking like this would make it stop. I don't even know why this came to mind. But that is what it came to my mind to do. To not fight, to just give in so it would end quickly. Oh God. You don't know what I went through."

I didn't know what to say at this point. I mean—would you? There was something spectacular in the violence, in the cycle of revenge, that I didn't want to acknowledge. And there were also questions I wanted to ask. Like how she got out of there and did she see a doctor or call the police. And then I realized that these were questions of a normal kind and that what I'd just heard about was—for want of a better expression—something else.

I had to go. I had to go. And I said this: "I really have to go."

She looked down at the floor and replied, "Go on."

When I got to the door I turned back to say goodbye and she held her hand up for me to wait, then she came over. We hugged again. And something happened in that moment that had never happened before. While holding a woman, I wanted a kiss.

I led her down the short hall to the room from which she'd rescued me, lay on my back in my white dress, and took her in my arms and used my fingers to massage her scalp and took the weight of her frail body—which was not too much to bear.

She cried. In the pitch of a little girl, she cried.

"And you know what was the worst part?" she said when she'd composed herself.

"Oh, my sweetie," I said, "do tell," while thinking, *This can't possibly get worse.*

"It wasn't a 'rangutang. It was just that fucker in a monkey suit!"

* * *

A few years later, while traveling through Heathrow airport, I picked up the *Guardian* and saw a small obituary. Seminal reggae producer Joe Haddad had died. Yes, he'd worked with everyone he'd mentioned and more. Yes, he'd built a lot of the original equipment that gave the industry its start. But he wasn't credited as inventing dub. However, he got partial credit for something else: the possible inspiration for a hit released in 1969 by Toots and the Maytals and a bigger hit for the Specials ten years later:

> *I see no sign of you*
> *I only heard of you*
> *Hugging up the big monkey man.*

ABOUT THE CONTRIBUTORS

UC Riverside/Carlos Puma

CHRIS ABANI is a Nigerian poet and novelist and the author of *Song for Night* (a *New York Times* Editors' Choice), *The Virgin of Flames*, *Becoming Abigail* (a PEN/Beyond Margins Award finalist), and *GraceLand* (a selection of the *Today Show* Book Club; winner of the 2005 PEN/Hemingway Award and the Hurston/Wright Legacy Award). His other prizes include a PEN Freedom-to-Write Award, a Prince Claus Award, and a Lannan Literary Fellowship. He lives and teaches in California.

Makonnen Fouché-Channer

COLIN CHANNER is the father of two children, Addis and Makonnen. He is also a fiction writer, occasional essayist, and university professor. His fiction includes the national best-selling novel *Waiting in Vain* (a Critic's Choice selection of the *Washington Post*) and the novella *The Girl with the Golden Shoes*. He was born in Kingston, Jamaica, in 1963. He founded the Calabash International Literary Festival Trust in 2001, and received the Silver Musgrave Medal in Literature in 2010.

Rachel Eliza Griffiths

KWAME DAWES is an award-winning Ghanaian-born Jamaican poet. He is author of sixteen books of poetry and numerous books of fiction, nonfiction, criticism, and drama, and has edited nine anthologies. Dawes is the Glenna Luschei editor of *Prairie Schooner*, a chancellor's professor of English at the University of Nebraska, and associate poetry editor for Peepal Tree Press in the UK. He is also the programming director of the Calabash International Literary Festival.

Avani Fachon

MARCIA DOUGLAS grew up in Kingston, Jamaica. She is the author of the novels *Madam Fate* and *Notes from a Writer's Book of Cures and Spells*, as well as the poetry collection *Electricity Comes to Cocoa Bottom*. Her one-woman show, *Natural Herstory*, is based on her fiction and features the voices of seven Jamaican women. She teaches creative writing at the University of Colorado, Boulder.

Kate Simon

CHRISTOPHER JOHN FARLEY was born in Kingston, Jamaica, and raised in Brockport, New York. He is the author of a number of books, including the novel *Kingston by Starlight* and the biography *Before the Legend: The Rise of Bob Marley*.

THOMAS GLAVE is the author of *Whose Song? and Other Stories, Words to Our Now: Imagination and Dissent* (2005 Lambda Literary Award winner), *The Torturer's Wife*, and editor of the anthology *Our Caribbean: A Gathering of Lesbian and Gay Writing from the Antilles* (2008 Lambda Literary Award winner). He is a 2012 Visiting Fellow at Cambridge University.

MARLON JAMES was born in Kingston, Jamaica, in 1970. His second novel, *The Book of Night Women*, was a National Book Critics Circle Award fiction finalist, a NAACP Image Award finalist, and winner of the 2010 Dayton Literary Peace Prize and the 2010 Minnesota Book Award. His first novel, *John Crow's Devil*, was a finalist for the *Los Angeles Times* Book Prize and the Commonwealth Writers' Prize. James teaches literature and creative writing at Macalester College in St. Paul, Minnesota.

KEI MILLER is a poet, novelist, and essayist. His most recent books are *The Last Warner Woman* and *A Light Song of Light*. Miller is also series editor of Heinemann's Caribbean Writers Series and he lectures at the University of Glasgow where he recently completed his PhD.

PATRICIA POWELL was born in Spanish Town, Jamaica. She is the author of *Me Dying Trial, A Small Gathering of Bones, The Pagoda*, and *The Fullness of Everything*. Recipient of a PEN New England Discovery Award and a Lila Wallace-Reader's Digest Writers' Award, Powell lives in Northern California and teaches in the MFA program at Mills College.

LEONE ROSS grew up in Kingston. She is an award-winning novelist and short story writer. Her work has been published by Penguin, Random House, Picador, Farrar Straus & Giroux, Tindal Street, Canongate, Sceptre, and Dutton/Plume—and translated into French and Slovak. Her second book, *Orange Laughter*, was named one of *Wasafiri* magazine's most influential novels in the last twenty-five years. Leone teaches fiction writing at the University of Roehampton in London.

Sidney Fleminger Thomson

IAN THOMSON is the author of *Bonjour Blanc*, an acclaimed book about Haiti, and *Primo Levi: A Life*, which won the Royal Society of Literature's W.H. Heinemann Award in 2003. His book on Jamaica, *The Dead Yard*, was awarded the Ondaatje Prize in 2010. He lives in London with his wife and children, and is a fellow of the Royal Society of Literature.